I0706017

NIGHT OF THE WITCH

THE CROOKED TALES SERIES

In reading order:

The Rising

Night Of The Witch

Children Of The Shadows

Dawn Of The Demon

The Reckoning

(Coming: June 2026)

NIGHT OF THE WITCH

CROOKED TALES
BOOK TWO

CHRIS HARRISON

WICKED INK

PUBLISHING

This is a work of fiction, and the views expressed herein are the sole responsibility of the author. Likewise, characters, places, and incidents are the product of the author's imagination, and any resemblance to actual persons, living or dead, or actual events or locations, is entirely coincidental.

Night Of The Witch (Crooked Tales Series) : Book 2
Copyright © 2024 by Chris Harrison

Published by Wicked Ink Publishing Ltd.
www.wickedinkpublishing.com

Cover and book design © 2024 by Wicked Ink Publishing Ltd.
Editors: Raymond Griffiths & Adam Bamford

All rights reserved. No part of this book may be scanned, uploaded, reproduced, distributed, or transmitted in any form or by any means whatsoever without prior written permission from the publisher.

First Edition: October 2024
Printed in Canada

Night Of The Witch / Chris Harrison. — Calgary, Alberta : Wicked Ink Publishing Ltd., 2024.
ISBN 978-1-998278-08-4 (paperback)
ISBN 978-1-998278-05-3 (ebook)
1. Haunted houses fiction. 2. Supernatural fiction. 3. Young adult fiction. 4. Horror fiction. I. Title.
Book 2 of the Crooked Tales series.
Text in English. Audience: Young adult and general adult readers.
This is a publisher-supplied cataloguing record.

For Scott

**In the shadows of the past
a witch's curse is reborn...**

NIGHT OF THE WITCH

PROLOGUE

Molly winced in pain as she removed the thorny branch that gouged its way deep into her ankle when she took cover.

A cold sweat flushed across her brow, as she clamped down hard on her bottom lip to contain the whimper she felt welling in her throat. Twisted in the shadows of the hawthorn bush, Molly stared with grim satisfaction as the very tip of gnarled wood exited her flesh and released a steady stream of warm blood. It glistened in the moonlight as it raced down her heel and onto the dry, crumbly earth beneath her bare feet.

They were close now. She could hear them echoing in the woods as they beckoned her to surrender to their hatred.

"Molly Harding! We know you're out here, we can smell your evil stench. Show yourself! Face trial for what you have done, so the lord may take mercy on your soul!"

The dreamy glow of distant flames danced and flickered amongst the trees like tiny fireflies, painting their barks amber as the outraged mob fanned out in their search for her.

Fenced in, there was only one route left if she wanted to make it to Cold Christmas alive.

Molly tore the hem from her dress and tied it tight around her wounded ankle. The light of her pursuers was not close enough to expose her...yet. She drove the ball of her right foot into the ground to test her pain threshold. A sharp pang crawled up her leg but ran out of steam as it reached her calf, she had definitely felt worse.

It was now or never.

Slowly hobbling backwards away from the rustling trees, Molly did her best to stay low and out of sight. She knew once she'd crossed the border, her accusers would flee back to the village that was once her home.

With its dangerous reputation, Cold Christmas would be enough to deter the witch-hunter and his men.

Once the voices grew faint, she turned towards her intended direction. A light south-westerly breeze picked up and Molly wondered if there might be a clearing further ahead. As much as she would welcome a break from the unforgiving terrain the woods had shown her, a clearing would surely leave her vulnerable.

"I can see ya, Molly!" the voice bellowed without warning.

It was far closer than the others and took her by complete surprise. Frozen to the spot, Molly wrestled with her composure as she tried to steady her weary legs from trembling.

Her mother had always told her panic was her enemy. A weakness that would surely be her undoing if she ever let it in.

She crouched lower, holding her breath, trying to observe her surroundings without making a sound. There was no torchlight to be seen, only row upon row of alder and oak trees.

Whoever her assailant was, he had broken away from the pack and was stalking her under the light of the moon.

"I can smell ya blood," he sneered, "like old pennies left out in the rain."

This time, the voice came from behind her and was even closer. An icy shiver scampered its way up Molly's hunched back as she cowered in the shadows. She'd heard no movement between his taunts, and the woods were littered with autumn leaves.

The heavy aroma of mulch and dried-out foliage surrounded her, yet all she could hear was the gentle breeze as it softly whispered in her ears. It was impossible for anyone to have gotten so close to her without detection.

"Got ya!" Frosty breath glanced her cheek as a hand landed firmly on the nape of her neck, gripping her with icy fingers.

Panic finally kicked down the door of Molly's self-control and a shriek broke out as she spun in blind desperation to evade her captor.

Wriggling free, she ran in the only direction available to her. Each step triggered a shooting pain in her ankle until her sprint descended into a pathetic limp.

Barbed branches slowed her down further, clawing at her skin as she fought her way through the trees and shrubbery.

A cluster of voices broke out behind her; the pack was closing in on its prey.

All she could do was shamble and hobble forward hoping to stumble upon somewhere else to hide, and stumble she did. As soon as she reached the clearing, she tripped over a large stoney path.

What little energy she had left soon abandoned her as she lay sprawled on the ground, but she had to keep going.

She had come too far to quit now.

Molly raised her head as she picked herself up from the ground. Her palms were stinging, fresh from her scrape with the rough stones she had fallen on. She knew exactly where she was now. Even in the dark, the building in front of her was unmistakable.

"Crooked House," she gasped.

Molly clambered up the path towards the broken door ahead. She knew if she made it over the threshold, she would be safe.

Crooked House was well known in her village, as was its curse. Originally, a family home, tragedy and murder had marred it ever since it was built. Now left derelict, it was only ever frequented by passing criminals looking for shelter as they travelled to and from Cold Christmas with their spoils.

"There she is!" The mob had caught up with her. A swarm of angry faces and flaming torches all seeking retribution, but they were too late.

Molly threw herself beyond the busted doorframe and disappeared into the shadows. A tight-lipped discomfort befell the group of men outside; they knew too well where their hunt had led them.

Inside, Molly sat with her back to the entrance wall and tried to catch her breath. She was safe in the knowledge their superstition would prevent them from entering, but she needed a plan all the same.

"Light it up!" barked the general, shattering the silence like a sledgehammer and destroying all hope along with it.

An amber glow radiated beyond the splintered

doorframe as flames hissed and snaked their way inside, devouring anything that stood in their way.

Molly's head slumped into her hands at the crushing realization of her impending death.

There was nowhere left to run.

It was over.

She either burned alive within these abandoned halls or burned at the stake out there.

The rhythmic crunching of dried leaves and dirt underfoot served up an ominous countdown, as Molly remained slouched in defeat. Sick to the pit of her stomach, her head throbbed, but something else was drastically awry. This was more than a symptom of her distress, it was the onset of another of her seizures.

A whistling vibration emanating from the base of her skull began to grow and intensify, tingling her nasal cavity as it paralyzed her senses. Her vision began to bend and warp as an unknown force from within stirred her eyes around and around like a hot cup of coffee.

Molly's head jerked sharply to the right, straining her slender neck, whilst the rest of her body succumbed to rigor mortis. A splintering pain sliced through her brain, and she could feel the dizzying consequences as her spinning eyes jerked and juddered before rolling back into their sockets.

The dreary hallway dissolved into a hazy-white blur as Molly, the humble servant girl, made way for Molly, the witch. Casting a harsh, crooked silhouette of jagged angles, she floated across the hall to face her aggressors. The tips of her toes gently skimmed the floor as she drifted into the doorway like a macabre puppet suspended by unseen strings.

Her expression twisted in pain, like a fresh corpse who had been terrified to death. She scowled at the handful of middle-aged men standing outside and revelled in their gasps of horror.

"Accipe has animas et conbures eas in inferno inferiori," her rasping voice was barely audible over the crackling fire which now surrounded her, but she didn't need anyone to hear her murderous hex.

One by one, the men burned as flames of blazing magenta corkscrewed from the ground beneath them. Their bodies entangled like fiery weeds until they each fell, screaming and writhing in agony, to their deaths.

The stench of charred wood and burnt flesh saturated the night air and Molly breathed it all in, basking in her glorious and violent swan song. Trapped and resigned to her fate, she finally turned to face the monster that had been watching her from the shadows since she'd arrived.

"We've been waiting for you Molly." came the clumsy, crackling voice from deep inside the burning building.

"Welcome home."

I

Wave upon wave of horizontal rain ruthlessly attacked the rear of the Wilson house. The only respite from its vehement rattling came when it was momentarily eclipsed by the ferocious howling wind.

Meridia pulled her marshmallow duvet up around her ears and stared at the replica moon floating in a glass ball of amber light beside her. She desperately yearned for some rest, but the harder she tried, the more elusive it became.

Over the past week, four hours of broken sleep had whittled down to three, then two, and now this. The events at Crooked House had taken their toll, and as much as she tried to lose herself in the warm and soothing orange hues that softly illuminated her room, she couldn't prevent herself from being pulled back to that wretched place. In an attempt to regain control of her own thoughts, she shifted her focus away from the detailed craters of her Luna nightlight to her faint reflection in the glass that encased it.

"God, I look old," she mumbled in disillusionment.

Anyone who hadn't been privy to recent events would be forgiven for thinking she had developed some kind of habit. Dark circles encompassed her jaded blue eyes that were once so bright and full of life, whilst her freckled face looked pallid alongside her vibrant auburn curls.

Her room, once a haven in times of turmoil, no longer offered any sense of security. That was the real problem here...she wasn't safe anymore. None of them were, and no magical duvet or nightlight, no matter how soothing, could ever change that.

A fleeting shadow swept across the globe from left to right. The sight of it triggered a wave of prickly heat, which engulfed Meridia's body in seconds as she battled to control her fight-or-flight response. She had a visitor.

She swallowed, a dry, painful swallow, as she tried to muster up enough courage to investigate. Peering over the top of her covers, Meridia anxiously examined every soft toy on her bedroom shelf, as if she scrutinized a police line-up. Her eyes remained bleary as she struggled to adjust from her nightlight to the shadows of her tiny boxroom.

Nothing.

She was alone.

The tension in her shoulders loosened and, without thinking, Meridia closed her eyes. Then, just for the briefest of moments, she felt at peace.

BANG!

She sat bolt upright in shock as the window burst open, letting the violent wind and rain in. A second wave of panic coursed through her body as Meridia gasped to catch her breath. Slack jawed, she stared at the retro alarm clock beside her as its angry digital display screamed 3:00AM.

"The witching hour," she thought, riddled with worry.

However, as her eyes came to terms with the suffocating darkness, one sobering detail struck her with the force of a sledgehammer; she didn't own an alarm clock.

"Whe...where am I?" she whispered, her head spinning in search of answers.

A heavy, putrid stench of mold nested in the back of Meridia's throat as she struggled to decipher her new surroundings. The familiar smell and a deep, instinctive sense of dread told her exactly where she was, but still her eyes needed proof. She slowly followed the light of the alarm clock, letting its modest rays ease her into the darkness that now enveloped her.

A kaleidoscope of shadows began to separate and assume more recognizable shapes. A table, a wardrobe, and a door.

Meridia shuffled to the edge of the lumpy mattress and flinched at the ice-cold slate tiles underfoot. She took a moment to steady her nerves, unsure if this was a dream or something more sinister.

Crooked House had snatched her once before and this felt every bit as real as it had then, but something was different. This wasn't room 6, and there was no ghoulish child to greet her.

The wind and rain had quietened, and the steady beating of Meridia's blood pumping around her head was the only sound she could hear.

Click!

She'd spoken too soon.

The door softly creaked ajar, letting a thin trail of opaque light seep into the room. Tiny flecks of dust ambled around in the air of their newfound spotlight, floating aimlessly like the walking dead.

A tall shadow scurried past the open door, sending the dust into a spin and Meridia's panic into overdrive. The pattering of fleeing footsteps followed, echoing as they ran down the hall outside and were soon accompanied by the sound of a woman sobbing.

Meridia crept towards the open door, knowing all too well the danger of being in Crooked House without the protection of sunlight. Aside from the gentle sobbing, all seemed perfectly still. A beguiling light emanating from deeper within the house danced and flickered beyond the confines of the room.

"*A fire?*" she wondered. Resigned to her situation, Meridia stepped out into the dilapidated hall.

"So that's what room 5 looks like," she muttered as she tiptoed past the brass number nailed to the door.

The light source and sobbing were both coming from her left, room 2. Its door stood wide open, and waves of amber and gold gently skimmed the rugged grey floor.

CHINK!

A sharp clank echoed behind her as a loose shingle ricocheted across the stony ground.

Meridia stopped in fright and spun around just in time to catch sight of a cloaked figure disappear down the gloomy corridor.

"*The monsters,*" she thought. But it was unlike them to run and hide.

Whoever or whatever she'd seen, she could still feel their eyes boring into her from the shadows. Steadying her nerves with a deep breath, she pushed herself forward in search of a way out. Although the exit lay just yards from where she stood, Meridia felt compelled to explore whatever secrets were hiding inside room 2.

Her intuition told her the mysterious figure she'd caught a glimpse of was more voyeur than assailant, and so she cautiously proceeded towards the source of light.

As she crossed the narrow passage leading to the back

door, she hesitated, but whilst questioning her decision to stay, the sobbing intensified and cried out to her kind nature; Meridia had to know more.

Peeping around the doorframe, she watched as a young woman sat perched on the end of a bed, with her head resting in her hands. She had seen this mystery guest countless times when studying the files on Crooked House, and now here she was in the flesh. Her dress was that of an old maid, tattered and torn at the hem. She was covered in that all too familiar soot and didn't seem to notice Meridia standing in the doorway.

"Are...are you ok?" Meridia stammered.

The woman kept her face cradled in her lap and whimpered,

"*I never did nothing wrong...sniff... that... that boy... sniff...I never...*"

Meridia took a tentative step into the room and felt the warmth of the fire's embrace. An old fireplace on the wall opposite the woman looked like it had recently been lit and illuminated the unassuming room. Sparse, yet functional, it matched all the others she had seen. A large oak wardrobe dominated the furthest corner and across from that, on the other side of the bed's ornate headboard, was another door which Meridia assumed led to a bathroom.

She took another step closer towards the weeping stranger and paused at the graffiti plastered across the room's door in white spray-paint

'BURN IN HELL'

"*What if this is another trick?*" she wondered.

But the woman's sorrow seemed genuine, and this was one guest they knew nothing about.

"How did you get here?" Meridia asked softly, as she ventured closer to the edge of the bed. Still, the woman kept her face covered whilst she cried.

"They forced me...sniff...those monsters forced me..."

Meridia reached out a consoling hand which hovered over the woman's shoulder in another moment of hesitation. Looking over her hunched back, she saw a shadow at the window. A man in a hood was staring directly at her. His eyes were bright, but human, and his stare was intense, like that of a crazed madman. Meridia's gaze was transfixed, frozen in the headlights of his stare until he eventually stepped back out of sight.

"W...we...we need to get out of here now!" she said, touching the woman's cold bony shoulder.

"I never did nothing wrong...that boy...he got what was coming...and so did them monsters too..." The woman's delicate, melancholy voice became harsh and jagged, crackling in tune with the fire. Her neck cracked like a dried-out branch as she lifted her head away from her hands.

Meridia froze on the spot, overwhelmed by fear and confusion at what she was now witnessing.

Thin black veins raced up the woman's spindly fingers and traversed her shoulder where Meridia's hand was resting.

She recoiled back in shock.

This was a trap!

"I burned them...sent them all straight to hell...straight to hell...straight to hell..." her twisted voice whipped through the air, razor sharp and maniacal.

With that, the fire went out, plunging everything into pitch-darkness. The room fell deathly silent.

Meridia knew the only way out was directly behind her,

so she skulked backwards one baby-step at a time, her arm outstretched and waving behind her like a tail as she tried her best to navigate the abyss.

Just as she started moving, the fire reignited and roared into the room. The bed was empty, and the woman had vanished. Flames licked and kissed the edge of the mattress, igniting it and turning everything a vibrant yellow.

As Meridia turned to make a bolt for the door, she was confronted by the woman floating in front of her, contorted like a puppet with tangled strings. Black sinewy veins lay exposed as her eyes rolled back in their sockets, and her mouth remained fixed mid-scream.

"You will all burn in hell....ALL OF YOU..." her head twitched from side to side in a pigeon-motion with each word.

Meridia felt the fire at her back as sweat poured down her brow, stinging her eyes. All the while, thick black smoke snaked around the room, swallowing everything in its wake and obscured what little vision Meridia could muster. The fumes scorched her lungs as everything around her turned to ash, all to the tune of a wicked, cackling laugh that came from the very depths of hell.

Overpowered and blinded by smoke, Meridia fell to her knees. Somewhere in the distance, a pale ball of light floated into view. Coughing and spluttering, she used all her strength to crawl towards it.

"Burn in hell...burn in hell...burn...in...hell..." the words slowly faded into the background as Meridia got closer and closer to the light.

The closer she got, the brighter it became, shifting from grey to white to yellow and eventually amber. Gradually the smoke subsided, and she was reunited with the familiar craters on her Luna nightlight.

Everything was calm.

Drenched in sweat, she sat up and surveyed her boxroom. There was no evil witch. No mysterious watcher at her window.

She was home.

She was safe.

"A dream...it was just a dream..." she gasped as she began kicking her duvet off to cool down.

Gravity soon took over and the weight of her heavy cover did the rest of the work for her, dragging itself to the floor at the foot of her bed. Her hands were clammy, still trembling from fear, so she wiped them dry on her pyjama top.

"What the..." Meridia looked down, baffled by the dirty black streaks that were smeared across her chest.

At that moment, she caught sight of her legs, covered in soot and ash.

This was far beyond a simple dream.

She had to warn the others.

2

It was just another gloomy Wednesday morning at St Swithun's. Framed by a rusty wire fence, its grey asphalt playground stretched as far as the eye could see and mirrored the dreary clouds gathered overhead. But the drizzling rain didn't deter the usual suspects from their ritual pre-school game of football. Their boisterous roars soared high above the humdrum murmurs of those who preferred to wait for the bell in anonymity.

Zach, Kane and JJ watched on from a lowly bench in the furthest corner, away from their peers. Their faces were as sombre as the melancholy sky above them. Hoods up, they sat silently watching the gate, waiting for Meridia and Izzy to arrive.

An entire month had passed since the events at Crooked House, and despite staying well clear of the area, the lingering threat continued to hang over them like a long, dark shadow.

"Here they come," Zach announced, as he saw both girls hurriedly walking across the zebra crossing beyond the school's boundaries. The hairs on the back of his neck suddenly rose to attention underneath his heavy winter parka, "Something's wrong," he added "They never walk that fast, and we've still got ages until the bell rings."

All three boys stood up in unison as if they were cheering on the scrappy football game between the self-proclaimed cool kids and those not-so-cool.

Meridia was first through the gate. Her freckled face was stern, as she dictated the pace.

Izzy just about kept in touch behind her, but it was a struggle. The wind and rain smeared her tortoiseshell glasses as she marched headlong into it, and so every four or five steps she would need to slow down and cuff them, then break into a light jog just to catch up again.

They walked around the ongoing game and past a group of popular girls who were busy with their own morning ritual of ogling boys and looking at TikTok.

"What's wrong?" Zach blurted as soon as they were within ear-shot; his elfin face wrought with worry beneath his furry hood.

"I was there last night, in my dream...at least I thought it was a dream..."

"What do you mean, you were there? Wh...where?...How?" Kane nervously cut across his younger and significantly smaller brother. His mind was racing and riddled with questions.

"Crooked House, I was there...but it was different this time. The monsters...they weren't there, or at least I don't think they were. I was in room 2 and saw her...the woman in the photo. She's a witch...I'm sure of it! She's an evil witch...There was a man there too...at the window. He was dressed in black and wearing a hood. He kept staring at me with these crazy eyes. Then the witch set everything on fire....she said we're all going to burn in hell!"

"I knew it wouldn't last. What do you think caused it? The dream I mean..." Kane's stomach sank at the prospect of a new monster to contend with.

"It wasn't a dream! I was there, I could feel and smell everything, and when I woke up I was covered in dirt and ash...she locked me in the room and set fire to it!"

"Did she hurt you?" Zach began tearing up as he listened and placed a comforting hand on Meridia's elbow. Quickly retracting it when he realized everyone else might be staring at him.

"She didn't, but she wanted to. She said we're all going to burn in hell..." an uncomfortable hush befell the group as this new development sunk in.

No new incidents had occurred since that fateful weekend, but Meridia's news instantly transported them back to that harrowing day.

"We need to speak to Peter at lunch," Izzy broke the spell of silence as she tightened the hairband that was keeping her mousy brown ponytail in check. "Maybe he can make sense of it all."

"I wrote as much detail as I could remember, so I'll explain it all then. Something bad is coming though, I can feel it."

JJ's mouth twitched as if he was going to chime in, but all he did was let out a muffled sigh. His big hazel eyes diverted to the ground as he retracted back into the safety of his shell. Often regarded as St Swithun's answer to the Fresh Prince, JJ had been a shadow of his former self lately and his usual buoyant sense of humour had all but deserted him.

"I know mate." Kane draped an arm over JJ's shoulder whilst tucking his shaggy chocolate-brown fringe deeper inside his hood so as not to ruin his perm.

"We're going to get through this, I promise. Peter will know what to do."

The school bell loudly interrupted their solum moment of reflection.

A few muted cheers came from the budding footballers who'd won their one-sided match for the umpteenth time. Clusters of children of all shapes and sizes responded like robots and congregated around the myriad of doors leading into the school, whilst heavily outnumbered teachers tried their best to mould the rowdier ones into orderly lines.

A customary wave of laughter and whispery gossip swept across the crowds as Kane led the group to their favoured entrance via the library. It had always been the least popular option because it passed by the headmaster's office, but these days, it spared them any direct confrontation.

Scarytales was a laughingstock since its last video had flirted with controversy. Eventually deemed an ill-conceived prank, the group had all been branded freaks or geeks, depending on their level of involvement.

For the first week, Kane had often longed for the ground to swallow him up; something Meridia took great offence to, for some unbeknown reason. When his parents didn't agree with his numerous pleas to move house, he'd resigned himself to his new existence on the outer limb of school-life. The rest of the group suffered a similar fate by association. Despite how trivial it all seemed in the grand scheme of things; Kane still struggled with his newfound exile from time to time.

"Can't be an influencer if there's nobody alive to influence," he thought to himself as they all skulked through the large glossy blue door.

3

"And that's all we have time for today, guys." Peter concluded, as he sat perched on the edge of his desk. Running his hands through his dirty-blond hair, he closed his eyes in contemplation after another enthralling debate about the second world war.

A frenzy of shuffling papers followed as his students all clambered to vacate the classroom and secure a good seat in the school cafeteria.

Peter was now a fortnight into his new position as guest lecturer at St Swithun's and was relishing every minute. It wasn't every day a famous author moved to the sticks to teach lower 6th history, so his arrival had caused quite a stir. He still couldn't believe his luck when the opportunity landed in his lap, it was the perfect setup. His income comfortably covered the costs of the modest house he was now renting on the edge of town, whilst his teaching schedule allowed him to stay close to Kane and the rest of the group, without arousing any suspicion.

Every lunchtime, they assembled under the guise of a 'special research project' and spent a solid hour using the school's resources to find out all they could about Crooked House and its mysterious inhabitants.

Peter gently rolled off his desk and onto his feet, then casually strolled back to his chair and started riffling through his bag. He looked more like a stereotypical drama or PE teacher with his tall athletic frame and chiselled movie star good looks.

"Hey!" Izzy did her best to sound upbeat as she entered the classroom. Since she was in a different maths group, she was the first one to arrive, ahead of Zach and Meridia.

Peter remained buried in his bag with his back to the door, "Hi Izzy, how are you today? Feeling any better?"

Izzy had been struggling with the lack of progress they'd made recently and was pretty flustered when she'd left their previous session.

"I'm ok thanks. I think I just needed a good night's sleep."

"Don't we all dear."

"Hey!" JJ entered next, with Kane in tow.

They joined Izzy at the nearest desk whilst Peter finally turned around holding a black lever arch folder.

"Good afternoon chaps."

Both boys grunted in response as they began hungrily tucking into their sandwiches. Meridia and Zach completed the group when they arrived and immediately dictated the agenda.

"We need to talk, Peter," exclaimed Meridia as she pulled up a chair closest to the front of the classroom. "I was there last night...at Crooked House. I met the woman in room 2."

A frown gathered on Peter's brow as he placed his folder back down on the desk next to him and gave her his full attention.

"Why don't you start from the beginning in that case dear and I'll just grab my notebook."

Meridia pulled her own journal out of her schoolbag, stood up, and told everyone about her terrifying encounter. A wall of open-mouthed faces, all frozen in shock, greeted her detailed account.

SNAP!

Meridia snapped her fingers to wake them from their trance.

"I'm done now guys..." she announced.

Peter wasted no time jumping in with his thoughts on what she had shared, "Thank you for revisiting what must have been quite an ordeal. That was incredibly brave. If it's accurate, this is the most information we've ever had about the guest in room 2, providing us with a fresh perspective. Based on your description, and what we already know, I would say it places her in the early 1700s. If we work on the assumption, she was indeed a witch, then we are looking at no later than 1727, which was around when the last of the witch trials ended. We know Crooked House was originally built at the beginning of that century, which means it's highly likely the guest in room 1 dates back to a similar time."

"How do we know that?" Kane asked.

"Because all the other guests appear to run in chronological order, with Zach being the last and most recent addition in room 10. It's therefore safe to assume the guest in room 1 was the very first soul acquired and this witch, or whatever she is, followed shortly after."

"Are there any records of the witches during those trials?" asked Izzy enthusiastically.

"Sadly not, I'm afraid. A great deal of the records from

that period were lost, and even if they weren't we'd struggle without at least a partial name."

"What about the boy she mentioned? It sounds like she may have done something terrible. Would that be on record?"

"That's great thinking Izzy, and may well yield something. Again, we'd be relying on whatever records were available, but it's certainly worth a visit to Cold Christmas. There's a quaint little museum in the village that I stumbled upon back in '09 when I had my first brush with Crooked House. They have a modest archive which could provide us with some answers."

"When can we go?" Zach was eager to identify their latest adversary.

"It's probably best I go alone at this stage. I'm free of lessons tomorrow afternoon so I can set off after our meeting and report back on Friday. I'll just tell the museum I'm doing research for my latest book and then soften them up with a credit when it's published."

"What about the man in the hood? Any ideas who he could be?"

"Impossible to say at this point, dear. He doesn't fit the description of any other guests we've seen so far, and you said he looked human. I'm fascinated by the way you were able to tell he wasn't a threat, and that he was more an observer. What gave you that impression?"

"It's hard to explain...it was just a feeling I had at the time. Even when I couldn't see him, I could feel him watching me from the shadows. It was more like he was hiding from me."

"And you're sure you didn't see any of the creatures?"

"No, they weren't there. I couldn't see or feel them anywhere."

The creatures' absence made everyone uneasy. Their working theory was they were plotting something big and perhaps this was the start of it.

Peter massaged his chin for a moment, deep in contemplation, and then rose to his feet.

"I'm still not entirely sure what a 'seer' is, Meridia. So far, my research has taken me on a merry goose chase, but something clearly triggered your gift again last night the same way Jessica did. We must assume you are in real danger when you enter these states, but for now, let's just be thankful you made your own way back safely this time. If you're willing, I'd like to arrange a sleep observation here at some point in the future?"

"Of course, if you think that would help?"

"It can't hurt, that's for sure. The more we can understand about your condition, the better equipped we'll be to help you cope with it. I'll have a chat with the head and see what I can arrange. I don't want to scare you, but I don't think you should be alone tonight M. Is there any chance you can arrange a last-minute sleep over with Izzy? I know it's a school night, but I think it would be wise until we know more about what's going on."

"My dad is in London this week, so I'm sure my mum will be fine with you coming over."

"Thank you Izzy. Meridia, see what you can do. You all have my number if you need me."

With that, the bell sounded for the end of lunch.

"I'll see you all tomorrow. Stay safe guys...please. You all know where I am if you need me."

As the group dispersed, Peter waved a finger in the air, signalling for JJ to hang back so he could have a quiet word.

"I'll catch you up in a minute, mate," JJ gestured at Kane to go on without him.

"I'm worried about you JJ. You're increasingly quiet and withdrawn. Is anything else going on you want to talk about?"

"I'm fine. Just tired, and the fact we're all living on edge is doing my head in. I'll snap out of it."

"The others need you, JJ. We all do. My door is always open if you ever want to chat...about anything. Ok?"

"Thanks Mr Higginsworth."

Peter looked at the door and saw a few pupils from his next class loitering, unsure if they could enter. He patted JJ on the shoulder and waved them in.

4

THE RAIN HAD EASED BY THE TIME THE LAST BELL rang, but its earthy aroma remained ever-present.

After battling their way through the stampede of pupils vying to be first out of the gate, a wave of serenity washed over them all. St Swithun's Road glistened beneath a lingering veneer of drizzle, as cars ferrying children did their best to avoid puddles collecting in the gutters.

"You do know it's not your fault, JJ. None of this is anybody's fault. I mean it. You've got to let it go."

As much as JJ knew Kane was right, something was still holding him back. He was getting cabin fever from being trapped in his own thoughts for so long, but no matter what he tried, he couldn't break free of the hold Crooked House had over him.

"I hear you. I just wish I'd never found that bloody article online...none of this would've happened if it wasn't for me."

"I thought that too for a while. I was the one pushing for a big break, remember? Now look at us. Sodding outcasts, the lot of us! Looking over our shoulder all the time. Skulking around school trying not to make eye contact with anyone...and don't even get me started on Zach. I even brought him and his mates into this nightmare..."

"But still, if I hadn't shown you that article..."

"Stop mate, just stop. These things were always going to find us. If Peter's right, then they've been planning this for hundreds of years, maybe longer. And they're still coming for us, according to Meridia. Sounds like they've even got a witch on the case now...what's next? Flying monkeys?!"

"Maybe we should head over there with a bucket of water and end this thing right now," JJ quipped with a wry smile.

"There you are!" Kane beamed and jumped on JJ's back in celebration. "You can't let this thing beat you. I miss you, man."

JJ felt himself tearing up and pulled his cap down a little to hide his face.

Kane acknowledged the moment with a gentle shoulder barge. "It's going to be ok. We've already stopped them once. We can do it again."

"I hope so, mate. I just want to get on with life, you know?"

As they reached Kane's gate, it was time to go their separate ways for the day.

"Are you sure you don't want to come in for a bit? Watch a movie or play some Xbox?"

"Maybe tomorrow, yeah?" JJ and Kane had repeated the same patter for the last four weeks, but this was the first time JJ had offered a ray of hope to his best friend. The breakthrough wasn't lost on Kane and left him grinning like a Cheshire cat.

"That works for me," he replied, trying his best not to add any pressure. "C'mon Zach, we haven't got all day."

They both waited for Zach, Meridia and Izzy to catch them up as they said one more goodbye.

JJ then carried on with his daily duty of escorting the girls the rest of the way home.

5

"Thanks for walking us back, James." Izzy and JJ were standing outside the Wilson's house, waiting patiently for Meridia to pack an overnight bag.

"No worries. You're on the way to mine, anyway."

"Kane's right, you know. None of this is anyone's fault. Nobody is to blame for anything that's happened," said Izzy.

"I know. I just wish we could all go back to how things were before, you know?" JJ avoided making eye contact with Izzy as he answered. He did that a lot these days.

Izzy was familiar with the trait, as her dad would do the same whenever he was trying to protect her from something. She figured JJ just needed more time to heal, so she didn't press.

"Sorry guys." Meridia's return interrupted the expanding silence, stopping it from becoming awkward. "I couldn't find my PE kit for tomorrow." She rolled her big blue eyes in feigned exasperation as she barged through the wooden gate at the end of her front garden. She was carrying far too many bags for a single sleepover, but luckily they didn't have far to walk to Izzy's house.

"Let me take that," JJ did the gentlemanly thing and grabbed the large blue rucksack Meridia was dragging along the ground behind her.

Izzy closed the latch on the gate and waved goodbye to Mrs Wilson at the window.

In the reflection, she noticed a van race past and the sudden flash of white revealed a man standing on the other side of the street looking out at them. His abrupt appearance was jarring at first, as Izzy hadn't noticed anyone else there a moment ago. Keeping her back to him, she used the window to get a better look before alerting the others.

He was an elderly man, dressed in a navy waterproof jacket and tweed flat cap which covered his white hair. There was a small portable shopping trolley by his side, and he looked perfectly ordinary at first glance, like any other pensioner waiting for a bus into town. However, his expression told a very different story; his gaunt, cadaverous skin was contorted, teeming with acrimony and malice. Scowling, deep-sunken eyes glared at Izzy unblinking, boring a hole into her reflection. It was a look of pure hatred, as if he was teetering on the brink of violence.

"Guys..." Izzy whispered from the corner of her mouth, trying her best to get JJ's or Meridia's attention. "Guys... look".

They were both too busy joking about the weight of Meridia's rucksack and oblivious of Izzy, who was now locked in a spine-chilling staring contest with the ominous reflection.

The old man's menace intensified as he slowly raised his right hand and a pale tremoring finger shakily extended, pointing at where the three of them were standing. Baring his teeth to reveal a tobacco-stained yellow snarl, Izzy was certain she heard him growl the word "*you.*"

With a stomach full of dread, Izzy turned around to face her agitator, half expecting to find him right in front of her. Instead, she found him steadily walking away from them, shopping trolley in tow, as if she had imagined the entire thing.

"You ok?" JJ was the first to notice Izzy's face.

She looked panicked and confusion by the old man waddling away from them on the opposite side of the road.

"He...that old man...he was staring right at me. I could see his reflection. He just kept staring...he looked so evil... and angry." Izzy glanced nervously back at the window in case the old man's reflection was still there.

"Who, Mr Richards?! He's a sweet little old man who lives around the corner. I can't imagine him saying boo to a goose." Meridia sounded surprised.

"But he looked furious with me...or us...I couldn't quite tell. I'm serious. He looked like he was about to charge over here."

The three of them watched on as Mr Richards nonchalantly dragged his shopping trolley around the corner without so much as a glance back.

"I believe you...with everything that's happened, I believe anything these days. Whatever it was, it's getting dark now, so let's get you both back to Izzy's. It's been a long day, and we can pick this up again when we see Peter tomorrow." JJ set off, hoping the girls would follow.

Izzy knew very well what she'd seen, but JJ was right, it was getting dark.

The best thing they could all do now was go home.

6

Meridia had been to Izzy's house countless times since they'd known each other, but the sheer size of it was never lost on her.

The guest room was not only three times bigger than her boxroom, but it also had an ensuite bathroom with a huge walk-in shower. It always felt like a night away in a luxury hotel whenever she stayed, although today she wished it were under better circumstances.

So far, the group had kept the mounting pressure hidden from their parents, but tonight, both girls were visibly on edge.

Izzy's strange and unprovoked encounter with Mr Richards had really gotten under her skin, whilst all Meridia could think about was how much she was dreading going to sleep that night. Having bolted their food at dinner, they opted to head upstairs and get on with their homework before getting an early night. Mrs Di Salvo relaxed downstairs watching TV, blissfully unaware of the stakes involved in tonight's assignment.

"All settled in?" Izzy asked as she peered around the guest room door.

Meridia had just plugged her nightlight in next to the bed. Despite her best efforts, her marshmallow duvet wouldn't fit in her rucksack.

"All set," she replied in a jaded tone. JJ was right, it had been a long day and Meridia's sleep deprivation was finally taking its toll.

Izzy wandered into the room, dragging an inflatable mattress behind her.

"I won't be of much use if I'm in the next room, will I? Hope you don't mind."

"Of course not, I was hoping you'd offer."

"Great! Can you help with my pillow and duvet in that case?"

Once they had finished setting up Izzy's bed for the night, they both settled down to talk through the day's events.

"So, what do you know about Mr Richards?"

"My mum knows him. His name is Albert, I think, or Alfred...I can't quite remember. His wife is really sick in the hospital. She's been there for a couple of years, apparently. I think her name is Valerie. She had a stroke one night, and she's been in a coma ever since. It's really sad, as my mum said they've been together since they were teenagers."

"I still don't understand what happened earlier. One minute the road was empty, and the next he was there, staring at me like a crazy person."

"That's what I don't get. He's always been sweet and polite whenever I've bumped into him. My mum says he gets the bus to the hospital every day to visit his wife. I didn't even notice him standing there when I first came out."

"I didn't see him at all when I was talking to James. It must be connected to what's going on, I just don't understand how or why..."

"We can talk to Peter at school tomorrow and see what he makes of it. That's assuming I wake up in the morning." Meridia's words were starting to slur from sheer exhaustion, but her morbid half-joke riled Izzy.

"Don't say that, I'm going to be right here with you. The first sign of any trouble and I'll wake you up, I promise."

As Meridia smiled at Izzy's concern, her eyes softly closed, and she finally succumbed to tiredness. Somewhere in the distance she heard Izzy's voice fade into a comfortable drone, and then dissolve, as she curled up into the fetal position and drifted off to sleep.

THE NEXT SOUND Meridia heard in her slumber was a slow rhythmic clacking of wood striking wood.

"Izzy, what's that noise?" Meridia mumbled as she pulled her covers up around her ears. "Izzy?"

No answer came except for the increasingly annoying sound which was now reverberating around the room.

Pulling the covers down, Meridia tentatively opened her eyes, expecting her nightlight's glare.

Nothing. She was in total darkness.

Crisp, cold air greeted her nose and cheeks as she emerged from the warmth of her duvet in search of something familiar she could anchor herself to. Meridia's heart sank like a lead weight as she realized the darkness encompassing her belonged to Crooked House.

"Not again," she whispered, sitting up to take in her new surroundings.

The darkness seemed impenetrable as Meridia strained and squinted her eyes to make sense of anything to help find her bearings. She could feel the air nipping at her face and ears now, whilst the smell of old burnt wood clogged her lungs.

A light breeze brushed against her right ear. It was warmer than the brisk night air and carried a rancid smell which stung Meridia's nostrils.

"Welcome home little one," came the crackling voice.

Meridia's eardrum vibrated, and she flinched away in a knee-jerk response.

The witch was there with her, hiding in the blackness, and she was close.

"Get away from me!" Meridia screamed as she leapt off the bed and stumbled over something solid and sharp beside her.

A shooting pain surged from her knee, flooding the nerve endings in her shin as she limped back to her feet, fumbling for something to steady herself on.

"Boo," the witch whispered in Meridia's other ear, sending her tumbling over in the opposite direction.

Sprawled on the floor, Meridia froze and held her breath as she tried desperately to see where the voice was coming from. The relentless clanking noise continued to rattle around the room like children chanting in a playground fight.

"There's no escape Meridia."

This time, the voice came from overhead. Meridia frantically scampered across the ground on all fours in an attempt to flee her tormentor.

Thud!

She crashed headfirst into a wall. Searing pain rippled

from the top of her skull to the base of her neck, and she let out a pitiful whimper.

"Why are you doing this?" Meridia cried, her head throbbing and eyes overflowing with tears.

Reaching out into the dark, she sensed the presence of the wall she had just collided with and sat with her back to it. The flat smooth surface was ice-cold to the touch, just like the stoney ground beneath her.

Still the clanking circled and swirled around her like a sneering tornado.

"*No one is coming to save you Meridia,*" came the harsh, rasping voice.

Meridia closed her eyes tight, her mind racing to find a way out of the nightmare she was trapped in. She had to wake up and fast. Her thoughts raced towards Peter and his offer of help earlier that day. He would know what to do. The throbbing in her head intensified, as did the unknown clattering in the room as if they were tuning into each other.

"Help me!" she screamed. Her voice was close to breaking under the weight of despair.

A surge of warm air swept over Meridia, and the room fell silent. All she could hear was her own breathing in the darkness. The clanking had subsided, and the witch was quiet.

"Hello?" A man's voice was coming from outside the room; its muffled tone sounded familiar.

"Peter?" Meridia tried to figure out what direction the voice was coming from. "Peter, is that you?"

A thin crack of light emerged to her left. It slowly expanded, illuminating the room as a door gently opened.

"Meridia!" Peter burst into the room and helped her to her feet. "You're hurt. What happened? Where are we?"

A thin trickle of blood slinked its way down Meridia's

forehead, and she felt a sudden head-rush as she stood, causing her legs to wobble.

"Easy there. You've taken quite a bash to the head."

"The witch, she's here...is...is this a dream? How did you get here?"

"I don't know. The last thing I remember was sitting in my chair reading student essays on the battle of Hastings... the next thing I'm sitting in the hallway of this place. This must be a dream."

BANG!

The door behind them slammed shut and the fireplace next to it erupted, painting the room bright amber.

Meridia wilted under the sudden rush of heat as it engulfed the room, and she snatched at Peter's arm to stay on her feet. Heart racing, the newfound warmth only amplified the chill she felt when she heard the crackly voice echo behind her.

"*Welcome back Peter.*" The witch was floating gracelessly in the room's corner, as if she was gripped by some kind of seizure. Her scrawny arms were gnarled and twisted, flailing wildly above her like branches in the wind, whilst her head violently snapped back and forth with each venomous word she spat, "*Tonight you die...Tonight, you burn in hell!*"

Peter instinctively shielded Meridia from the witch's view and scanned the room for a weapon. The fire was raging now and seemed to ebb and flow with the witch's movements as if she was its conductor. Beside the old brick fireplace was a rack of rusted pokers.

"Who are you?" Peter probed as he edged his way closer to the fire. "What do you want with us?"

The witch's jaw unhinged, and her mouth widened as she broke into a chilling cackle, which filled the room. Like a floating corpse, she moved to within touching distance and loomed over Peter.

He balked at the stench of her breath as she whispered, "*I want your soul.*"

Peter's hand wrapped around the handle of the nearest poker, and he lashed out at the witch's head. The blow connected flush with her bony cheek, sending her head reeling in the opposite direction with an emphatic *crack*.

"Run Meridia! Get out now!" But fear had already taken hold of her and Meridia stayed firmly rooted to the spot.

The witch's head continued to turn away from Peter's gaze. A sickening crackle of bone grinding against bone accompanied each jerk until her neck wrenched a full 360 degrees to face him again. A gruesome tendril of waxen skin amassed under her jawbone, as if she was made from elastic.

Meridia watched on in horror as the witch, locked in a death stare with Peter, then twisted her entire body to untangle herself.

"*Wakey, wakey,*" she barked at Meridia whilst firmly clasping Peter by the shoulders.

The witch hoisted him off the ground with supernatural strength, sending the poker clattering to the ground.

"Meridia!" he cried, as his face twisted in anguish.

As he opened his mouth to call out again, the witch pulled him closer, pressing her withered lips tight against his. Peter's eyes opened wide in shock as he frantically tried to wriggle loose from her grasp, but as he pulled himself away, something grotesque and slimy remained connected, tying them together at the mouth.

At first glance, Meridia thought it was the witch's blackened tongue, but as Peter twisted his head further away, she could see it was something far worse.

The snake-like creature, covered in gloopy white mucus, was working its way deeper into his mouth, filling his throat. Within a matter of seconds, the tail left the witch's mouth, lashing and whipping against Peter's chin until it disappeared completely between his lips.

An ungodly laugh echoed throughout the room as the witch celebrated her victory, whilst Peter retched and gagged to regurgitate whatever abomination he had just swallowed.

"Meridiaaaaa....." his voice began to drag and slur as time slowed.

The fire's flames burned murky red, and a thick black smoke filled the room, engulfing everyone.

Meridia felt the ground beneath her begin to melt, slowly devouring her like quicksand.

"PETER!" she cried out in desperation, but the more she struggled, the faster she sank.

All she could do was watch helplessly as Peter writhed in pain whilst trying desperately to break free from the evil witch. Darker and darker, the room faded into nothing as Peter's sluggish calls for help dropped to a lowly whisper and then disappeared completely.

"Meeeridiaaaa....Meridiaaaa....Meridia! Wake up!" It was no longer Peter she could hear calling to her, the voice was Izzy's.

Meridia noticed a persistent tugging at her shoulder, nagging her out of her slumber.

"Meridia, wake up! Your head's bleeding."

7

By the time Meridia and Izzy reached St Swithun's playground on Thursday morning they were both soaking wet and gasping for breath.

Exhausted, and with her head still pounding from her latest visit to Crooked House, Meridia tried to call Peter one more time as they entered the school grounds.

"Voicemail again," she puffed. "What are we going to do, Izz?"

"Maybe he's just in a staff meeting...or prepping for class?" Izzy countered, trying her best to pacify her, but the alarm bell sounding in Meridia's head continued to grow louder and louder.

The previous night was so much more than a dream, and she had the gash on her head to prove it. She knew in her gut Peter was in some kind of trouble, and it was all her fault.

Once again, Zach was the first to react upon seeing the girls amble past the gate.

"Something's wrong again, guys. Look!" He alerted Kane and JJ before abruptly fleeing the anonymity of the 'losers bench' and hightailing it across the ongoing football match to greet them.

"Streaker," came the immediate response from Jacob Alman, the most popular boy at St Swithun's. He was a gifted footballer for his age, and painfully handsome. With his poster-boy good looks and immaculately groomed blonde undercut, he had the attention of most of his peers. Looking every inch the small-town big deal as he stood in the pouring rain with his foot firmly on the ball he smirked at his audience, prompting a chorus of spurious giggles from the group of girls on the side-line as they all competed for his attention.

Zach, however, remained oblivious, refusing to be caught up in the tedious spotlight of high school politics and popularity contests. His only concern was Meridia, and judging by the look of anguish she was carrying, he knew something bad had happened.

As Zach jumped over the make-shift goalpost made up from a mountain of school bags, he felt a ball whistle past his ear and clatter into the wire fence ahead. Another round of giggles erupted from behind him, accompanied by a few oohs and aahs.

"Piss off, Alman!" Kane had caught up with his brother and began remonstrating on his behalf.

"Whatever weirdo. Why don't you go back to your bench with the rest of your little freaks before you get hurt."

As tempting as it was for Kane to walk over and square up to Alman, a boy he dwarfed in stature, he sensed he had more urgent matters to tend to with Meridia. Before he could make up his mind completely, he felt JJ's arm around his shoulder, gently steering him back towards the group, and the blood that had started bubbling in his veins swiftly reduced to a simmer.

Kane took a deep breath and turned his attention to Meridia, trying his best to ignore the encore of laughter and jeers coming from Alman and his cronies.

"What's wrong?" he asked, "And what happened to your head?"

"It's Peter...have any of you seen Peter yet?" Still struggling to catch her breath, Meridia's eyes were wide with worry.

"Not yet. Why? What's happened?"

"I keep...I keep trying to call him, but...he's not answering. I think...I think he's in trouble...I think the witch has got him." Kane paused for a moment to let Meridia's rambling sink in.

It was no wonder they had all been labelled freaks given what he'd just heard. Alman didn't know the half of it, and thank God he didn't. Yet despite how far-fetched Meridia sounded, Kane had seen how powerful her visions were. If it wasn't for her gift, they would all be dead, Alman included.

"JJ, we've got eight minutes before the bell goes. Call Peter now while I think." JJ responded and circled the group with his phone to his ear.

"Nothing. It rang out to his voicemail." Now it was Kane's turn to pace, as he knew the chances of Peter ignoring all of them, particularly after yesterday's events, would be slim to none.

Something was definitely wrong.

"Meridia, how certain are you he's in trouble? On a scale of one to ten."

Meridia glanced at the ground for a moment as she pondered Kane's question.

"Nine!" she stated with authority. If she wanted to fully utilize her newfound gift, she needed to start trusting it.

"Ok, so I have the spare key to Peter's rental, the one he gave us in case of an emergency. When the bell rings, I need you guys to go in as usual and see if he's in school. I think his tutor group is 10F..."

"It's 10E." Izzy corrected.

"Thanks Izz. So, you guys head in and I'll start making my way over to his place. If you see Peter in the meantime and everything's cool, then just text me and I'll come straight back here. I'll just say I had a dentist appointment or something."

"Shouldn't we all go? In case something bad has happened..." Zach challenged.

"It'll be too suspicious if we all go. Besides, we need someone to make sure he's not just forgotten his phone or been pulled into a meeting or something. I'll go. I can be there in fifteen minutes, and if anything's wrong, I'll call."

Kane's reasoning was sound given what they knew, which was very little.

"Everything will be fine, guys. I'll just slip out when the bell rings."

The group agreed and when the bell sounded, Kane discreetly backed away from the playground and disappeared through the gate. In the hubbub of pupils making their way to the school doors, nobody was any the wiser.

All that was except for Alman.

8

When Kane arrived at Peter's house, everything appeared normal.

A plain two-up, two-down house marked the end of the terrace, unremarkable in appearance. The house had a bland, grey, pebble-dashed rendering and a nondescript frosted glass door. A tiny front garden framed them, leaving just enough room to store two large plastic rubbish bins.

However, it was the location which appealed most to Peter, and he'd converted the second bedroom into a provisional study where he could keep tabs on the camera streams at Crooked House.

Kane checked his phone one more time before opening the gate.

According to JJ, nobody had seen or heard from Peter since he left school the day before. Satisfied there was no further update, Kane rang the doorbell and waited.

After a few moments of silence, he cupped his face to the frosted glass in order to see inside. When that yielded nothing, he considered looking through the letterbox and then stopped himself.

The last thing he needed was a nosy neighbour calling the police.

"Be cool Kane. Just open the door and walk in. Nothing to see here," he whispered to himself as he fumbled around in his pocket for his keys.

Kane turned the lock and nervously entered.

"Peter? Peter? It's me, Kane." he called up the stairs in case this had all been a huge misunderstanding.

The house remained silent, and a sense of dread washed over Kane, forcing him to venture further inside.

If Meridia was right, then who knew what he might discover in here. More to the point, who knew what might find him.

He figured the best place to start was upstairs and then work his way back down. If something bad had happened, then it would have been more likely to occur during the night when Meridia was asleep and dreaming.

Tiptoeing up the narrow, beige carpeted staircase, Kane paused when he heard a floorboard *creak* above him.

The unexpected sound rendered him dry-mouthed and teetering precariously on the edge of the fourth step as Meridia's words came flooding back to him, *'the witch has got him'*.

Whoever he'd heard upstairs, he was sure it wasn't Peter, and they had the higher ground. Kane stood rooted to the spot as he weighed up his options.

Another *creak* sounded above him, this time louder, closer.

There was no doubt in his mind now, someone or something else was in there with him.

"I'm calling the police!" Kane shouted up the stairs.

He wasn't even sure where the words had come from. It was a stupid bluff, but one he had committed himself to.

"Police please...yes, I'd like to report an intruder. My name is Peter...Peter Higginsworth... 67 Willow Road..." before Kane could finish, he heard a scrambling clatter upstairs followed by a dull *thud* in the front garden behind him.

On the other side of the opaque street door stood a tall, dark figure. If Kane hadn't known better, he'd have sworn they were wearing a cloak of some kind.

The brown shadowy mass lingered for a moment, staring Kane down, before pressing both hands against the glass in protest and then running off into the distance.

With his heart now firmly in his mouth, Kane turned and galloped up the remaining stairs.

"Peter?! Peter!"

9

Meridia stared blankly at Mr Seth's whiteboard.

The equations he'd scribbled in marker looked like gibberish at the best of times, but today they seemed completely illegible. Maths was not Meridia's strong subject, and on this of all days, she could have used a more enjoyable distraction.

Her battered and bruised head was yet to stop throbbing, and the weight of her eyelids kept threatening to pull her face-down onto the desk in front of her. The drone of her teacher's monotonous voice gently lulled her to sleep as he wittered on about abstract algebra and the value of x.

"Am I boring you, Ms Wilson?"

Meridia snapped to and felt her cheeks flush with embarrassment as the rest of her classmates burst out laughing.

"Sorry sir...my head hurts. I think I might need to see the nurse."

"The nurse can't help you, Ms Wilson...Nobody can." Mr Seth's voice was suddenly cutting, carrying with it a spiteful undertone which brought Meridia out of her trance.

Theatrical canned laughter erupted, echoing around her in the stark classroom, but as she surveyed the horde of children facing her, she found them all tight-lipped, eyes-closed, and emotionless, as if they were in a trance of their own.

Disorientated by the macabre histrionics, Meridia grappled with her thoughts as she tried to regain her composure.

The oppressive laughter continued its assault, ferociously bellowing at her from all angles and reigniting her pounding head. Just as the pain bordered on excruciating, the bedlam subsided, and her classmates abruptly opened their eyes in unison.

A sea of raven orbs sparkled under the fluorescent lighting, all encased by the ashen, lifeless faces of her peers.

"*We're watching you Meridia,*" their voices were as one, reverberating in Meridia's ears as she frantically searched the room for Mr Seth.

She found him to her left, bent at the knees with his bloated face in hers.

His eyes were white, as if rolled back in their sockets, and running alive with dark threadlike veins. He looked more like a corpse, with blanched skin that sagged around his gaping mouth. A waft of putrid breath filtered out from between his tawny decaying teeth as he barked,

"*There is no escape from me, seer! Not for you, and not for your precious Peter. You will all burn in hell!*"

Meridia tried to stand, but she found herself glued to her chair, unable to move.

Mr Seth jerked and twitched as he gawkily lumbered even closer. A contorted smile etched its way across his gruesome face as he took his twisted pleasure from the fear he was forging in Meridia's eyes.

"You will all burn in hell..." he whispered, and with that, vibrant flames of purple and lilac sprouted from the ground, engulfing the classmates that surrounded her.

The blistering heat melted them like wax, exposing flesh and bone as their blood-soaked faces cried out in pain and begged for mercy.

Meridia screamed with them, a desperate scream, distraught at the torturous atrocity searing her tearful eyes.

Revelling in his dark and deadly work, Mr Seth cackled over her in victory whilst the surrounding fire steadily flickered and flamed, painting the washed-out classroom deep magenta.

"Stop!" Meridia screeched, "Let me go!" but the maniacal laughter continued unremittingly.

As she wrestled to break free from her chair, Meridia felt something softy land on her head. She fearfully looked up at her tormentor and immediately gagged.

Within his cavernous mouth, she could see something wet and slimy crawling inside.

Long brown antennas emerged, slowly followed by the shiny dome of a cockroach as its prickly forelegs pushed its bulbous body all the way out of Mr Seth's mouth and onto his cheek. Scuttling around his corpse-like face, the vile insect was swiftly joined by another, and then another, until a steady swarm of them leaked out of her deranged maths teacher and bled onto the desk she was trapped beneath.

With nowhere else to go, the relentless stream of invasive cockroaches scampered and clambered all over her, tangling in her thick, wavy red hair and slinking down the back of her neck as they burrowed their way under her jumper.

Meridia screamed, a hysterical, blood-curdling scream, as she convulsed in her seat and frantically yanked at her hair. Wave upon wave of fresh cockroaches piled on top of her, tickling the crevices of her ears and creeping towards her lips as they tirelessly searched for a way in.

Suddenly, she felt someone shaking her by her shoulder.

"Meridia! What's wrong?" she opened her eyes and Emma Jenkins, her partner in maths, was staring at her fraught with worry.

Meridia looked around, and the entire classroom had her under its microscope, rubbernecking as if she'd just beamed down from Mars. Mr Seth was standing at his whiteboard, slack jawed, without a single cockroach in sight.

"Ms Wilson, please excuse yourself."

"But..."

"Get out Ms Wilson. You can do your explaining to the headmaster."

10

Kane reached for the banister as he climbed the top step and used it to launch himself towards Peter's study.

When he entered, he could see someone had ransacked the room, scattering school papers and numerous historical books all over the dusty-grey coloured carpet.

Peter was sitting at his desk, slumped over his keyboard and motionless.

Stopping in his tracks, Kane felt the blood drain from his face as the room began to swirl and spin around him. Steadying himself on the doorframe, he closed his eyes and counted to ten in the hope he didn't pass out from the shock.

"Snap out of it! Peter needs you." his inner voice cut through the crackling interference buzzing in his head and Kane staggered over to where Peter was sitting.

He hesitated, then touched his slouched back to check his breathing.

"Thank god!" he yelled in relief, although Peter was clearly in a bad way.

"It's ok, I'm going to call for help," he sobbed as he dialed 999 for real this time.

The operator immediately asked Kane to check Peter's airway to ensure there were no obstructions to his breathing. Kane felt his mouth go dry again as he edged around the desk to get a look at Peter's face.

Convincing himself Peter was merely in a deep sleep proved a rookie mistake, and Kane leapt out of his skin when he discovered the disturbing truth.

Peter's glazed eyes were wide open, as was his mouth. The expression carved into his face was sickening. His chiselled jaw was crooked, fixed in a silent scream, as if he'd been scared into a coma by something truly terrifying.

Kane's knees buckled momentarily at the sight of him before the operator cut in, "Mr Jackson? Is there anything obstructing the airway?...Mr Jackson?"

"Err...sorry...I...let me just check. Hold on."

Kane leant in a little closer to establish where Peter's tongue was and found it flaccid, languishing in the bottom of his mouth. Ducking down lower, he looked for signs of anything foreign lodged in his throat. He could hear Peter's rasping breath as he drew closer, but there was nothing obvious limiting his air supply.

"I can't see anything...I can hear him breathing though."

"Ok, that's great. You're doing great, Mr Jackson. The ambulance will be with you very soon. Without disturbing him, can you see any signs of injury?" The operator's voice barely registered with Kane, who couldn't tear his eyes away from Peter's horrifying expression. "Mr Jackson?"

"I...I can't see anything...wait..." Kane noticed the briefest of movement, a subtle flicker in Peter's eye.

At first he thought it was a twitch; another sign of life,

so he waited and watched intently, praying it happened again.

"Peter...can you hear me?"

Peter remained unresponsive. His face was still deranged and frozen in torment whilst his desperate eyes wildly stared out into space.

Kane continued to switch his attention from the left-to-right eye and then he noticed it again. The sight of it sent him reeling backwards in terror, colliding with the bookcase behind him as he wrestled with the scream that was now threatening to tear its way up through his vocal cords.

Within the white of Peter's eye was a shadow, swimming erratically as if trapped behind the sclera and trying to break free.

Kane watched on in horror, mesmerized by the disturbing spectacle, as the snake-like creature slithered and pushed against Peter's eyeball the way a goldfish tests the boundaries of its bowl.

"Mr Jackson? Is everything ok?"

Kane's trance was broken by a banging at the front door.

Glancing out the window, he could see the bright yellow roof of an ambulance parked directly beneath him. After pausing for a moment, he turned back to look into Peter's eyes and saw that whatever had been stirring within him had subsided.

An icy shiver worked its way up Kane's spine as he took one more grief-stricken look at his debilitated friend and then staggered downstairs to let the paramedics in.

II

"It's ok Mr Jackson...we're here now..."

The stranger's voice floated in and out of Peter's consciousness as if he was dreaming. Every muscle in his body ached as he lay paralyzed in the unfamiliar, murky room.

"I just found him like this...I don't know..."

The second voice sounded vaguely familiar, but the fog in Peter's mind felt impenetrable and cloaked its owner.

"It has the hallmarks of a stroke, but we can't say for sure at this point..." the effort it took to understand each word was exhausting and so Peter let the conversation wash over him.

"Aw...poor Peter."

This time, a woman's voice addressed him directly, full of mock-sympathy sailing on a venomous undercurrent. Peter tried to raise his head, but his neck flat-out refused to comply. He felt imprisoned in his own redundant body; a befuddled and bewildered spectator in whatever nightmare he was now stuck in.

"It seems you're going on a journey, my dear Peter... aren't you a lucky boy?"

Flashes of blue light swirled around the room, illuminating a white ceiling riddled with cracked plaster and sporadic patches of dark green mould. The flashing subsided as quickly as it had begun, plunging Peter back into the unknown darkness.

"Don't worry, Peter, it will all be over soon," the woman seductively whispered in his ear. Her voice triggered a tingling sensation, which danced from the tip of his earlobe all the way down his jaw.

"And then you'll be mine."

12

Kane's knee bounced up and down as he anxiously perched on the edge of his seat in Chase Side Hospital's waiting room.

He'd hated hospitals ever since his nan had passed when he was ten, and the smell of disinfectant had instantly transported him back to that dreadful day. It was the first time he'd ever seen his father cry, and for some strange reason, he found that far more difficult to process than the loss of his beloved grandparent.

He'd done his best never to step foot in another hospital since, but here he was, yet again on tenterhooks, with another potentially dire prognosis lurking just around the corner. A stroke carried a grave severity, and based on Peter's condition upon their arrival, Kane wasn't exactly brimming with optimism.

Having answered all the paramedic's questions, he was now relegated to the side-lines whilst the doctors conducted a more thorough examination. His pent-up nervous energy was making him hungry, so he saw what the vending machine had to offer. It was still too early to raid his lunchbox, so he figured a chocolate bar would suffice.

As he bent down to collect his pimple-inducing reward for a torrid morning, a familiar voice rang out behind him, "Darling, what are you doing here? Is everything ok?"

Kane turned to find JJ's mum staring at him, her face laden with worry.

Alice Jordan was a nurse at Chase Side and a sight for sore eyes after the morning he'd had. She was a short, rotund woman in her mid-fifties with light blonde hair that was tied back tightly into a bun. Always immaculately turned out, Alice took great pride in her appearance as she felt it helped reassure her patients.

She'd often say to JJ, 'nobody will trust you to take care of them if you can't take care of yourself.'

Both she and her husband Derrick had conceived JJ far later than they'd hoped and consequently found the age gap tricky to navigate, particularly when JJ was at prep school. These days, they were both heavily focused on their careers, which often involved working long hours.

Kane had always felt torn over their work ethic as he saw the impact it had on JJ, however on the plus side it meant he got to spend more time with his best friend.

"Hey Mrs Jordan. Things aren't great, I'm afraid. It's one of my teachers...they think he might have had a stroke. I was the one who found him."

"Oh, you poor dear. Shall I call your mum to come get you?"

"It's ok thanks. I'm going to wait and see what the doctors say. He doesn't have any family here, so I'm all he's got today...thanks though." Alice gave Kane's elbow a reassuring squeeze.

"He's in the best possible hands, Kane. Let me see what I can find out when I've done my rounds. What's his name?"

"Peter...Peter Higginsworth."

"Oh snap, that gorgeous writer? I'd heard he was staying in town. Leave it with me and I'll see what's happening. Do you want anything to eat, sweetie? I can make you a sandwich if you want?"

"I'm good thanks, I've got my lunch with me in my bag. Just thought I'd top up on some sugar whilst I wait." Kane lethargically waved his chocolate bar for Alice to see before she gave his elbow another squeeze and hurriedly left for the next ward.

Kane checked his phone to find it was 10:28am. It was approaching first break at St Swithun's, which meant JJ would call any minute, so he returned to his chair and devoured his snack whilst he waited. Sure enough, at 10:32am Kane felt his phone vibrate in his pocket.

"Hey mate, I've got you on loudspeaker here. Any news on Peter?"

"Nothing yet. I saw your mum a minute ago, and she said she'd see what she could find out for me. It was horrible guys...his face... he looked like he's seen a ghost. The doctors think he may have suffered a stroke, but they're still running tests. There was someone else there when I arrived though; a man, I think. He bailed out the window the second I entered, but it looked like he'd been searching for something in Peter's study. There were books and papers everywhere."

"Did you see what the guy looked like?" JJ continued as the group spokesperson.

"Nah, I was halfway up the stairs and couldn't see much through the glass in Peter's door. That's not the only thing that happened though, mate. Peter's eyes…first they were wide open, which was freaky enough, but when I looked closer, there was something moving inside of them! I nearly shat my pants when I saw it."

The line went quiet for a moment while Kane's words sank in.

"Have you still got his keys?" Izzy piped up.

"Yeah, I locked up when I left with the paramedics. Why?"

"I don't think the break-in was a coincidence. We should probably go back after school and look around." Izzy was right in her thinking, but her decision to jump straight into hatching a plan grated with Kane, who was still shaken up from the morning's events and worried about Peter.

"I hear you, but I think we should take a beat while we wait to find out how Peter is first. A stroke is serious Izz, and he was in really bad shape when I found him."

"Sorry, I know…I wasn't undermining that. I just remember him reaching for a folder yesterday and then putting it away when Meridia told us all about her dream. What if he found something?"

"That's a pretty big leap Izz, but you're right. I remember seeing him do that too. I meant to ask him about it after, but we just ran out of time." Kane stared at his shoelaces whilst he pondered their options. "Ok, let's aim to meet at Peter's after school. It can't hurt to take a look, and if nothing else, we can make sure the rest of the house is secure while he's in here. I'll let you know if I hear anything in the meantime, ok?"

"Cool. We'll be there unless we hear anything different. Hang in there bro, Peter will pull through."

Kane knew JJ was just being his usual optimistic self,

but when Meridia spoke up and reiterated the sentiment, he almost believed them both.

"Later guys," and with that Kane was alone again in a place he loathed almost as much as Crooked House.

13

It was a little after 2pm when Doctor Chapman emerged from the double doors leading into the hospital waiting room.

He was a tall, thin man, cleanly shaven, with receding grey hair which he kept closely cropped to his scalp. Bushy salt-and-pepper eyebrows protruded over a pair of maroon-framed glasses that were precariously perched on the end of his nose.

Glancing down at his clipboard, he robotically called out, "Mr Jackson?"

Kane felt his legs turn to jelly the moment he heard his name. This was the moment he'd been dreading since arriving. Raising his hand in response, Kane lumbered up from his chair and followed the doctor into a private office.

"Take a seat young man. I hear you've had quite the day."

Kane sat on the edge of the padded blue polyester seat and listened intently as Doctor Chapman continued.

"So, your friend has given us quite the mystery to solve today, but I think we can now rule out the possibility he suffered a stroke. His MRI results show a tiny lesion on the parietal lobe, but we believe this is some kind of infection. Has you friend visited anywhere exotic recently?"

"I'm not sure. Definitely not within the last couple of months, if that helps?" Doctor Chapman nodded and made a note on his clipboard.

"I see. He appears to be suffering from encephalitis, which is doctor-speak for inflammation of the brain. It's common for this condition to trigger seizures, which is why your friend looked the way he did when you found him. Usually, a virus picked up overseas would show up within four to six weeks, so I think we can rule out anything infectious. We've placed him in an induced coma whilst we treat him intravenously to reduce any swelling. I'm hopeful we'll see an improvement over the next twenty-four hours, but I'll be keeping him in the ICU overnight as a precaution. His condition is still critical, but stable. Mr Higginsworth is very lucky you arrived when you did."

Kane breathed a silent sigh of relief, thankful there had been no mention of parasites swimming around in Peter's head, or black magic. Whatever he had, it was treatable at least.

"Can I see him?" Although the prospect of a trip to the ICU filled him with even more dread, Kane didn't want to leave without letting Peter know they were all rooting for him.

"I'm afraid not. Maybe tomorrow if he responds well to treatment. I suggest you go home and get some rest in the meantime. Here's my card and we'll contact you if there's any change in his condition. Alice said she'd look in on him at the end of her shift, too. She tells me you're a friend of her son. Do you have any more questions?"

"If he responds to the medication you're giving him, will he make a full recovery? I mean, will he be as he was?"

"Right now there is every hope of a full recovery, but we're not out of the woods yet. Matters of the brain are always complicated and some things we won't know until he is conscious again."

Doctor Chapman didn't realize just how apt his choice of words had been. They really weren't out of the woods yet, and Peter's condition was just the tip of a terrible iceberg.

Kane followed the doctor back to the waiting area and then left to navigate his way to the exit via a maze of indistinguishable and blandly decorated corridors. When he eventually breathed in the cold, damp air of freedom, he felt a tiny sliver of hope for the first time that day.

He texted JJ the positive news and agreed to meet them all at Peter's house straight after school. Kane figured if he headed there now, he'd get a half-hour head-start on the others and hopefully uncover some clues as to what the mysterious home invader had been looking for.

14

"*His vitals have stabilized...where's the boy?*" the elusive voice flickered its way into Peter's mind, darting in and out of his consciousness.

"*He's gone now...back to the house, I think.*" Confused by the cryptic thread he was pulling on, he felt what little energy he had diminish once again.

"*Good...*" The conversation faded away into the void, like the remnants of a dream, and Peter succumbed to exhaustion.

A violent stabbing pain woke him from his lull, like a hot needle poking and prodding inside his abdomen.

"*How much time had passed?*" he thought, "*Minutes? Hours? Days?*"

Punch-drunk and unable to move so much as an inch, Peter suffered in silence as the pain intensified, swelling within his gut and clawing at his chest. He tried with all his might to scream, to call for help, but still his body refused him.

"*I'll not deny you, Peter,*" came the woman's voice,

cutting through the static in his mind, as if in answer to his thoughts. *"We are one, you and I."*

"Who are you?" He wasn't sure if he had asked the question aloud or it had remained just a thought inside his murky head.

"I am Lilitu." She croaked.

The more she spoke, the harder it was for Peter to tell where her voice was coming from. It was as if she had nested somewhere in his muddled mind.

"What do you want?" He probed, wondering if the voice was a figment of his addled imagination. Another sharp spasm rippled through his body, winding him as it rattled under his ribcage. The pain was now intolerable, and Peter felt his sinuses tingle as he fought to stay conscious.

"Behold..."

The woman's answer tore a hole in Peter's skull, filling it with torturous sights and sounds from centuries gone by. The ruins of an old, abandoned church burning beneath the winter sky, its courtyard littered with the bodies of mutilated children, all piled on top of one another.

Decades of suffering, all combined to form a river of blood which flooded Peter's neural pathways, overloading his senses with intense scenes of anarchy, murder, and devastation. Each violent memory embedded itself, forging with his own, until Peter could no longer tell where he ended and Lilitu began. The screams of her victims echoed through the corridors of his mind, chasing him away into the darkest depths of his subconscious until...

Peter was no more.

15

As Kane approached Peter's house for the second time that day, he could feel the curtain twitchers watching his every movement. Willow Road was a sleepy residential estate and seeing the local celebrity carted away in an ambulance was sure to set tongues wagging.

Ignoring his newfound audience, Kane let himself in and wasted no time making his way to the study to rifle through the books and papers strewn around the room. Aside from an empty syringe packet the paramedics had missed when cleaning up after themselves, he found nothing out of the ordinary.

He methodically made two piles from the deluge. One of exam papers, which it looked like Peter was in the process of marking, and one of books he guessed had been taken directly from his bookcase. Each time he added something new to the pile, he shook the item out over the carpet in case anything useful was hiding inside.

Once he finished, Kane eliminated the exam papers from his investigation and tucked them neatly underneath Peter's desk. He looked at the stack of reference books he was left with and mulled over the titles in case they triggered any ideas. Again, he drew a complete blank, unless the mysterious intruder had been looking for detailed insight into 18th Century England.

Frustrated by his lack of progress, Kane walked over to the middle of the room and surveyed its contents in their entirety. It was modest, but no boxroom, and housed a vast collection of Peter's books in two identical black MDF bookcases. A matching black desk sat against the furthest wall from the door, nested under a large window which overlooked the diminutive front garden. On top of that was Peter's laptop, which had been closed, a large monitor and a mini desktop printer.

Kane's mind drifted back to earlier that day and the haunting image of Peter's face came flooding back to him. A slight shiver escaped down the back of his neck, turning into a full-blown fright as his phone vibrated in his pocket.

Looking out into the street, he could see JJ staring back up at him, waving with his phone pressed to his ear. Zach, Meridia and Izzy gathered behind him as they all walked towards the front door.

"Hey guys, thanks for coming." Kane greeted them nonchalantly, as if it was his house.

"I've been looking in the study as that's where I found Peter this morning, and I think that's where the creepy guy was too."

One by one, they bundled through the front door and up the stairs Kane was gesturing to.

"I haven't seen the black lever arch folder Peter had in class though, or his bag for that matter...it's the first room on the left, just opposite the stairs."

Once upstairs, the group caught up on the day's events.

Kane gave them a brief recap of what he'd learned at the hospital, and Meridia shared her ordeal in maths.

"I still don't understand why everything has suddenly kicked off now. We'd had a few weeks of nothing, and now Peter's in intensive care. Every time Meridia nods off, someone attacks her, and there's a hooded home invader roaming Willow Road." Kane was flummoxed by the way things were unfolding.

"Hooded?" Meridia's colour drained from her face as she jumped in.

"Sorry, I thought I'd mentioned it earlier. The guy that was here earlier looked like he was wearing a brown cloak with a hood. Bet the neighbourhood watch missed that though." Meridia's blood ran cold as Kane's words sank in.

"The guy in my dream...my first dream, when I was at Crooked House...he was wearing a brown hooded gown."

"Shit, I forgot about him." Kane conceded, "That's my bad M. I must've forgotten to mention the whole hood thing when we spoke earlier. So, are we thinking he's more than a burglar, or was that just a premonition of some kind?"

"Right now, I have no idea. I feel like I'm missing clues in my dreams that are important. I'm sorry guys, I'm still trying to figure this all out." Meridia trailed off.

She could feel the growing pressure on her to make sense of her gift, but since saving the world her only achievements were bagging herself a detention and putting Peter in hospital.

"It's ok, you're not in this alone." Zach placed a reassuring hand on Meridia's shoulder. "It's up to all of us to make sense of what's going on."

"Zach's right guys, I think we may have taken Meridia's dreams...or whatever they are, too lightly..."

"Wait!" Meridia cut across Kane with another

realization. "I've seen people in hoods before that. In another dream...just after our first visit to Crooked House. There were hundreds of them chasing me through a dungeon."

"A dungeon?" Zach exclaimed.

"It was something like that...dark and dingy. I don't really remember much now, other than there were loads of them, all dressed exactly the same in brown hoods and cloaks, chasing me. I remember someone else being there too, a boy's voice, but I couldn't see him."

The tension in Meridia's face suddenly eased, relinquishing the strain on her memory.

"I wasn't journaling any of my dreams back then. I just passed that one off as a nightmare after what we'd seen."

"Sounds like a cult to me," Kane quipped. "Just what we need on top of everything else."

"There was that girl who lured Archie into Crooked House, so I don't think we can rule anything out at this point. Let's come back to the burglar once we've finished looking around here, as I don't think any of us want to be walking home in the dark after what's happened today." JJ provided the voice of reason, pulling them all back to the task at hand.

"Good shout mate. Let's go room to room and see what we turn up." Kane added, ushering everyone out onto the landing.

In his rush to follow everyone out, Zach clumsily bumped into Peter's desk with his school bag. The innocuous nudge was just enough to jog the dormant mouse and wake the large monitor.

"Err...guys. You need to look at this..."

Displayed on the 30inch monitor behind everyone were the camera feeds to each of the rooms in Crooked House, all neatly presented in split-screen format. Nine of the ten rooms were occupied: their guests floating dead-centre of the room, as if being suspended from the ceiling by invisible bondage. Each one of their faces was a stop-start frenzy of volatile expressions, rapidly shifting from one to the next. Some were twisted and consumed by hatred, whilst others writhed in agony.

"Holy shit!" Kane was the first to race back to the desk so he could get a better look. His blood ran cold the moment he locked eyes with all the tormented souls on display, their anguish was palpable.

Each of the nine echoes were present and accounted for except one: the witch from room 2.

"Oh god, it's Peter!" Kane pointed at the feed from the witch's room and in her place, squirming and twitching like a struggling escapologist, was Peter. His face was freakish, contorted by whatever pain and suffering his captors were subjecting him to.

"We have to help him!" Meridia gulped, her eyes already welling with panic and guilt.

"I don't understand...he's at the hospital. I saw them take him in. This has to be a trick." Kane muttered, still unable to pull his gaze from the horror on show. "If Peter is there, then where is the witch?"

"I was in two places at the same time, remember? What if this is just a vision...or a warning?" Zach was trying his best to pacify his brother and steady his own nerves.

"He's right, this might not be what it looks like. Nothing is in that bloody place." It was JJ's turn to interject, and although he lacked his usual optimism, he made a valid point. "Maybe this is a trick, or some kind of trap trying to lure us back to Crooked House."

"We have to do something though...look at him!" Kane reached into his pocket and fished out his phone.

"This is all my fault..." Meridia fretted, spiralling at the site of Peter on screen. "I brought him into this when I had my dream. There must be a way I can help him..."

"Hello, can I speak to Doctor Chapman, please?" Kane was doing the only proactive thing he could think of, which was calling the hospital number he'd been given earlier. "I'm checking on my friend, he was admitted earlier...I just wanted to know if there has been any change to his condition?"

The rest of the group stopped languishing in their despair and all turned their attention to Kane's conversation.

"Peter Higginsworth...my name? It's Kane...Kane Jackson. I'm the one who found him this morning...Doctor Chapman...he said he'd keep me updated, but I just wanted to check..."

Kane nervously tapped his leg whilst he waited for the nurse to report back.

"He is...That's great. Thank you so much...really? Ok I'll be there after school in that case. Thanks. Bye."

Kane put his phone away and brought everyone up to speed. "Well, he's still in the hospital, so that's something. He's responding well to treatment, and we should be able to visit him tomorrow afternoon if things continue. They said they'll be discussing when to bring him out of his coma then too."

"That's great news! So maybe this was all a trick like JJ said," Zach added, with one eye on Meridia, who was dabbing her eyes dry with the cuff of her school blazer.

"Look!" Izzy had returned her focus to the monitor, only to find all the rooms were empty again.

"Where did they go?" Kane quizzed.

"I don't know. I was too busy listening to you on the phone." Izzy was clearly irked, cross with herself for being distracted so easily.

"It's ok Izz, maybe that's a good thing. Maybe their plan didn't work, so they gave up?"

"Speaking of giving up, I think we should head home now guys. It'll be almost dark by the time I get to mine after walking the girls back."

JJ was right. Staying there any later wasn't worth the risk, and although they hadn't found what they were looking for, whatever that was, at least they'd received some encouraging news about Peter from the hospital.

They all made their way back downstairs whilst Kane checked the rest of the house was secure before locking the front door and setting off home.

16

Exhausted and overwhelmed, Meridia reached her front gate, feeling an immense pressure on her shoulders.

Like everyone else in the group, she felt responsible for the mess they were now in, but the fear of making anything worse petrified her. Since her first dream involving the witch, things had progressively become more dangerous, and the thought of what might be in store for her that night filled her with dread.

It had unsettled them all that the witch was absent from the video feed they'd seen at Peter's house, but the more Meridia had mulled it over on her way home, the more her stomach tied itself in knots.

"Thanks JJ. I guess I'll see you both tomorrow then..." Izzy was too preoccupied to hear Meridia.

Instead, she was nervously taking in her surroundings, half expecting to see Mr Richards scowling at her from the shadows. After the recent events, they were all spooked.

"No probs M. Listen, I was thinking about the whole

sleep issue and reckon you should try setting a repeat alarm to break up any bad dreams. I saw it in a film once. Even if you set it for every hour, at least you'll get some rest."

"Did it work in the movie?" Meridia was touched by JJ's concern and was willing to try anything to recharge her batteries.

"Err...not quite. They all died, but that was just a movie." JJ chuckled at his own honesty. "Look, just try it tonight, and if you run into any trouble, then just think of me. I'll give that witch a run for her money."

"This whole week feels like a bad dream. I just wish I knew how to fix it. This gift I have feels more like a curse at the moment."

"We'll figure it out M, I promise. It's almost the weekend, so we'll put our heads together and come up with a plan then. Go get some rest and we'll see you tomorrow." JJ placed a reassuring hand on Meridia's shoulder and then called out to Izzy, interrupting her paranoia. "C'mon Izz, just one more stop on the JJ express. I need to eat."

Izzy glanced up at the dusky sky and jumped when the streetlights turned on. Darkness was approaching, and they had to get moving.

"See you in the morning M," she mumbled, her head still on a swivel, and then both she and JJ hurried away down the road.

As much as they were all very much in this together, Meridia couldn't help but feel alone as she watched them both disappear into the distance. Whatever fresh horrors lay in-store for her that night, she knew she'd have to face them on her own.

WHEN MERIDIA STEPPED inside her front door, the first thing that greeted her was the warm, enticing smell of homemade lasagne. The irresistible scent led her to the kitchen, where her mum was setting the table for two.

"Hey hon, how was school?" Emily Wilson looked up over the table and then struggled to contain her shock when she saw Meridia standing in the doorway. "God, you look exhausted. Everything ok?"

She placed the last of the cutlery down and walked round to give her daughter a hug.

The moment Meridia felt the warmth of her mother's embrace, she broke down in tears, sobbing into her apron.

"What is it M? What's wrong?" Emily rubbed Meridia's back the same way she did when she was a baby and needed soothing.

"I'm sorry," she wept. "I've just had a tough couple of days...I've not been sleeping...*sniff*...and I fell asleep in class today...and everyone laughed at me...then I found out one of our teachers is in hospital...*sniff*...I've just wanted to come home and have this hug all day."

"Oh, you poor thing. I had no idea you haven't been sleeping. I always get teary when I'm tired. It probably didn't help staying at Izzy's last night either. But what happened to your teacher honey? Why are they in the hospital?"

"It's P...err...Mr Higginsworth. We don't know what's wrong with him, but it sounds pretty serious and we're all really worried. He's helping a group of us with a local history project..." Meridia stopped herself from saying any more. She longed to bury herself in her mother's arms and confess everything.

"Oh dear, I'm so sorry. That's the famous author, isn't

it? I'd heard he was teaching at your school, but didn't realize he was teaching you. That poor man...I wonder what it could be. He looks so young. If he's at Chase Side, then he's in the best possible hands. They'll get to the bottom of whatever's wrong, I'm sure."

With that, the timer on the oven sounded and Emily pulled away to silence it.

"Why don't you go wash your hands while I serve up. I've made your favourite, lasagne...that always makes you feel better, and it might even help you sleep later too."

"Thanks mum, that's perfect. Don't worry, I'll be fine... be right back." Meridia cuffed her tears away as she walked back out into the hall to hang her blazer up.

As she tiptoed to reach the brass hook, she noticed something out of place from the corner of her eye and immediately froze.

On the other side of her street door, beneath the dim light of the porch, she could see a hooded figure staring in at her through the frosted glass. Completely motionless, his hood cast a long dark shadow, obscuring his face as he intimidatingly filled the door frame with his sinister presence.

Gritting her teeth, Meridia swallowed the scream that had instinctively formed in the pit of her throat and allowed her anger to take the wheel. She'd had enough now and wanted answers. Turning to face the watcher in the window, she forced herself forward, shuffling her right foot a couple of inches towards the door.

All she could think about was the shitstorm they had all been trapped inside ever since visiting that wretched house with all its monsters. The more she pondered, the angrier she grew, making it easier to edge towards the door.

Her unwanted visitor continued to stand his ground, unflinching, until Meridia reached for the door handle.

The second she felt the smooth brass latch between her thumb and forefinger, the figure backed away beyond the light of the porch, disappearing into the darkness behind him.

"No! I'm not having it," Meridia muttered to herself, raging now at the thought of all the pain both she and her friends had endured.

"I'm sick of living like this!"

She twisted the latch and brazenly opened the door in contempt, but her garden was empty, and the road beyond quiet. A dozen yards ahead of her, the wooden gate to her garden clattered against its post as the wind batted it back and forth, in and out of the streetlight's glare.

The man had gone.

A mix of relief and disappointment washed over Meridia as she raced down the path to secure the gate. When she reached for the catch, she noticed a throbbing in her palm. She had been clenching her fist without even realizing it. A tiny row of white indentations peppered the pads beneath her fingers and strangely, she found that more disconcerting than the creep outside her front door.

She had always hated violence, more so since the issues with her dad. The last thing anyone needed was her following in his footsteps.

"M? Dinner!" She heard her mum calling from inside.

"Saved by the bell," Meridia muttered, and then took a deep breath of the cool evening air before trudging back indoors.

"Coming mum!" she replied as she entered the hallway.

Once inside, she clicked the deadbolt into place on the inside of the front door and paused for a moment to gaze through the glass again. She looked up at the yellow haze from the porch light as it cascaded down, illuminating the tiny ripples and twirls in the glass.

"No more visitors tonight," she whispered, turning the light off and, with it, the outside world.

17

After dinner, Meridia made her excuses and retreated upstairs to her room. She figured if it was going to be a long night of disrupted sleep, then she might as well get a head start on proceedings.

As always, her mum understood and took up her usual spot in front of the TV. Since the incident with Meridia's dad, her mum had become quite the recluse, shunning her friends, and ducking out of social gatherings in favour of hibernating on the sofa. Although they had a restraining order in place, Emily Wilson was still apprehensive he might one day return and look to finish what he'd started that fateful afternoon. Whilst Meridia had witnessed nothing that happened on that terrible day, she carried her own fear and paranoia of winding up just like him.

Gregor Wilson had a notoriously short fuse, even as a child growing up in the backstreets of Glasgow. Outraged by the indifference the universe had shown him, he spent most of his formative years downtrodden and living hand-to-mouth.

An only child of a young prostitute, he'd seen his fair share of hardship and brutality, until at the age of eleven he lost his mother to her heroin addiction. Homeless and without a family, he then spent the rest of his adolescence bouncing around inside a broken child support system, littered with unsavoury foster parents whose only interest in him was financial. It was no surprise that by the time he was sixteen, he'd been kicked out of more schools than he'd eaten hot dinners and had very little in the way of career prospects.

That was until he met Elizabeth and Richard Saunders, a middle-aged and respectable couple from London who owned a car dealership on the outskirts of town. Having seen potential in Gregor, they gave him something nobody had ever given him before: a chance. With that chance came a place to live and a job in their garage, servicing and fixing cars. Richard taught him everything he knew about the automobile industry, and Gregor soaked it all up like a sponge, always eager to learn more.

By the time he turned twenty, he found himself promoted to the front office having shown great promise in sales, and that's when he met Emily. Even though his fiery temper remained simmering beneath the surface, Emily was the only person since his mother to ever melt it away.

For Gregor, life was finally something worth living, and just like the fairy tales his mother had read to him as a young boy, the two lovers were soon married. Moving to a quaint little village near Cold Christmas in order to start a family, the Wilson's welcomed Meridia into the world a year later. Gregor swore he'd give her everything he never had as a child, and that was where his troubles began.

Working all the hours under the sun to provide for his young family, he made his case to Mr & Mrs Saunders that he had what it took to run the business and let them both retire to enjoy the fruits of their labour. However, when Mr Saunders discovered he had pancreatic cancer on the eve of his sixtieth birthday, it forced the matter, and Gregor assumed responsibility for the entire operation. But the added stress took its toll.

Over time, the angry boy slowly reared his head again, as tough market conditions and underperforming staff chipped away at his composure. The more time he ploughed into remedying his mounting problems, the worse the business faired and the more agitated he became. Without his mentor, and lacking any experience in an economic downturn, the company was eventually forced to fold, taking with it Mr & Mrs Saunders's retirement and everything they had worked so hard for all their lives.

The day the bank foreclosed was the day ten years of relentless pressure finally caught up with Gregor. He drove home drunk that afternoon while Meridia was at school, overcome with rage. Everything he'd carried with him since he was a child, every single injustice and grievance with the world, all came spilling out and the only person there to vent his fury on was Emily.

When he eventually sobered up in his cell, he told the police he'd blacked out and had no memory of even getting home that day.

Emily spent the best part of a month in the hospital, recovering from the beating she had taken. Suffering a fractured orbital socket and two cracked ribs, Emily also had several of her teeth strewn across the kitchen floor where she had crawled to seek refuge. That was eighteen months ago now, and Meridia had not seen or heard from her father since his release.

———

When Meridia had finished brushing her teeth, she entered her bedroom to find one of her mum's famous hot chocolates waiting for her beside the bed. The rich chocolaty aroma was every bit as welcoming as the soft glow of her amber nightlight, combining perfectly to melt away the feeling of overwhelm she'd just carried all the way up the stairs.

As JJ suggested, she set her phone's alarm to sound on the hour before snuggling down into her duvet. She yearned for a peaceful night, willing to settle for an hour's rest at a time. Gazing at the tiny craters in her moon lamp, she searched for comforting shapes to occupy her imagination, but she needn't have bothered. Within a matter of seconds, Meridia felt her eyes tingle as she wrestled with the weight of her eyelids, and then, in true Wilson fashion, she fell fast asleep.

Beep...beep...

Meridia awoke to the first alarm of the night and found herself still safely tucked up in her own bed. Squinting to make out the time, she sluggishly silenced her phone, let out a drowsy sigh of relief, and then turned over to go back to sleep.

Beep...beep...

What felt like seconds later, the alarm sounded again for 1am and she looked around her boxroom with bleary eyes for any signs of trouble but found nothing untoward. The orange hue that engulfed her left no room for any unwelcome visitors to hide.

Satisfied she was still quite safe, Meridia deleted her next alarm to capitalize on the quiet spell she was enjoying. Once again, she turned her back on her phone and nuzzled into the warm duvet bunched up around her head.

Beep...beep...beep...

Each electronic chime of her alarm felt like a dagger to Meridia's heart. Dreamless and drama-free, that had been the best sleep she'd had in days.

Desperate to return to it, she reached out and silenced her phone. The dim display said 3am and Meridia considered chancing the rest of the night without any further interruptions. The temptation of four hours of blissfully uneventful rest proved too much to resist and so giving in to the impulse she hit delete.

She wondered if the broken nature of her night was preventing the witch from getting her claws into her, but whatever the reason, she would be sure to thank JJ in the morning.

Meridia rolled onto her back and took in a deep breath of satisfaction as she felt the smooth contour of her memory foam pillow gently cradle the nape of her neck. For a fleeting moment, she felt as if she was lying on a cloud. That was until she opened her eyes.

Floating just inches above her, as if suspended from her bedroom ceiling, was Peter.

His face was aghast, consumed with pain and turmoil, whilst his jaw moved awkwardly up and down, never quite closing, as if he was trying to speak.

Meridia jumped and then instantly froze, caught in the headlights of his haunting stare as he tried desperately to will the words out that were stuck in his throat, but the only sound to escape was that of a death rattle.

A thick globule of saliva slowly oozed out of his gaping mouth, landing on Meridia's cheek before slithering down the side of her face.

Grossed out, she tried to wriggle her way onto the floor but found herself completely paralyzed. Whatever dark forces were keeping Peter dangling above her were also keeping her pinned to the bed beneath him.

"Peter, I'm so sorry." Meridia wept, distraught at the sight of him.

He looked ten years older. His face was gaunt and grey with dark circles strangling milky eyes that had lost all their sparkle. His expression of total despair chilled Meridia to the bone, as he continued to struggle and groan overhead.

"What is it Peter?" she pleaded, as he persisted in grappling for control of his jaw.

In the meantime, Meridia tried with all her might to break free from whatever spell she was under, but all her defiance yielded nothing.

Her temper bubbled and boiled with each failed attempt, until eventually she snapped, letting out an ear-splitting screech of pure frustration, which then turned into a wail.

"I hate you!" she shouted at the rafters, "I fucking hate you! Let me go!"

Fiery tears of rage streamed down her face as she continued to scream obscenities at her unseen adversary. Looking up through bloodshot, blurry eyes, she could see Peter had quit fighting. His face was one of sorrow, limp with resignation.

"Don't you dare give up Peter!" Meridia shot up at him, "Don't you dare! I know you're in there."

Her bright blue eyes glared at him, cutting through the

warm afterglow of her nightlight. Beneath the glimmer of her replica moon she could see tears beginning to well in Peter's eyes, but he remained inert, like a worn-out rag doll that merely resembled her friend.

The two captives exchanged a brief look of surrender, impotent against the witch's evil dominion, and then Peter became animated again.

His eyes suddenly bulged wide in shock as he began to retch and choke.

Meridia saw a shadow around his throat, and then it swelled, as if something else was alive inside him. Powerless to move, her mind immediately raced to the cockroaches that had poured out of her maths teacher and she braced herself for the worst. It started with a tiny drop, as a black tar-like substance slowly trickled from Peter's mouth, dangling over Meridia like elastic, until landing on the tip of her chin. The glistening filth felt warm and heavy on her skin like treacle, but its smell was anything but sweet. Its revolting odour assaulted her nostrils, stinging the back of her throat as the trickle became a stream, and the stream became a gushing deluge, dousing Meridia in her bed.

Peter continued to spew his sticky, black mess of putrid slime all over, clogging her airways until she could barely breathe.

"*Wake up Meridia! Wake Up!*" she told herself, eyes clenched, and head cowered away from the splattering onslaught of gunk that entombed her.

And then it stopped.

Beep...beep...beep

The alarm rang out to her left, and she tentatively risked opening one eye. The familiar glow of amber infused with the slender shaft of daylight that was creeping its way in through the gap in her blackout curtains greeted her.

Silencing her 7am alarm, Meridia breathed a heavy sigh of relief when she found there was no sign of Peter or his vile discharge. Somehow, she had survived another night.

18

Kane felt his phone vibrate in his pocket and looked to see who was calling him.

"Caller unknown," he shouted ahead to Zach. "I think it's the hospital."

Zach backtracked towards his brother and hovered around his elbow while he took the call. The gloomy rain that had pelted their town all week had finally given way to some patches of blue that Friday morning, and for once, both boys were eager to get to school.

"Hello, Kane speaking."

"Ah, Mr Jackson. This is Doctor Chapman...we met yesterday at the hospital."

"Hi doctor. Is there any news about Peter?" Kane slowed down a little so he could concentrate better.

"Well, yes there is actually, and I'm pleased to report it's all good. Mr Higginsworth has responded very well to his treatment and came to of his own accord in the early hours this morning. I've just finished conducting a neurological assessment, and he passed with flying colours."

"That's amazing!" A sudden rush of relief flooded

Kane's senses, which swiftly spread its way to Zach who could hear the conversation. "So, what does that mean doctor?"

"Well, he's still exhausted from his ordeal so I'd like to keep him in just one more night for observation, but if he's ok and shows no signs of a relapse, then I'll be happy to discharge him tomorrow morning...I can't tell you how lucky your friend is...I've never seen a recovery like it if I'm honest."

"Fantastic. Thank you so much. Does that mean we can visit him later, after school?"

"Of course, I see no reason why not. We have strict visiting hours here though, so you'll need to be away by 8pm so he can get his rest."

"That's fine with us. We'll be there around 4pm in that case, and thanks again for calling. It's such great news he's going to be ok." Kane was beaming from ear to ear as he hung up the call. Finally, something positive to go into school with.

"Thank god he's going to be ok!" Zach chirped as they both picked up the pace. "Meridia will be so relieved to know he's on the mend."

"Yeah, everyone will be. He had us all really worried there. Hopefully, he'll be able to shed some light on what happened that night. So far, he's the only one of us to turn up in one of Meridia's nightmares so I just want to know if it was a vision she had and Peter was already ill, or if she somehow put him in danger the way she thinks she did." Kane was terrified it might be the latter.

If Meridia was responsible for Peter's condition, then it meant none of them were safe, regardless of the wide berth they'd been giving Crooked House. The last thing any of them needed was a trip there, real or not, especially Zach, given his role in the madness they were now entangled with. Kane had elected not to share his fears with anyone, even JJ, so as not to risk word getting to Meridia. He wasn't as worried about upsetting her as he was unintentionally planting the seed of Zach in her mind.

By the time the brothers arrived at St Swithun's, the rest of the gang were patiently waiting for them on their adopted bench. Slipping past the popular girls undetected, they had almost made it to the halfway line of the wannabe footballers when Alman barked.

"Oi, Jackson! Where did you sneak off to yesterday? Run home crying to mummy?" The juvenile taunt incited rapturous laughter from the usual suspects, the football goons littered across their make-believe pitch, and the assortment of groupies watching from the sideline.

Kane felt a hot flush as his temper simmered and then released it into the cool morning air as he continued walking with Zach in tow. He wasn't about to let Alman ruin the good start he'd had to the day and besides, it wasn't as if he had any kind of reputation to protect these days. Crooked House had already tarnished that irrevocably.

"Just ignore him mate." JJ offered a voice of reason when the brothers reached their place in the school pecking order.

"I know, he's such a prick," Kane responded. "Anyway, forget Alman. I've got some good news. Peter is out of his coma and on course to come home tomorrow." His announcement brought relief and jubilation to everyone.

"I saw him again last night...in my dream." Meridia sheepishly declared once the celebrations had died down. "He was in my room, floating over my bed...he looked like he was trying to tell me something but couldn't speak...and neither of us could move. It was awful. He looked...awful.

He just kept moving his mouth like he was trying to speak and then all this black stuff came pouring out...he threw it up all over me."

"That sounds gross," Zach fumed. "I'm so sorry everything keeps happening to you. Was there any sign of the witch or the shadow monsters?"

"Not this time. It was just Peter, and he came to me. It felt real like the other dreams, but there was no trace of anything when my alarm went off." Meridia could still taste the disgusting black vomit but spared the group of that minor detail.

"Any idea what it meant?" Zach pressed a little, eager for them to get a head start on whatever dangers might be waiting for them around the next corner.

"No idea. Like I said, neither of us could move and Peter couldn't speak." Meridia shrugged.

The dream had left her baffled, but something in her gut hadn't felt right since she woke up from it. Figuring she might need more time to unpack it, she looked to the others for suggestions.

"Maybe it was just connected to Peter's recovery, and the vomit represented him getting it out of his system?" Zach's interpretation was as good as any, but felt too cut and dry to be on the money.

If they'd learned anything from their dealings with Crooked House, it was that nothing was ever as it seemed.

"Hopefully we'll find out after school. He'll be open to visitors this afternoon." Kane had been holding that news back for effect before they got sidetracked by Meridia's dream.

"Typical," Meridia exclaimed. "I can't make it today guys. I've got detention for falling asleep in class. My mum will be picking me up when I'm done."

"Bummer."

"Yeah, I thought I'd gotten away with it once I'd blamed the bump on my head, but apparently Mr Seth was 'deeply offended' by my behaviour...I mean, who even likes maths anyway?" Meridia blushed the moment she finished her sentence and could feel Izzy's eyes on her.

"Ahem." Izzy added, refusing to let her off the hook.

"Sorry Izz, you know what I mean. He's only making an example of me because he can't control the rest of the class. Luckily my mum didn't seem to care much when I told her and now we're going out for pizza after. Maybe I should get Friday detention every week..."

Meridia was interrupted by the morning bell, so the group gathered their bags and shuffled off to join the playground zombies, all mindlessly looking for a way into the building. There was a different energy at St Swithun's on a Friday and people seemed far more eager to get inside when school started.

"Catch you at break guys," JJ shouted, before being swallowed up by the crowd.

19

It had been a slow day at St Swithun's, and when the last bell echoed throughout its languid, chartreuse halls, Meridia couldn't believe she still had another hour of detention to get through.

"What are you going to do?" Zach asked, as he hastily stuffed his French book into his rucksack.

"I'm going to read through my journal again. The last few days have been pretty intense, so I've barely had time to process anything. I figured if I look at it all now with fresh eyes, I might make more sense of it...at least that's the plan anyway." Meridia swung her bag onto her shoulder and followed Zach towards the classroom door. "Will you tell Peter I'm sorry I can't be there today, but I'll definitely be there tomorrow?"

"Sure. I'll text you when I've seen him just to put your mind at ease."

Zach brushed Meridia's arm as they parted ways in the corridor, and she felt a trademark rush of blood fill her freckled cheeks.

"Er...enjoy detention and don't put yourself under too much pressure to figure stuff out. Chat later."

"Be careful Zach." She wasn't even sure where the sentiment had come from. Something deep inside her had remained fearful for him ever since they'd learned of the dark prophecy of Crooked House, but this was different. Her gut was nagging at her again as he walked away, and she had no idea why.

"Will do." He chirped back as he disappeared into the sea of children flooding the exit.

Meridia closed her eyes and feverishly rubbed her forehead with both hands in order to break up her train of thought. The racket of rowdy pupils welcoming the weekend in unison made her dizzy and, for a moment, she felt the floor beneath her sway as if she'd inadvertently stepped onto an airport travelator.

"C'mon Meridia, get it together." She muttered before steadying herself and reluctantly setting off toward room 3.

Somehow Meridia beat everyone to detention, including the teacher on duty.

Room 3 at St Swithun's was used for geography and conveniently placed next to the staffroom, which allowed whoever was tasked with supervising it to flit back and forth between locations. Aside from the large map of the world pinned to the wall, it looked like any other classroom. Beige painted walls carried a decade of battle scars, whilst a neat grid of functional grey MDF desks concealed the durable cobalt carpet beneath them. The banal décor was capped off by bright blue stackable plastic chairs with shiny black metal legs, which were scattered around the room in the rush of the previous class to escape.

Meridia claimed the most coveted seat in detention. A back row desk in the leftmost corner, which created plenty of space between her and the teacher, whilst also allowing her to see anyone new entering the room.

Unless detainees had homework due to the teacher on watch, they were mostly left to their own devices. Fortunately, Meridia was up to date with all of hers, which left her free to study her journal for clues she might have missed. As she pulled the book from her bag and sat down, the door opened, and Mrs Hayward stepped in.

She was a plump lady in her fifties with auburn hair that was a few shades darker than Meridia's. Rumour had it she was the head teacher's mistress and pupils often saw her with him at lunch, enjoying a coffee at the local café. She surveyed the room and looked at a slip of paper she was clutching before clip-clopping her way to the front of the room. She always presented herself well, typically favouring a dress or skirt over trousers, regardless of the weather. Today she was wearing a fuchsia jacket and matching skirt, with a white blouse underneath, which left her looking like a shoe shop assistant.

"Ms Wilson, I'm surprised to see you here," she said with a feigned frown of disappointment. "It looks like we're just waiting for one other to join us..."

Right on cue, the door opened, and Jacob Alman entered the room.

"Ah, Mr Alman, so nice of you to make it. Please take a seat..." Mrs Hayward gestured to the abundance of empty desks in front of her and Alman strutted over the one nearest the doorway he was loitering in.

"It's just the two of you today, so unless you've got any outstanding work, I would suggest you spend the next hour reading or reflecting on why you're here. I will check in on you from time to time, but I'll only be next door and these walls are deceptively thin, so no messing around!" Mrs

Hayward trotted out of the room, her head held high like a show pony.

"What are you in here for?" Alman asked as he slumped back in his seat and propped his foot up on the corner of his desk. His green eyes peered expectantly out from under his tousled blonde fringe as he pulled a phone out of his pocket.

"I fell asleep in maths." Meridia fired back curtly.

She had nothing against Alman. In fact, she wondered if this was the first time either of them had spoken, but she saw the way he enjoyed goading Kane and there was no question where her loyalties lay.

"Haven't we all..." Alman replied.

His thinly veiled attempt to appear cool flew right over Meridia's head as she dived into her journal.

"I'm in for throwing an apple at Jimmy Holt. It hit him right on the back of his melon head. I thought it was pretty funny, but Mr Shipford didn't see it my way." He doubled down on the cool stakes, but Meridia remained unimpressed.

"Why'd you do it?" she challenged deadpan, glancing up from her book to emphasize her point.

"He was bugging Kelly Smith in 10F, staring at her funny and stuff. Teachers wouldn't do anything about it, so I did." He shrugged nonchalantly and returned to his phone screen.

That wasn't quite the answer Meridia was expecting based on what little she knew of him, but she decided not to press any further. She had far more important things to think about.

Starting with her first encounter with the witch, Meridia studied every line she'd written about her recent dreams. Upon reading them, it surprised her how vivid each ordeal still felt to her. Akin to a 4D IMAX experience in her mind, she relived each experience, reconnecting with the heat in room 2 when the witch set it ablaze, and the smell of the cockroaches as they scuttled over her face during her run in with Mr Seth. The thought of them made her shudder, and she nervously twiddled a lock of hair, half expecting to find a roach still nesting in there somewhere.

By the time she'd finished reading her notes, half an hour had passed, and she reasoned the group should now be at the hospital. Her anxiety levels spiked the moment she thought of Zach, just as they had out in the hall, and a sudden burst of prickly heat danced and tickled its way across the back of her neck.

Something felt wrong, and the more she pondered, the worse she became. A cold sweat followed, swamping her forehead and she felt queasy from its clammy grip.

Closing her journal, she swapped it for her phone, compelled to reach out to Zach.

```
Hey, hope u all got there ok.
My spidey-senses are tingling,
so just thought I'd check in
and make sure you're alright.
Hope Peter is feeling better
and tell him I said hi x
```

As soon as she hit the send button, her stomach cramped up again, tightening like a clenched fist and taking her breath away.

Something was definitely off, and her gut was now screaming at her that Zach was in danger.

20

Zach was about to hit send on his phone when Meridia's message came through. He chuckled to himself at the coincidence and then felt a flush of colour surge to his cheeks when he saw she'd signed off with a kiss.

```
I was in the middle of texting
u. Just arrived and walking to
Peter's ward now. I'll text
again once we've seen him.
Hope you're enjoying
detention x
```

He second-guessed the kiss, deleting it at first and then adding it again before tapping reply. He and Meridia had sent hundreds of messages to each other since they'd been bought their phones, but the kiss was unfamiliar territory.

"What are you looking all coy about spud?" Kane teased as he gave his little brother an affectionate shoulder barge.

"Nothing...Meridia just texted, that's all. She said her spidey senses were tingling, whatever that means."

The relayed message dampened everyone's spirits as they followed the green painted line on the floor towards the recovery ward at Chase Side Hospital. The new navigation system was a trial, inspired by the London underground network and Zach found it every bit as confusing to follow as their path weaved in and out of red lines for A&E along with yellow lines for the X-ray department.

"Does anyone else think this is a lame way of signposting things?" Zach blurted to break the awkward silence.

"Everyone preferred it the way it was apparently, but head office told them they had to give this a couple of months to bed-in." JJ repeated one of his mum's recent gripes from the rare time they'd sat down at the dinner table together.

"I like it," Izzy countered as she gleefully tracked the green line up ahead. "It's like Hansel & Gretel."

"Hopefully there isn't someone at the end of this looking to stuff us all in an oven," Kane quipped, dragging them all back to more ominous territory.

"We're perfectly safe here guys. Not sure what Meridia felt, but last time I checked, the witch only comes out at night." JJ attempted to settle any nerves as their path led them to an open elevator, and they all bundled in.

The recovery ward was on the third floor of the hospital and, as they exited, a small, unmanned reception desk greeted them. On the wall behind it was a whiteboard with a list of names and numbers written beside them in blue marker pen.

"There! Higginsworth, cubicle six." Izzy was the first to make the connection, pointing at Peter's name on the board before leading the way.

The ward seemed deserted as they quietly crept down its bleached corridor. Cubicles on each side of them were closed off by blue privacy curtains, with the dozen or so patients no doubt resting in their beds behind them.

"Excuse me, can I help?" A stern matriarchal voice ricocheted off the shiny linoleum floor, shattering the sterile serenity and stopping them all in their tracks.

Zach, who was bringing up the rear, turned to face a tall, middle-aged nurse who had materialized from one of the cubicles close to the ward's entrance.

"Sorry, we're just here to visit our teacher, Peter Higginsworth?"

"Doctor Chapman told me we were ok to see him when we spoke this morning." Kane backed up his brother's response with an air of authority.

"Oh, yes...he said you might be coming." The nurse's voice softened slightly as she gestured ahead of them. "He's just up there on the left. Number six, I believe."

"Thanks." Zach gave the nurse a thumbs up and followed the rest of the group onward.

When they reached cubicle six, they found the curtain drawn, just like all the rest.

"Peter?" Kane whispered into the rippled royal blue fabric. "It's Kane. Is it ok to come in?" He presumptuously poked his head through whilst the others waited patiently in the hall.

Kane briefly disappeared into the cubicle before re-emerging and pulling back the curtains.

The moment Zach caught a glimpse of Peter, his heart sank.

Propped up in his hospital bed, he was the very definition of death warmed up. His hair, usually glossy and impeccably groomed, looked dishevelled and lank, whilst his face appeared gaunt and pallid.

Peter scanned the group through waning eyes, as if he

was searching for someone in particular. He was just as Meridia had described him in her dream, minus the black vomit, and looked a shadow of his former self.

"No Meridia?" he asked rather croakily. "You'll have to excuse me, my throat is a little sore from all the tubes they had in me."

"Meridia says hi. She had detention after school, so couldn't make it today." Zach explained.

"How are you feeling?" Kane jumped straight in with the question that was on everyone's lips.

"Tired." Peter replied, as he gave a slow blink. "Which is odd given I've just awoke from a coma."

He gave a wry smile and pushed himself a little more upright in the bed as he continued, "I don't really know what happened if I'm honest. One minute I was marking papers, and the next I woke up in here. The doctors tell me I have you to thank Kane and that I most likely owe you my life."

"It was all Meridia really. She had a dream...and you were in trouble. Then when you didn't show up for school that morning, she made me go check on you. You really don't remember anything about what happened?" Kane pressed, keen to understand the significance of Meridia's dream.

"I'm afraid not. The doctor said that's normal though and I might remember more over the next few days. They've been pumping me full of drugs, so my head's still a little foggy." Peter's eyes found Zach's, and he offered him a half-smile. "I take it you've all managed to stay out of trouble then?"

"Meridia's had a tough time since you've been in here. The witch hasn't left her alone, and she's really freaking out over everything. She got in trouble at school...it's like every time she falls asleep something bad happens." Zach wrestled to keep his voice intact as he blurted out everything he'd been bottling up.

The constant worrying about Meridia collided head-on with his relief at seeing Peter alive, and it all became too much to control. Hearing his brother's composure was crumbling, Kane jumped in.

"We've had easier weeks, that's for sure. We won't bog you down with it all now though. I'm sure that's the last thing you want after everything you've been through." Peter's eyes sharpened a little, as if he was weighing up Kane's offer of easy passage.

"Tell me more about Meridia's dream...I'd like to know what she thinks she saw..."

"She said the witch got you." Zach had recovered from his wobble and felt duty bound to tell Meridia's story.

"Meridia said she thought of you, and then you appeared in Crooked House. You tried to fight the witch, but she was too strong...and that's when Meridia woke up. She said you told her you'd been marking papers in her dream...and then when Kane found you, he said you were slumped over your desk. Meridia thinks it's her fault you're in here...she feels responsible, and she's been scared to sleep ever since." Zach felt his voice wavering again and swallowed his frailty down with a shot of anger.

He'd been suppressing lots of his emotions lately, to appear outwardly stronger than he was, but this time he used one feeling against the other, hoping they would cancel each other out.

"That's fascinating...her gift is impressive, although I don't recall encountering the witch. I expect it was just a vision that something was wrong. A coincidence maybe. Did she tell you the last thing she remembered seeing before she woke?" The mystery seemed to breathe new life into Peter, and he pushed himself even further up the bed until he was bolt upright.

"She said the witch picked you up and trapped you in the corner of the room, I think. Then Meridia fell through the floor and the next thing she knew, she was back in her bed...guys?"

Zach looked around for assurance that he hadn't missed anything important and received a choir of nodding heads in response.

"She saw you again last night...in her room. She said you were floating above her at 3am and looked like you were trying to tell her something, but you couldn't speak. You ended up throwing up all over her apparently...some kind of black sticky gunk. She said it was gross."

A look of concern flashed across Peter's face as if Zach's account had touched a nerve, but it was fleeting, and his eyes swiftly softened again, as if his energy had taken a sudden dip.

"Do you remember anything about that?" Kane jumped in, noticing his reaction.

"No...I'm afraid not," Peter chuckled, "perhaps it was somehow connected to the time I woke up here? I think these dreams might be Meridia's way of tapping into her gift. I'm sure they feel very real to her at the time, and they sound terrifying, but I don't think they should be taken literally."

"They seem pretty real. She still has a bump on her head from one of them...She's trying to make more sense of them while she's in detention, but we've told her not to put herself under too much pressure." Zach felt a little defensive at Peter's remark, as if he was trivializing the episodes Meridia had been experiencing.

"I'm sure we'll find a logical explanation for it all. Perhaps you can all come to my house tomorrow and we can talk more about it then? They're letting me out in the morning, all being well."

"Nothing is logical as far as Crooked House is concerned," Izzy vented her discomfort under her breath.

Something about her choice of words lodged in Zach's mind, stirring up his paranoia. Izzy was right, and Peter knew that just as well as the rest of them. Perhaps he was tired, or it was the just setting they were in, but if Zach didn't know better, he could have sworn Peter was being intentionally dismissive, as if he was hiding something.

21

Meridia had been watching her phone like a hawk, willing it to illuminate with an update from Zach whilst she twiddled her pen back and forth between her thumb and forefinger.

It had been almost twenty minutes since she'd last heard from him and any attempts to distract herself had failed miserably. All she kept gravitating back towards was the powerful sensation of dread that was steadily turning the screw on her abdomen.

"Somewhere else you gotta be?" Alman called from the other side of the classroom. "You've been fidgeting and checking your phone for the last ten minutes now. If you want this to pass quickly, then you need to play a game or watch YouTube. Trust me, I've been here enough times to know."

Meridia found Alman to be annoyingly nice, and as much as she wanted to tell him to get lost, he had a point.

"Thanks. I'll do that."

She trawled through an endless conveyor belt of brightly coloured apps until she landed on the familiar red of YouTube and opened it for inspiration. The algorithm thoughtlessly offered her an array of haunted house videos with a smattering of reaction shorts to the latest horror movies. Just what she needed.

Slumped over her phone in defeat, she allowed her eyes to close for a few seconds longer than a blink. Once again, an image of Zach flickered and flared in her mind's eye, painting her thoughts with washed out shades of green and royal blue, before a subtle hint of disinfectant slinked its way up her nose.

Meridia opened her eyes, expecting to see her phone staring up at her from the desk, but instead she found herself floating above a dimly lit hospital cubicle, swimming in an ocean of obscurity. A fluorescent light pulsated somewhere beneath her like a nightclub strobe, revealing snippets of carnage. Clawed, bloodstained curtains gently rippled and waved, pulling her attention down towards the shadows on the floor.

There, crammed within the cell's tiny confines, littered around an empty bed, she could see the bodies of her friends. Mauled by some kind of wild animal, their bloodied corpses lay strewn across the ground like rag dolls, bathing in a crimson pool that sparkled under the volatile spotlight. Meridia's eyes unwillingly galloped around, circling the carnage of blood and bone in search of Zach, but both he and Peter were nowhere to be seen.

"This can't be true..." she mumbled, as her heart plummeted into the icy depths of shock and her body went numb.

"Zach?!" she cried into the echoing abyss, but there was no sign of him.

The pristine white bed in the middle of the room shone like a beacon in the darkness, tugging at her gaze and dragging her attention away from the bloodshed surrounding it. As Meridia stared more intently, she noticed something moving beneath the sheets.

Soon the bed was alive, its covers twitching and writhing as a snake-like creature slithered towards each corner in search of a way out. The seductive, sinuous motion held Meridia in a trance as the creature traversed the soft cotton terrain, growing larger with each circuit until finally coming to a halt in the centre of the bed.

From there it rose toward her, mutating to the muffled sounds of dislocating bones and ripping flesh, until it stood tall, transforming the bedsheet into a Halloween ghost costume. Slender, blood-soaked fingertips slowly emerged from beneath the folds as the ominous spectre began dragging its cover down towards the floor.

An overwhelming sense of foreboding gripped Meridia as she watched on from her celestial viewpoint.

Inch by inch, the sheet fell to the ground until gravity took over and completed the ghoulish unveiling. Atop of the bed stood a young woman, naked and bathed in blood.

"What have you done?!" Meridia cried.

The mysterious woman looked up sharply and scowled, a petulant scowl consumed with rage and resentment. The whites of her eyes burned unnaturally bright against their crimson backdrop, glistening under the fluorescent light that flickered overhead, as they bored a hole in Meridia.

"*Yoooou!*" she bleated, her rasping voice was immediately recognizable as belonging to the witch of Crooked House.

Overcome by panic and confusion, Meridia fought to catch her breath amidst the coppery odour assaulting her lungs. She reeled backwards with what felt like every fibre of her being, sending the bloodbath below and its architect spiralling into the darkness from where they both came.

Meridia's heart stuttered as she floundered, momentarily lost in a void of nothingness, until she clocked an object hurtling towards her in the distance. The drab grey surface of her school desk reached her at supersonic speed, causing her to flinch in her seat as she reconnected with reality.

Her heart still racing, she anxiously scanned the room to find everything as it was. Alman, hunched over in the opposite corner, immersed in his phone, hadn't even noticed her latest episode. Fumbling for her own phone, she frantically dialled Zach's number.

22

Zach was more than a little miffed at how their hospital visit had gone so far.

There was an unfamiliar tension in the air that he couldn't quite put his finger on, and the easy-going dynamic they usually enjoyed when they were all together now seemed stilted somehow. JJ and Izzy were strangely quiet and had hardly taken part in any conversations, whereas Kane seemed to have his own secret agenda.

Zach looked at the dated, oversized white clock on the wall and reasoned Meridia would be leaving school for her dinner date soon. As his brother's voice faded into white noise, he flirted with the fantasy of going with her. What he wouldn't do for a large pepperoni pizza right now with extra pepperoni.

Allowing his mind to wander, he noticed a familiar smell drift under his nose. Lemon and mint, he thought to himself as he breathed in its sweetness. He was thankful for a break from the bitter disinfectant that had dominated since their arrival. It was an unmistakable scent. In fact, it was a signature scent and one that belonged only to Meridia.

He looked around the cubicle, half expecting to see her standing beside him, but there was no sign of her. It was as if she was standing right next to him though. The smell was intoxicating and the perfect tonic to a challenging afternoon.

"Can you smell that?" he whispered to Izzy, who was closest to him.

"Smell what?" she replied, puzzled. Zach was just about to explain when he felt his phone vibrate. Meridia was calling.

"Meridia's calling guys. I'll be back in a sec." Zach slipped out into the hall and answered the call as he walked back toward reception. "Hello?"

"Zach, Thank God! Where are you?" Meridia sounded distressed.

"We're still at the hospital. What's wrong? You sound upset..."

"Get out of there...now! I don't care what you tell them, but you need to get everyone out of there right now. You're all in danger!"

"Wh..what? How?"

"I had another vision...a real one! You need to get everyone out of there now."

"A vision? What kind of vision? Wh...what about Peter?" Meridia's state of panic was infectious and spread to Zach in an instant.

"I'll tell you when you get out, but please Zach...you've got to leave now. It's you they're after, not Peter. Just get as far away from that place as you can..."

"Ok...ok, I'll get the others and text you when we're out!"

"Please Zach, Hurry! I don't know how much time you have."

Meridia's choice of words shook Zach to his core, and he ran back to Peter's cubicle, his legs trembling in fear. Time was something he had been acutely aware of ever since discovering he was doomed to be the final piece of a centuries old apocalyptic puzzle.

He burst through the curtains like a bat out of hell, making everyone else jump out of their skin.

"We've got to go guys! Meridia needs us...I'm sorry Peter. C'mon guys, we don't have much time...I'll tell you all on the way." Zach was on the verge of crying as he hocked the curtain back to fashion an exit and emphasize the urgency.

The rest of the group looked on in stunned silence, still processing Zach's rambling appeal.

"What's wrong?" Izzy asked as she hoisted her schoolbag onto her shoulder.

"I'll tell you on the way. We don't have much time!" Zach's reply was desperate and stirred everyone else into action.

Peter watched on from his bed as the once peaceful ward descended into a crescendo of hustle and bustle as everyone collected their things and gathered around the exit. There was a slight pause as the group waited for Peter's approval to depart whilst he weighed up his response to the sudden disruption.

"It's ok. You go and I'll catch you all tomorrow. Kane, let me know what's going on as and when." Peter politely shooed them away, and his blessing acted as a starter pistol as all four children raced down the corridor towards the elevators.

"Thanks Peter, I'll message you as soon as I can," Kane

called back as they disappeared out of sight to the rumble of thunderous footsteps echoing down the hospital hall.

"What's going on?" Kane demanded as he repeatedly pressed the down button to call the elevator.

"Meridia had a vision. She said this place isn't safe and we've got to get out." Zach's head bobbed from left to right as he answered, preoccupied with the empty corridors on either side of them.

Once again, there was no nurse at the reception desk and the ward was unnaturally quiet since they'd all stopped running. Although Zach had no idea what Meridia had seen, her call had left him on edge to the point he was now gearing up for some kind of confrontation.

"But we're at the hospital...and it's still daylight. What exactly did she say?" Kane prodded as a sharp chime sounded at the lift's arrival.

"She said she'd explain when we were out. She wasn't joking around Kane, she said it was me they wanted."

"Who's they?" Kane probed.

"She didn't say. Maybe it's that creep in the hood...I don't know..."

"Damn...I left my coat on the back of the chair in Peter's cubicle," Izzy interrupted.

"You go get it and we'll try to hold the lift for you." Kane barked, frustrated by his increasing lack of control over the situation.

"No, you take that one. There's another on its way down. I'll grab that and meet you on the ground floor."

"I'll go with you." JJ slipped out of the elevator's metal jaws as they began to close, "I'll call the next lift while you get your coat."

"Hurry Izz!" Zach pleaded as Izzy scuttled her way back towards cubicle six.

"It's fine. We'll be right behind you." JJ's well intended promise offered little reassurance before he disappeared behind the two tired stainless-steel doors as they lumberingly scraped shut.

Both brothers glumly looked at each other in recognition of the old horror trope as Kane warned, "I've got a really bad feeling about this…"

<h1 style="text-align:center">23</h1>

Izzy's HURRIED FOOTSTEPS REVERBERATED throughout the muted ward as she made her way back to cubicle six. As she passed row upon row of sealed blue curtains, Chase Side felt more morgue than hospital, so Izzy eased up from a light jog to a quiet tiptoe.

Spooked by Meridia's prediction, there was something eerie about the ward and its hidden occupants now that sent her imagination into overdrive.

When she reached Peter's bed, Izzy found that someone had drawn his curtains, but she didn't recall seeing anyone else on the ward when they had left him. She turned back towards the elevators and saw JJ at the other end of the corridor, some hundred yards away, pointing at an imaginary watch on his wrist.

"Stop being silly." She muttered to herself under her breath and then softly called out, "Peter? It's Izzy...I forgot my coat so just stepping in to get it, ok?" Izzy tentatively reached out and felt for the edge of the curtain.

BANG!

As her fingertips grazed the rugged fabric, she jumped

at a loud clatter from the other side, as if something metal had been sent crashing to the floor.

"Peter? Are you ok?" She plucked up the courage to slip between the curtains and enter the cubicle.

To her surprise, Peter's bed was empty and there was no sign of him anywhere.

"Peter?" her voice reduced to a whisper as she felt her nerve abandon her.

BANG!

Another loud clang came from her right, somewhere behind the adjoining cubicle, and Izzy leapt out of her skin again. She grasped the collar of her coat and dragged it away from the seat it was slumped over. The metal buttons scraped against the hard plastic chair, slicing through the tense silence, and giving away her position.

Izzy lifted her coat to avoid any further racket, keeping her eyes locked on the neighbouring curtain as she backed away towards her exit. As she felt the thick fabric brush up against her back, she saw the curtain opposite her twitch and swell as if someone was pressing up against it from the other side. Following its pleats all the way down to the floor, she saw two bare feet gradually emerge, one by one, from beneath the blue hem. They were not Peter's, and most likely a woman's, although they looked grubby and neglected.

Izzy forced her leaden legs to peddle backwards and lug her herself out into the hallway, but as she retreated, the mysterious patient on the other side of the curtain responded and shuffled closer. Taking in a deep breath, Izzy's knuckles whitened on the collar of her coat as she dug deep within herself to get away.

She made her move, spinning sharply into the curtain at her back to make her escape, but all she managed to do was wrap herself up like a taco. Feeling her balance desert her, she frantically tried to unravel herself from her obstinate cocoon, floundering within its rigid embrace. Woozy from her spin and choked by the overpowering smell of hospital soap, Izzy stumbled back inside the cubicle.

From there, she frantically set about the curtains again in her search for an opening. Glancing over her shoulder as she fumbled amongst the wall of fabric, a pair of emaciated arms protruded above the opposite side of the bed, swaying aimlessly as their host ambled forward like a lumbering zombie.

"Finally!" Izzy bleated in triumph as her fingers clasped onto an edge, and she used it to drag herself out into the empty hall.

The instant she escaped into the corridor, the florescent light above her flickered and died. In the shadows behind her she could still hear the slow, methodical shuffling of feet edging their way towards her and so she ran, but as she did the darkness followed. One light at a time.

"James!" she cried, but JJ was nowhere in sight.

With each desperate stride she made towards the elevator, another light went down as the gloomy stampede tried its best to swallow her whole. A strange inaudible whispering joined in the hunt, nipping at her earlobes as she puffed and panted in her attempt to pull away from the ominous blackout.

"What's wrong?" JJ emerged from behind an alcove next to the abandoned reception desk.

"Call the lift James!" Izzy screamed, the shadows hot on her heels as she raced toward him. "Call the lift!"

JJ responded in a flash, bashing the call button repeatedly in a state of panic until Izzy clattered into him and the darkness engulfed them both. Welded together and gripped by fear, a chilly breeze whistled past their ears, carrying with it the eerie whispers that had chased Izzy along the corridor.

The melodious chant grew louder as layer upon layer of murmuring voices joined the aural assault, cocooning them in incantations the way cotton candy clings to a stick when being spun.

Ping!

The elevator doors casually opened in front of them. Piling in, Izzy and JJ pressed the button marked 'G' and anxiously bounced up and down whilst they waited for the doors to close. With a matter of inches to spare, a woman's face emerged from the shadows and tried to force herself into the gap.

Peering in at them with eyes wide and wild, she flashed an unhinged toothy grin that spread from ear to ear like a gruesome Cheshire Cat.

Izzy recoiled in fear as the doors closed flush, keeping the spectre at bay, but before she could utter a word to JJ, she noticed another figure within the dull reflection of their steel vessel.

Someone else was in the elevator with them.

Squeezing JJ's hand, she turned and saw an old man standing with his back to her in the opposite corner. Her heart sank the moment she recognized his flat cap and jacket: it was Mr Richards.

Izzy squeezed JJ's hand even tighter as she tried to make out his face from the reflection in the control panel he was facing. The lift had an identical set of doors on either side, and it looked like Mr Richards was gearing up to leave in the opposite way they had entered.

Both friends watched on silently as the elevator

numbers slowly counted down from '3' to 'G', all the while Mr Richards didn't move a muscle.

Izzy wondered if he was scared, and perhaps that was why he hadn't turned around since their noisy arrival.

Ding!

The elevator chimed and to Izzy's surprise, the door behind her was the only one to open. Mr Richards remained facing the opposite corner, seemingly uninterested in leaving.

"There you are, what took you?" Zach complained from the ground floor reception where he and Kane had been patiently waiting, but Izzy didn't even turn to acknowledge his question.

She just remained focused on the inside of the lift, watching and waiting for god knew what.

"C'mon Izz."

She felt JJ gently lead her by the hand towards the exit. Backing her way out, Izzy continued to watch the old man in the elevator like a hawk until the doors began to close again.

Just before Mr Richards disappeared altogether out of sight, he turned his head towards Izzy and delivered a snarling sideways glance of contempt. Izzy continued to stare at the closed doors, indignant and more than a little miffed at the old man's grievance with her.

"C'mon guys, we need to go," Zach snapped her out of her trance and ushered everyone to the safety of the street outside.

"But what about Peter...he's still inside." Still shellshocked, Izzy obediently followed the rest of the group into the crisp winter air as she continued her plea. "He wasn't there when I went into the cubicle...what if something happened to him? What if that thing got him?"

"Wh..what thing...what happened up there?" Zach stuttered, unsure what he'd missed in the short time it had taken them to catch up.

"The lights went out and something started chasing me...it came from the cubicle next to Peter's...I think it was a woman, but then there was this weird whispering...and a face... then the old man was there, staring at me again..."

JJ placed an arm on Izzy's shoulder, giving her the chance to take a beat. She was rapidly losing control and her nerves were making her ramble.

"There was something else up there with us, for sure. I didn't see anything, but I heard it. It was like the darkness chased us all the way out of there." JJ looked up towards Peter's floor in search of answers, whilst Izzy stood dejected, lost for words as she tried to rationalize everything.

Neither of them were doing a great job explaining what had just happened, and she wondered if it was their minds playing tricks on them. Her eyes caught up with JJ's and what she saw changed her mind.

Halfway up the hospital's tired exterior, she could see a row of lights flickering on and off erratically. A slender silhouette of a woman was standing bold as brass in the middle of one of the windows and appeared to be staring down at them.

"There! Look, is that...who is that?" Izzy asked, hypnotized by the mysterious figure watching them from above.

The rest of the group began squinting in response to get a better look.

"What's going on up there?" Zach asked, engrossed in the peculiar light show as it jumped and danced from side to side along the ward.

"We need to go back. He could be in trouble." Izzy

mumbled as she marched back towards the hospital entrance.

"Wait! Let me call Peter," Kane grunted, agitated by the confusion that was mounting around him. "It's ringing..." he added sarcastically.

They all returned their attention back to the shadowy voyeur and watched as it slowly placed a hand up to its ear, as if answering a phone. Kane recoiled, confused and placed his phone on loudspeaker so everyone could hear.

"Hi Peter...is everything ok?"

"All ok. There's been a power cut it seems. The whole ward is flickering like a nightclub up here. I heard a nurse say that a patient wandered off in all the confusion. They are just looking for her now."

Izzy felt herself blush at the prospect she had just been spooked by a confused old dear.

"Where are you now?" Kane asked.

"Right where you left me, resting in bed. Why?"

Peter sounded calm, but a little distant in Izzy's opinion. His charming inflections were still there, but something else was missing. He felt cold somehow.

"It's just that Izzy..." Izzy hushed Kane by placing a finger up to her lips, "er...Izzy thought she saw that missing patient when we were on our way out." Kane shrugged his shoulders in defence of his below-par improvisation as the line went quiet. "Peter? Are you still there?"

"Still here. But I'll be out tomorrow."

For a moment, Izzy detected a strange undertone to Peter's comment but didn't let on. She was feeling a little paranoid. The rest of the group seemed unconvinced by everything she'd seen lately, which left Izzy questioning her own sanity.

"I'll leave you to it in that case. Just text if you need

anything and we'll see you tomorrow." If Kane had picked up on anything out of the ordinary in Peter, then he certainly wasn't showing it.

He ended the call and put the phone back in his pocket. As he did, the stranger in the window lowered their arm and stepped back into the shadows.. "Well, that wasn't weird at all," Kane quipped.

"Let's get out of here guys." Zach began leading the group away from Chase Side as Izzy took one last glance back up at the building before joining them.

The flickering lights had subsided, and all was still.

24

Meridia felt her phone vibrate in her pocket as she walked briskly across the school carpark. Her strange vision was still dominating her thoughts, and she remained on edge.

The temperature had dropped a few degrees since she'd stepped outside at lunchtime, so she pulled her coat into her body to shield herself from the crisp winter air. Seeing a text from Zach on her phone, she sighed with relief.

```
Hey! We're out and ok, but
things got weird at the
hospital. First Peter was
acting odd and then Izzy and
JJ were chased out of there by
a whispering shadow!

The witch maybe?

It could all be nothing though
as Peter's tired and a patient
wandered off during a
power cut.
```

```
Anyway, we're all heading home
now and meeting at my place
tomorrow at 9. Kane said it
would be good to get together
before seeing Peter again. I
hope you have a nice time with
your mum and save me a slice
of pizza.

PS don't worry, we're all
fine x
```

Something about the tone of Zach's message cut through her nerves and forced a smile.

"You're looking happy for someone who just had detention." Her mum was standing at the gate waiting, just as she had promised.

"That was just Zach asking me to bring back a slice of pizza for him." Meridia blushed as she realized how that might sound, and her mum was quick to pounce.

"Aw...you two are so sweet. They do say the way to a man's heart is through his stomach..."

"We're just friends mum." Meridia did her best to deflect as she reached out and gave her mum a huge squeeze.

Emily Wilson was slightly taller than her daughter, but that was the only noticeable difference. Often mistaken for Meridia's older sister, Emily always claimed the only anti-aging treatment anyone ever needed was a good night's sleep, and boy, did she love her sleep.

Meridia let the hug linger a little as she buried herself in her mum's soft winter coat and took in a deep breath of her perfume. Its lavender scent always soothed her, and despite the mild distraction of Zach's message, she still needed soothing. It had been a long and challenging week, leaving her severely drained. Danger loomed ahead, and her intuition told her this was just the beginning.

"Hope you've worked up an appetite today young lady. I think I might treat us both to ice-cream after." Meridia's mum was excited at the prospect of her own little 'girls night'. It had been a long time since she'd shown any genuine interest in leaving the house, but Meridia saw her suggestion of a local pizza, and now ice-cream, as a gigantic step in the right direction.

"Can we stretch to a brownie if they have any? It's too cold for ice-cream."

"It's never too cold for salted caramel ice-cream M...but yeah, you can have whatever you want."

The two girls locked arms and shared another affectionate squeeze as they left St Swithun's behind them and set off towards town.

Borselino's was a local family run pizzeria and only a ten-minute walk from the Wilson house, but it made the best pizzas in Shawbrook.

Despite most of its business coming from delivery these days, the modest restaurant kept a handful of tables out back for the odd passerby looking for some authentic Italian hospitality.

As Meridia and her mum entered through the glass-paned door, the warmth of the traditional wood-fired pizza oven welcomed them in from the cold with open arms. Behind the grey, speckled granite counter Stefano was busy flipping pizza dough with his back to them. As it often was, the restaurant was devoid of customers, but within seconds Stefano's wife Sofia materialized from out back carrying a magnificent triple-layer chocolate gateau for the cake fridge which sat proudly on display in the shop's front window.

"Emily!" she exclaimed, hurrying to set the plate down. "How wonderful to see you."

Emily froze like a rabbit in the headlights. She'd forgotten just how tactile Sophia was, and it had been a long time since anyone other than Meridia had given her a hug.

Watching on in wonder, Meridia was unsure how her mum would react to the unwanted attention, half expecting her to flee the restaurant and retreat to the safety of her sofa. Thankfully, she stood her ground and took the physical contact on the chin, although Meridia couldn't tell if that was entirely her choice.

"How nice of you to come by. Are you dining in with us this evening?" Sophia was a tall, slender woman in her early thirties who bore a striking resemblance to a young Isabella Rossellini.

She and her equally attractive husband had come to Shawbrook after inheriting her uncle's shop when he passed. They saw a gap in the market and converted the struggling deli into a thriving restaurant, but, during the COVID pandemic, they were forced to introduce home delivery. It proved a game changer and they hadn't looked back since, beating out the high street pizza chains with their unique twists on traditional Italian classics.

"That would be lovely, thanks. We're just having a mini-girl's night to see the weekend in." Emily regained her composure and followed Sophia to a red and white checkered table opposite the counter.

Both girls caught a mouth-watering waft of freshly melted mozzarella and Italian herbs as Stefano spun a pizza around in the oven, and they eagerly took their seats.

"Let me grab you ladies some menus. Would you like some water for the table?"

"Yes please, that would be lovely." Emily took her coat

off and draped it over the back of her chair, whilst Meridia unravelled her scarf and did the same. "Do you want a soft drink M? I might have one of their homemade lemonades."

"I'll have one too. Can't wait to order my pizza though. I'm starving...next time I get detention I'll make sure I take an extra snack."

"Ahem...Next time?" Emily shot a disapproving look across the variety of condiments separating them.

"Here you go ladies..." Sophia provided the perfect distraction from Meridia's own goal as she placed a laminated menu in front of each of them, along with a tiny square of pizza. "This is a new creation Stef is testing at the moment: tuna and sweet chili cheese. I'll be back in a bit to take your order, but in the meantime, would you like any drinks?"

"Two of your homemade Sicilian lemonades please. We're both parched." Emily ordered for both of them as she searched the menu for the day's special. "Ooh...chicken and pesto pizza, sounds nice."

"I'm going for a pepperoni today with extra pepperoni. It's all I've thought about all day." Meridia lied, wishing she could let her mum in on all the secrets she'd been hiding from her lately.

Whilst her mum relayed their order, Meridia realized how easy it had become to deceive the one person she loved more than anything in the world. She wondered if Crooked House was really the cause, forcing her hand, or if it had simply shone a light on latent tendencies that were lurking in the shadows all along.

"Earth to Meridia..." Emily waved her hand back and forth in front of Meridia's eyes. "Do you want some olives while we wait?"

"Olives? Yuck!" Meridia grimaced at the prospect of those oily little suckers squelching around in her mouth.

"Just testing. You seem distracted...still thinking about lover boy?" Emily gave a wink as she pulled her daughter's leg once more.

"I know what you're doing...it's not working. We're just friends."

"So, what are you up to tomorrow?" Meridia blushed the moment she realized she'd played right into her mum's hands.

"I'm going to Zach's...with Izzy. Our school project isn't going to finish itself." Another lie wriggled its way free of Meridia's lips, and she felt the shadow of guilt loom over her once more.

Enough was enough. She had to tell her mum everything.

"Chicken and pesto..." Sophia arrived carrying two large rustic-looking wooden chopping boards and placed the first down in front of Emily, "...and one pepperoni with extra pepperoni."

"Thank you." Emily took in the fragrant smell of basil as it hitched a ride on the steam from the pizza, and Meridia held her tongue.

"*What am I thinking?*" she thought to herself, "*This is the first time in forever she's left the house and here I am about to ruin it all. Suck it up Meridia. Today is all about your mum!*"

"Dig in." Emily gave them both the green light to indulge in their thick and creamy mozzarella infused feast. And, for the hour that followed, Meridia felt twelve again.

25

As Meridia went to bed later that evening she could still feel the chocolate brownie and ice-cream sloshing around in her stomach, but that was a small price to pay for seeing her mum out in the world again.

As soon as she flicked her nightlight on the warm fuzzy afterglow from her girls' night out swiftly evaporated, making way for the stark realization it was bedtime. The comforting amber hue that once painted her room had recently turned into a corrupting force, instilling a sense of dread and foreboding in everything it touched.

She set her alarm for every hour as a precaution again, but remained hopeful that Peter's return signalled some sort of respite from her nightmares. Despite the weight of the world returning to her shoulders, the moment Meridia pulled her marshmallow duvet up to her chin she slipped into a carb-induced coma and, just for the briefest of moments, all her worries softly melted away.

When Meridia wearily opened her eyes, daylight was already seeping in through the window and her phone was nowhere to be seen.

Gripped by panic, she sat bolt upright and searched the room for the next threat, knowing deep down in her gut that a good night's sleep was too good to be true.

Aside from her door being ajar, which was a little unusual, the rest of her room was just as she'd left it. There appeared to be no witch in sight, no paranormal expert floating above her, and more importantly, she was still in her own house. Unsure of the time she slipped out from under the covers and checked her bedside table for her phone, but all she found was the end of its charger cable.

"Where's that gone?" she pondered.

She was certain she'd set it last night, unless she hadn't made it that far. She patted down her duvet, checking in case it had somehow gotten caught up in its ruffles, but again she came up empty-handed.

Shrugging off the remnants of her slumber with a gratifying star-shaped stretch, Meridia ventured downstairs in search of it. Wherever her phone happened to be, it had most likely been driving her mum nuts with its incessant beeping, so she picked up the pace a little, skipping her usual routine of making her bed, and wandered out into the hallway.

All the other doors upstairs were wide open and as she passed her mum's empty bedroom, she glanced in at her alarm clock which was flashing '11:37am' in neon red.

"Shit! I'm late," she gasped, and scuttled downstairs.

Reaching the bottom step, she could see the street door was wide open and letting in a gale. The sudden gust of cold air weaved its way through her fleece pyjamas and chilled her to the bone, carrying with it the bitter smell of dirty oil, along with creamy undertones of burnt plastic and rubber.

Placing one foot firmly down onto the pine-coloured

laminate flooring, she instantly retracted it in shock as the ice-cold plastic stung her bare sole.

"Too good to be true," she muttered to herself as her guard went up and she reached over to fish her soft sheepskin slippers from the porch. Doing her utmost to avoid any further contact with the floor, she retrieved both slippers and shuffled into them to investigate.

As she cautiously approached the door, visions of the mysterious hooded figure flooded to the forefront of her mind, but when she peeked around the doorframe into her tiny front garden, she would have gladly taken the creepy stalker over the carnage that now littered Nightingale Lane.

A torrent of tiny grey ash particles flashed past her face, galloping on the wind like a band of wild horses as they fled the crackling inferno that engulfed her street.

As far as her eyes could see, every building on her sleepy suburban estate was now consumed by fierce amber flames, pumping a steady stream of thick black smoke into the bright blue sky above. Mr Morrison's car, her neighbour opposite, was a smouldering wreck of mangled blue paintwork and shattered glass that dusted the pavement with its grey-green fragments as they flickered under the light of the raging fire.

The street itself was desolate, devoid of anyone, as if all the residents were either dead inside their demolished houses or on the run from whatever dark force was responsible. Mysterious star-like symbols decorated the ruins with thick red paint, like a graffiti artist's tag taking credit for the destruction and debris.

"MUM?" Meridia turned back into her house, overwrought with fear "MUM!...MUM!"

She raced towards the living room, becoming more and more desperate with every holler. "Mu..."

Meridia came to an abrupt halt the moment she reached her living room and stood slack-jawed in its doorway. The old red brick fireplace she had lazed beside every winter since she was a toddler, the antique cream wall adorned with a myriad of nostalgic pictures from her youth were both gone. All reduced to a lifeless pile of rubble.

"NO!" Meridia rushed to the mound of broken bricks and childhood memories the moment she saw it.

There, beneath the wreckage, was a dust-covered hand, its broken fingers contorted and caked in dried blood as they sprouted from their stony grave.

"MUM!" Meridia cried, fighting back tears and vomit as she fell beside the remnants of her best friend and mother.

Emily's hand was rigid and cold to the touch as Meridia comforted and cradled all she could cling onto, hoping to warm her back to life.

"I couldn't stop her...she was too strong..."

Meridia's head whipped sharply to her right to find Peter sitting on the remains of her broken sofa, his head hung low as he stared at the scorched herringbone floor at his feet.

"You must break it Meridia...you must find it and break it before it's too late..."

"WHAT IS IT?!" Meridia screamed at Peter in frustration, unable to let go of her mother's hand.

"Just tell me...tell me what to do...what do I have to break? Please...just tell me!" She sobbed. Her spirit crushed under the weight of her loss.

Peter wearily raised his head in response to her pleas. His once chiselled face was now gaunt and grey, awash with fear and guilt, whilst his eyes remained firmly shut tight.

"I can't..." he whimpered. "She won't let me..."

Peter slowly opened his eyes to reveal two black shiny

orbs glistening eerily beneath the shade of Meridia's broken home. There was a darkness within them, within Peter, that she had never seen before, and it sent her reeling back in horror.

As she flinched, the rubble gave way underfoot, and she tumbled backwards onto her pillow. The soft memory foam cradled her fall and gently guided her back to the safety of her bed.

Meridia was awake again, her phone clutched tightly to her chest on top of the duvet that swamped her trembling body. It was 8am and time to get up.

26

Doing his best to evade capture, Jacob Alman cautiously peered over the busted remains of a red brick wall on the corner of Nightingale Lane.

It had been almost a week now since the first catastrophic wave of destruction swept its way through Shawbrook, and it was abundantly clear that no-one was coming to rescue its surviving residents; if there were any.

Having travelled on foot for days without food, he was yet to stumble across another soul, as each estate he passed through had been reduced to nothing more than a smouldering graveyard.

The stench of death still hung heavy in the air as he surveyed the carnage surrounding him. Thick black smoke stung his eyes, blurring his vision, but he'd seen enough roads by now to know this place was just like all the rest. Burned-out ruins of a civilization caught unawares, still aglow from the murderous hellfire that had scorched their town, killing everything it touched.

"What the fu..." Using his grubby sleeves, Alman

hurriedly rubbed both eyes in disbelief as he made sure he wasn't hallucinating.

Across the street, beyond the wreckage of an old blue car that lay crushed at the roadside, he was sure he'd glimpsed a girl hiding amongst the debris.

"It can't be.." he muttered, although he'd recognized her instantly.

Her hair was unmistakable, cutting through the smog like a bright red beacon. But it couldn't be. Meridia Wilson vanished well over a year ago following the Cold Christmas tragedy.

He wanted desperately to call out, but he knew from the ominous symbols surrounding him it wasn't safe. Still, he needed to do something. If it was Meridia, then perhaps she had answers. Her reappearance couldn't be a coincidence. Before he could give it another thought, she re-emerged. It was her, but she hadn't aged a day since her disappearance.

Alman watched as she fell to her knees onto a pile of rubble and began screaming at the tattered remnants of an old sofa.

"Ssh... They'll hear you." He whispered anxiously to himself. His whole body tensed as his fight-or-flight system kicked in, and his eyes instinctively darted around in search of the first sign of trouble.

Click-clack...click-clack...

The bone-chilling sound instantly struck fear into his heart as he prepared himself for what was to come. He had to run as fast as he could. It didn't matter which direction, he just had to put as much distance between him and Nightingale Lane as humanly possible.

Across the road, Meridia abruptly went quiet and wobbled, as if about to fall backwards.

Click-clack…click-clack…

They were getting closer.

Alman felt a tingling sensation rise to the surface of his lip, followed by a coppery taste on the tip of his tongue. He'd bitten down so hard to temper his anguish that he'd drawn blood.

Click-clack…click-clack…

They were here, and Meridia was a sitting duck, just waiting to be torn limb from limb, just as his family had been. She finally flopped back, giving in to gravity, and as she landed on the bricks and mortar she vanished like a ghost, exactly as she had done that fateful winter afternoon.

27

DING DONG

The doorbell reverberated throughout the Jackson house like a scene from the Addams Family, almost shaking the pictures from their walls.

"I've got it!" Zach eagerly galloped downstairs to let Meridia in.

When he opened the door, she looked annoyed; angry even. Her thick auburn eyebrows were drawn tightly together, and her lips were pursed.

"We need to talk about Peter," she exclaimed, brushing past Zach and marching up the stairs to join the others in Kane's bedroom. "I had another bloody dream last night and something weird is definitely going on with him." Her voice bounced down the stairs in her wake as Zach scurried to keep up.

"We know...we were kind of hoping you could tell us what it was." Kane was waiting by the door as Meridia entered the crowded room.

JJ and Izzy were already there, having skipped knocking for Meridia on their way at her request.

"Sorry I'm late. I had another shitty night and just wanted to have breakfast with my mum before I left. I'm so sick of this crap. Peter was in my dreams again, but this one was different. My whole road looked like a bomb had hit it and Peter was one of 'them'. His eyes...they were black, like the others. He said we...or I...need to destroy it...no, break it. We need to find it and break it. Whatever 'it' is, I'm sick of this cryptic bullshit! Why can't he just tell me what 'it' is?" Meridia tore around the room like a hurricane, covering whatever floor space she could find as she ranted, whilst the others all looked on in stunned silence, waiting for her to take a breath.

"Hi." Izzy jumped in to fill the briefest of pauses before Meridia got going again.

"There were these creepy markings on everything...like upside down stars..." Meridia grabbed the open pad on Kane's desk and began scribbling, "Hi Izz. They kinda looked like this, and in the centre was a skull, at least I think, but it didn't look human..." She held the pad up for everyone to see. "Like this. Creepy right?"

"I'd say," JJ added, "That's a pentagram...it's occult, right Kane?"

"Yep. The inverted pentagram is used a lot in movies to depict cults or devil worshipers. I don't think I've seen it with the skull in the middle though...is that meant to be a goat?" Kane studied Meridia's sketch intently as he ran through the horror encyclopaedia stored in his brain.

"Devil worship? It was plastered all over the place... what does that mean? Why was it everywhere on my street?" Meridia finally ran out of steam as she placed the pad back on Kane's desk.

"Maybe Peter will know what it means. He's the expert...that's if it means anything at all. No offence M, it's just that not all your dreams make sense...at least not right away." Kane made a valid point, which Meridia acknowledged with a reluctant nod. "One thing you are right about though is Peter. Something is seriously off with him, and after our visit to the hospital, I'm not sure I entirely trust him."

"Really? But he's...Peter...surely it's not that bad...is it?" Meridia wrestled with her own instincts, despite knowing deep down Kane might be right.

"Kane's right M, Peter isn't himself at all, and whatever was going on at that hospital was more than just a confused patient wandering round in the dark." Izzy spoke up from the corner she was tucked into.

"Something chased us out of that place. I saw it. I felt it. Mr Richards was there too, giving me the chills again...there's something up with him. Yes, the creepy woman in the window might have just seen Kane pull his phone out and decided to mimic him, who knows...but there was someone...something else there yesterday...it was like being back at Crooked House. It was evil." Izzy's choice of words wasn't lost on the group; she was rattled.

"In my vision, at school, I saw you all in the hospital... the witch had killed you all right there. She saw me watching her from...from wherever I was. But I couldn't see Zach, or Peter...just the three of you. That's when I knew I had to warn you. It was just this overwhelming feeling like something terrible was about to happen...like a preview, the way it felt at Crooked House that day. I can't explain it...or control it and it's really pissing me off." Meridia felt her temper flare again as she relived the anguish and frustration of her stint in detention.

"I could smell you...just before you called, I could smell your perfume in the hospital. It was as if you were standing right next to me." Zach blushed as he made his confession, fearing everyone might laugh.

"I smelled it too." JJ jumped to his support. "It was brief, but I definitely smelled it."

The revelation left Meridia feeling even more perplexed, so she flopped down on the edge of the bed for a moment to process it.

"What were you doing M? When you had the vision, I mean." Izzy leapt at the chance to apply some logic to something.

"I was just sitting at a desk, twiddling my pen and the next thing I knew I was floating above the hospital ward. It wasn't like a dream...I was awake, like I was at Crooked House."

"You mean *my* pen...I gave you my pen in science because yours ran out, remember?" Zach's throwaway remark lit a fire in Meridia's mind, casting out the shadows surrounding her gift, and she jumped to her feet in excitement.

"That's it! That must be it. It was *your* pen I was holding...just like it was *your* torch I was playing with in my pocket that day at Crooked House...my gift must be triggered by whatever I'm holding."

"I've seen psychics do that on Most Haunted...they hold an item that belonged to a ghost and channel their spirit... maybe your gift works the same way?"

Meridia's excitement spread to Kane, and it was his turn to pace.

"Maybe we can test it...you know, like run an experiment or something, with an object and not tell you who it belongs to?"

"Or we could try it with something of Peters?" JJ's suggestion tackled a more pressing issue and instantly gained favour from the rest of the group. "Do we have anything of his here?"

"His key...I've got the key to his house in my pocket." Kane fumbled around in his jean pocket and pulled out a brass yale key linked to a rather basic blue plastic tag.

Eyes wide with anticipation, he handed it over to Meridia, who treated it like a fidget toy, playfully flipping it back and forth between her thumb and forefinger.

"Way to put me on-the-spot guys...I'm not sure if this is gonna work..." Meridia continued to play with the key in her hand for a while as her audience watched in mesmerized silence. "I think maybe we should try this another time...I'm not getting anything, and we need a backup plan if we're going to Peter's today. Maybe the fact I'm not getting anything means we're barking up the wrong tree?"

"Tell you what, you look after the key, and we'll just see what happens. No pressure, ok? Peter text me first thing to say he'd passed his assessment and is being discharged at some point this morning. I told him we'd head over after lunch, so that gives us plenty of time to figure out what's going on." Kane was eager to get brainstorming. "So, it seems we're all in agreement something is definitely up with Peter. It must be linked to Meridia's first nightmare so why don't we go over that again in case we missed something?"

"I don't know what else to say really. The witch locked me inside Crooked House. She was terrorizing me in the dark, but then Peter arrived and took the brunt of it all. The last thing I saw was her grab him...I think she lifted him up maybe as I sunk into the ground. That was when I woke up. I don't have my journal here so I can't really add much more detail than that...I think last night's dream is still too fresh in my mind." Meridia shrugged her shoulders in resignation as Kane weighed back in.

"What if Peter somehow got pulled into your dream for real, only he got stuck there? When we asked him about what happened, he said he didn't remember anything other than marking school reports. But what if he's lying?"

"Why would he lie about that though?" Izzy played devil's advocate. "Sorry, I didn't mean that how it sounded. I meant what reason might he have to lie about that?"

"That's the million-dollar question isn't it...maybe he's scared, or the witch has something over him we don't know about?" JJ entered the debate.

"I saw him again the night before he came out of his coma...he couldn't speak, but it looked like he was trying to tell me something...until he threw up all over me! Then last night when I saw him again, I asked him to tell me what was going on, but he said the witch wouldn't let him...at least I think that's who he meant. It's all so muddled in my head...I don't know what's important anymore. Maybe they're all bad dreams and nothing more." Meridia's commentary triggered something in Kane. A thread he needed to pull on.

"You said you saw us all at the hospital that day, but not Peter right?" Meridia nodded in agreement. "But you saw the witch. And then when Izzy went back to get her coat he was gone then too, but the witch was there...let's just assume it wasn't a random patient for the moment..."

"Who was it then?" Izzy was intrigued to see where Kane was going.

"So, the last couple of times the witch has shown up, Peter has gone AWOL. That can't be a coincidence, right?" Kane pressed his point a little, waiting for the others to catch up.

"Like superman," Zach finally got involved. "Whenever

superman shows up, Clark Kent disappears and vice versa... wait, does that mean Peter could be..."

"What if Peter is the witch...or the witch is Peter? Would that make sense of what you've been seeing, M? I mean, would that stack up?" Kane waved a finger at Izzy to wait while Meridia mulled the idea over.

"I guess...I mean, it would explain why I still saw him after he woke up in the hospital. But why is it always at night?"

"Maybe the witch is sleeping then..."

"Do witches sleep?"

"Maybe our one does...or maybe it's nothing to do with Peter and you're the one dictating things with your power?" Meridia began rubbing the key more intently as she listened to Kane's theories. "Whatever the reason, he keeps trying to communicate with you, which suggests he's still in there somewhere. There must be a way to help him...maybe we should just burn that bloody place down to the ground and be done with it!"

"We can't ever go back there, remember? Not even to burn it down." The very thought of Crooked House instantly wriggled its way under JJ's skin as he vetoed Kane's suggestion.

"Let's assume you're right and Peter's possessed by the witch..." Izzy rolled her eyes as soon as she heard the words leave her mouth, "what are we expected to do about it?! We're not exorcists, we're kids! Peter is the paranormal expert...how are we supposed to fix him?"

"I don't know, but we have to try something."

With that, Kane's phone beeped.

"Speak of the devil...or witch in this case...Peter's in a taxi and on his way home. He said we're welcome to have lunch at his...what do we wanna do guys?"

"I say we go and figure out a plan when we get there. For all we know he might be ok, and we're all worried over nothing." It was JJ's turn to play devil's advocate, suggesting that perhaps they were all getting ahead of themselves. "If he starts acting strange, then we make an excuse to leave and regroup, or we just leg it, but at the very least it gives us a chance to suss him out."

"But what if it's a trap and as soon as we get there he turns into a witch and kills us all?" Zach was nervous they might not have the luxury of leaving once they got there.

"We can scope the place out when we get there and just come back if we have a bad feeling about anything. I know that's not really a plan, but JJ's right, we still don't know enough. The last thing we want to do is go in and make anything worse. The first sign of trouble, I'll pretend to get a message and use that as our way out of there."

"I say we do it," Izzy shrugged, unable to come up with a better plan of her own.

"Show of hands?" Kane took it to the vote and raised his for all to see.

Zach instantly followed suit, swiftly joined by JJ and Izzy.

Meridia was slower to respond, mulling it over in her mind before tentatively raising hers at half-mast. She had a bad feeling about this.

28

As they approached the corner of Willow Road, a hush of apprehension descended upon the group. The winter sun that had staunchly followed them ever since leaving Kane's house had now wavered in its conviction and retreated behind a cluster of dense grey clouds. An ice-cold breeze quickly pounced in the sun's absence, causing Meridia to shudder as it tightened its grip on the back of her neck. It was as if Peter's road had its own weather system, and the smell of rain wafted through the pack of friends as they marched on towards number 67.

Meridia had been nervously kneading Peter's key in her coat pocket ever since they'd all left Kane's house, but so far it had offered nothing beyond keeping her fingers warm.

"Did you guys feel that?" She asked, breaking the ominous silence.

"Yep," JJ was quick to respond. "It's like the first time we went to Crooked House, the way the wind picked up and the temperature dropped. I've got a terrible feeling about this guys."

"Me too. Really bad…" Meridia's swift concurrence

only spooked them all further as she continued to garner her reputation as a walking barometer for the paranormal.

RAT-A-TAT-TAT!

The group jumped as an empty Coke can rattled past in the wind, cutting through the eerie stillness of Peter's street before resting in the gutter at their feet. With neither a person nor car in sight, it seemed as if the entire estate had been evacuated in readiness for their arrival.

"How are we going to scope the place out without him seeing us? There's literally nothing close enough for us to hide behind! Where are all the cars? Where is everyone?" JJ's observation threw a spanner in the works as they drew within sight of the house.

"Damn! There were plenty of cars and bins dotted around last time, so we might need to improvise." Kane was annoyed their paper-thin plan had fallen over at the first hurdle.

"You guys go in and I'll hang back a little. You can tell Peter I got held up at home or something, but that I'm on my way. That'll give me time to look around while you keep him talking." JJ's suggestion was as good as anything else they could muster at such short notice.

"Just be careful mate, there was a ton of curtain twitching going on the last time I was here." Kane's reply was filled with apprehension as he knew all too well there might be more to worry about than nosy neighbours.

"It'll be fine. I'll just have a quick look before joining you inside. Besides, the neighbours can't be that sharp if they missed a guy in a hood break-in, in broad daylight, right?"

"Fair point. We'll keep him talking in the hallway, which should clear a path for you to get around back. There's a side-gate to the right of the house that he keeps unlocked, so you'll have to head down there...Oh and I'll leave the garden gate unlatched as that can be noisy to open. Just make sure you call at the first sign of trouble, ok?"

"Deal."

And with that, the rest of the group wished him luck and made their way up the deserted street, leaving JJ loitering on the corner.

When Kane unlatched the front gate to Peter's front garden, he felt a sharp tremor rattle its way up his back. His last visit was traumatic, to put it mildly, and the thought of walking headfirst into danger again made his stomach churn.

"M, are you picking up on anything yet? Just thought I'd ask before I knock the door."

"Nothing specific I'm afraid. I just know something is wrong." She shot a nervous glance toward JJ.

"Not too late to back out guys." She followed, but it was.

Creeeeeak!

The front door swung open abruptly to reveal Peter lurking behind it wearing a wry smile. "There you are! Come in, come in...I've been waiting."

29

JJ watched as one by one the rest of the group disappeared inside Peter's house.

It was go time.

When he got there, he realized the dreary beige brick wall to Peter's garden was only knee height, leaving him totally exposed to the front of the house. For a moment, he considered continuing his walk straight past the house to buy himself a little more time, then he noticed that someone had drawn a set of blackout curtains inside, shielding the living room from any prying eyes.

"Strange," he muttered to himself, as he gently pushed on the wrought-iron gate and tiptoed down the short, dusty terracotta path towards the frosted glass door. Trying to balance nonchalance and stealth, he quickly sidestepped to the right of the house where he found a tall wooden side-gate just as Kane had described.

Creak!

JJ's heart bobbled up into his mouth at the sudden noise, and he felt a cold sweat seep into the fabric of his baseball cap. Fear of being caught rooted him to the ground, so he took a deep breath to steady his nerves before pushing again, slower this time, until he created a wide enough opening to slip inside.

"Phew," he whispered once he'd reached the other side.

Now he had enough cover from the surrounding walls to explore without attracting any unwanted attention. However, something about the blackout curtains still troubled him, so before he went any further, he checked his phone for any word from Kane.

His heart sank when he saw the message 'no network coverage' plastered across the top of his screen.

"Shit!" he snapped, caught in a quandary of what to do next. "Stick to the plan JJ. One quick look and then knock the door."

Creeping towards the back garden, a sudden burst of cold wind nipped at his ears as it whistled its way past him. Securing his hat, he continued making his way towards the far corner of the property where he found a stark shingled garden, populated by a very basic grey rattan table and chairs that had seen better days.

Without a blade of grass in sight, a handful of boldly painted plant pots lay strewn around the edges of an otherwise drab and depressing looking plot, providing the only splash of colour.

To his left, a narrow stone pathway tightly hugged the rear of the house and led to what looked like a set of patio doors, whereas all that lay beyond the gravel to his right was a tired, sun-bleached wooden fence. There was only one way JJ could go, and so he shuffled his way along the path until he reached the patio doorframe and gingerly peered inside.

THUD!

Izzy was cowering between a heavy set of emerald-green curtains and the glass pane of the door. Her face was knotted with fear as she grimaced at him, gesturing towards a key that was sticking out of the lock on his side.

Hastily, JJ turned the lock until he felt it click, then forcefully pulled back on the heavy sliding door handle. With one heave, he opened it as wide as it would stretch, and Izzy flopped out onto the path in front of him.

"Quickly," she whispered, "We've got to save the others...Peter is going to kill them!"

30

"Come out, come out wherever you are...you can't hide from me forever..."

Zach could hear the floorboards creaking nearby as Peter prowled the upstairs landing.

"All I want is Zach...give him to me, and I'll spare the rest of you."

The insidious offer rattled Zach, so Meridia gave his hand a reassuring squeeze as they both hid, trembling beneath Peter's bed. Her palm was soft and warm in his, providing the perfect tonic to their latest crisis.

Peter had shown his hand the moment they'd entered, locking the door shut behind them and swiping at Kane with a carving knife. They all scattered in blind panic, with Zach and Meridia bounding upstairs. It proved a rookie move as they now lay there trapped, with nowhere else to run.

The voice of his brother drifted into Zach's mind as he lay holding his breath. *Never run upstairs dude...the killer always catches the idiots who run upstairs...*

Creak!

Another floorboard moved just beyond the door that separated them from their psychotic, knife-wielding host.

He was close now.

All Zach could think of was Kane. He wasn't even sure if the knife had made contact. It had all happened so fast.

He had to be ok. Surely he would come and save them.

"I know you're up here Zach...you and that meddling seer. I can smell your fear. Come now, and I promise your death will be quick."

Zach's eyes widened in terror as he watched Peter take one step into the bedroom.

Meridia let go of his hand and silenced him by covering his mouth, knowing they would be found in a matter of seconds.

"I wonder if you'd be silly enough to hide under this bed..." Peter's voice softened to a playful whisper as he toyed with his prey. *"There's only one way out of this room I'm afraid, and that's past me..."*

CLATTER!

A chorus of metal pots and pans striking the stone-tiled kitchen floor rang out downstairs, causing Meridia to bash Zach's nose as she flinched. Through watery eyes, he saw Peter pause in the doorway.

"I'll get to you two down there later...I have who I want right here."

And with that, he suddenly swooped down low and stared directly at Zach and Meridia, startling them as they desperately tried to wriggle their way backwards. His eyes were ablaze, vivid green and full of glee as he wildly snatched a handful of Meridia's thick red hair and began dragging her out from under the bed.

"Argh," Meridia kicked and screamed as Zach pounded at Peter's hand to force him to relent, but he didn't budge.

"Stop! Let her go! Please! Somebody please...Kane!" Zach cried as he wrestled with Peter's arm, but he was too strong, and before he knew it, Meridia was already halfway out from under the bed.

CLANG!

A heavy saucepan connected sweetly with the crown of Peter's head, sending him crashing to the floor. He was already out cold when his head bounced off the edge of the bed, flipping him onto his back in a crumpled heap.

Kane had answered the call, shaking with adrenalin and still clutching the saucepan as he stood over his fallen mentor.

"Shit...Is he dead?" JJ emerged from behind him as Zach and Meridia both scrambled to their feet.

"I couldn't stop him M...I'm so sorry...I just wasn't strong enough." Zach was in tears as he anxiously checked over Meridia's scalp for damage.

"I'm ok...We're ok..." Meridia cradled him by his wrists and lowered his hands away from her. Heartfelt as his concern was, her head was still tingling from the pain of having her hair almost yanked out. "I'm fine."

"Is he breathing?" JJ pressed, growing more agitated behind Kane in the doorway.

Kane stood shellshocked, oblivious to the clamour going on around him and unsure what he'd just done. "He....he was going to kill us...I had to..."

"For fuck's sake guys. Is he breathing?!" JJ snapped, his words shaking Kane out of his trance.

Kane stared at Peter, who hadn't moved since being struck.

"Yes...thank god. Yes, he's breathing."

"Then we haven't got much time. You grab his arms and I'll get his legs."

31

Peter groaned as he opened one eye and surveyed the group of children standing around him.

"What?" He snarled with a jump, flexing his arms to push himself up, only to find them duct taped to his office chair.

Soft brown leather creaked beneath him as he writhed and struggled against his restraints, testing their strength. He quickly conceded and was still again as he took in a deep breath of contemplation. JJ had done an excellent job securing him, and he took a peculiar sense of satisfaction from the flash of irritation in Peter's eyes as he realized even his chest was tightly bound.

"Thank god! She's gone. Wh...what happened? How did you get rid of her?" His eyes darted around the group in search of sympathy, but he came up empty.

"You can't fool me," Meridia was quick to cut him down. "Who are we really talking to?"

"Wh..what do you mean? It's me. Peter. How did I end up here?"

Peter wobbled in his seat a little, still dazed from the blow to his head. A thin trickle of blood had snaked its way down the back of his neck and bled into the collar of his bottle green sweater.

"How long have I been out?" he asked innocently.

"You can drop the act. We know you're lying." Kane fired back. He felt a lot better knowing it wasn't Peter he'd concussed, even if he wasn't sure how that was possible yet.

"I know it's you witch…I'm a seer, remember?" Meridia waded back in, edging closer to their hostage. "I could smell you the second we walked in. What have you done with our friend?"

The duct tape let out a light crackling sound as Peter took in another mouthful of air.

"Well? Where is he?" she pressed.

"*Hahahahaha…you little shits!*" Peter's appearance changed before their eyes as his mask gave way to the evil hiding underneath.

It was subtle at first, almost like a trick of the light, but by the time he'd finished his sentence he was wearing a cruel twist on his usual movie star looks, revealing a dark and sinister version of himself that had been concealed somewhere within.

"*Just give me the boy and this will all be over. We won't stop until we have him…and you can't stop us!*" Veins protruded from his temple as he spat his venomous demands.

"*You think you are the first to challenge us? Hahahahaha…you pathetic pieces of shit! You are nothing!*" The more agitated Peter became, the more unearthly his voice became, as if it was being projected from the bottom of a well. "*You will all burn in your beds haha…you will all burn in hell!*"

His words served up the perfect trigger for Meridia, bringing the burning buildings back into her mind, and her mother's crumpled hand. Her composure melted in the heat of the moment, and she suddenly found herself lost in the room, flustered and floundering.

Peter's spiteful glare cut her to the bone and spooked everyone around her as the balance of power teetered precariously on the brink.

"Tape his mouth...I've heard enough of his bullshit!" Kane was quick to react, gesturing to JJ for the tape.

Peter bobbed and weaved in his seat, but was powerless to prevent himself from being gagged. The less control he had, the more animated he became, huffing and puffing his cheeks beneath the strip of tape that clamped his poisonous lips together.

"Don't listen to him M, he's full of shit." Kane offered Meridia the briefest consolation whilst pacing the office.

"W...what are we going to do?" Zach stammered. Things were spiralling and they needed a new plan.

"We could torture him?" Izzy piped up from the bookshelf she'd been loitering next to and everyone, including Peter, looked at her in shock. "What? We've already bashed him over the head with a saucepan. I think we're way past the point of no return."

"I don't think we need to cross that line today Izz." JJ provided the voice of reason, "but we could leave him here and come back once we've had time to think?"

"No way! I'm not leaving here until we have answers. I don't want another night of Peter haunting me in my sleep." A look of concern swept over Peter as Meridia insisted they stay, and he glanced up towards a corner of the ceiling behind them all.

"Guys, can we go into the hall for a minute?" Kane

spotted the odd reaction and had already clocked the patch of mould as they'd dragged Peter in from the next room.

Something Meridia said had drawn Peter's attention to it.

"Just humour me. I might have an idea." He shot a sideways glance at Peter as he ushered everyone out. "Did anyone see what just happened in there the minute Meridia mentioned him haunting her?"

"He looked worried...I saw it too." Izzy whispered.

"Exactly! But then he looked up at the mould in the corner." Kane continued, "That wasn't there when I first found Peter, I'm sure of it. That means it's new, and if Peter seemed interested in it, then it might be important somehow. I remember watching It's Behind You...I think it was either the first one or the sequel, when the detective kept looking for tells. He said most people who are guilty of something can't help but give themselves away. All you have to do is read the signs. I think we should take a look in the loft." He pointed at the narrow hatch above them to emphasize his point.

"I think there's something up there...maybe something he doesn't want us to know about." Kane's imagination kicked into overdrive and left everyone behind as he began connecting an array of dots, all stemming from the hundreds of horror movies he carried under his belt.

"There must be a stick or something to get the hatch open, that's what our grandad has." Kane busily looked around the hallway.

"Like this?" Izzy held up a wooden pole about a metre in length with a plastic hook on the end. "It was propped up against the banister."

"Hold your horses mate...what if Peter's dead body is up there or something?" JJ dragged Kane kicking and screaming from the multitude of outcomes he was cycling through in his head. "I'm all for getting some answers but…"

CLICK!

Kane poked the loft hatch with the stick he had swiped from Izzy, cutting short JJ's monologue in its prime.

CLICK!

Another more accurate attempt landed flush on the catch, prompting the wooden jaws to slowly open from the ceiling and reveal a dusty set of retractable ladders covered in cobwebs.

"Oh my god, what's that smell?" Meridia covered her nose and mouth with her cuff as a putrid stink of raw sewage and rotten eggs leaked out from above them.

Izzy heaved as the rest of the group followed suit before blocking out the ominous stench as best they could.

"Oh god, he's dead isn't he…he's up there dead, and whatever that thing is in there killed him didn't it?!" Zach was threatening to hyperventilate as he tried to talk through the palm of his hand.

"I'm going up guys. It's the only way we'll know for sure." Kane felt for the hook end of the pole and used it to fish for the steps that disappeared into the darkness of the loft.

"For all we know, that could be a bird we can smell up there, or a cat…bingo!" Kane hooked the bottom step and left the pole dangling while he directed his troops. "Listen guys, when I go up there, I'm gonna need someone to keep watch on Peter in case he tries anything."

JJ stepped up to the plate and assumed his position in the office doorway as Kane pulled firmly on the ladder. "Bro, I need you to hold the ladder still while I climb up, ok?"

Zach nodded like a zombie, still shellshocked from being chased.

"Ok then, here goes…"

32

The rickety old ladder creaked and rattled with each rung Kane grudgingly climbed.

"Hold it still! It's wobbling all over the place." Meridia joined Zach at the bottom and grabbed the base with both hands to help keep it steady, whilst Izzy remained straddling the office doorway and the landing to stay abreast of everything as it unfolded.

"God, it stinks so bad," Kane groaned.

Before his ascent he'd borrowed Meridia's scarf, using it as a makeshift face mask so he could investigate the loft without throwing up, however so far it was touch and go if his breakfast might make a surprise cameo. As he drew closer to the opening, the smell became more and more pungent, flooding his nostrils and making his eyes water as he gagged and coughed beneath the warm tartan wool.

"You'd better not throw up on that Kane! It was a birthday present from my mum." Meridia watched him intently as he reached the loft hatch.

"No light," he exclaimed. "I can't see a bloody thing up here."

"Use the light on your phone!" Zach called up, fraught with worry as his brother teetered above him.

"URGH!" Kane jumped as an enormous house spider made a dash for freedom, scampering across the back of his hand and tickling him with its thick, hairy legs.

Kane's balance abandoned him as he instinctively let go of the rung he was clinging onto to shake it off. The spider plummeted, landing on the top of Meridia's head with a light thud, and instantly began burrowing its way into her thick curls.

"Argh! Get it off me! Get it off me!" She could feel its legs scurrying around on her scalp as she panicked, shaking the ladder even more with her flapping.

"What?! What is it?" JJ darted past Izzy, who watched in fascination as the chaos escalated in front of her.

Despite JJ's best efforts, it took him three attempts to send the spider flying over the top of the banister. The contact made his skin crawl, and it was so big he could've sworn he'd even heard it land on the carpet at the bottom of the stairs. "It's ok, it's gone. Jeez, that thing was massive! You guys ok?"

"Thanks mate, we're good. I didn't see it until it was on me. Sorry M."

Kane looked like a reluctant bank robber as he stood perched halfway up the ladder staring down at them all. He activated the flashlight on his phone and turned back to face the dark cavity above him. Although there were only a dozen rungs, Kane wasn't great with heights at the best of times and struggled to climb something so flimsy. He hesitated a moment, gathering himself before directing his light up into the darkness and then cautiously peered inside.

"It looks like the floor's moving up here guys. I can't...

wait..." Kane took another step up so he could get a better view. "Cockroaches! Shit! There's hundreds of them...it's infested!"

"Close it Kane, just close it and come back down!" Meridia felt triggered again.

First the spider in her hair and now this. It couldn't be a coincidence, but her fear of being showered in roaches again was stronger than any desire she had for answers.

"Wait...something doesn't add up. Why didn't they just crawl out of the hatch when I opened it? They've had plenty of time." Kane took another step on the ladder, which carried him waist-high into the loft. He felt a rush of warmth from the rest of the house congregate around him, but the vile smell seemed to dissipate a little, or maybe he'd just become accustomed to it.

"They're marching around and around in a circle...it's so weird. They don't seem interested in me, or the open hatch. It looks like something is in the middle of them, but I can't make it out, it's too small. It's like they're drawn to whatever it is...or protecting it maybe?" Kane banded his flashlight around to see more of the loft space, but aside from the usual beams underpinning the roof, and the slightly less usual swirling sea of cockroaches, there was very little else to look at.

The floor was fully boarded, suggesting it had been used as extra storage space over the years. Thick cobwebs hugged every crevasse Kane explored, whilst a couple of battered old cardboard boxes marked 'Xmas' were tucked into the farthest corner from where he stood. Based on the layout, Kane guessed whatever sat at the centre of the bugs' attention was located directly above Peter's office.

"Guys, I hate to say this, but I think I need to go grab whatever it is they're circling."

"Seriously?!" Zach blurted beneath him. The thought of so many bugs was making him and Meridia twitch at the bottom of the ladder.

"It's got to be whatever Peter looked worried about, which means he probably didn't want us to find it. It's got to be important. I just don't see any other way. On the plus side, at least there's no dead body up here, right?"

"Find it..." Meridia mumbled, stepping away from her post in deep thought, "That's what Peter said in my dream... and the cockroaches I saw that day...it's got to be connected. Kane's right. Whatever that thing is, we need it. I think it might be the key to what's going on with Peter."

"Ok...just give me a sec to think this through. I've got two problems. The first is how do I get to it when it's surrounded by cockroaches, and the second is how are they going to react once I grab it?" Kane kept looking around the loft for inspiration but came up short. "I'm thinking maybe I just run and snatch it, then hightail it back. If they follow, then I can just close the hatch behind me...no wait, I can't do that because I have to fold the ladder back up first. Shit!"

Kane pushed his thick mop of hair away from his forehead to cool off while he thought.

"Ok, I've got it. I'm going to go all the way into the loft, and I need you to fold the ladder back up behind me. Once that's up here with me, I'll just make a run for it and get out as quickly as I can so we can shut the hatch. I can't see the cockroaches carrying on with their weird little dance once that thing has moved, so we'll need to be quick. I'll drop it down to you guys, then I'll hang and drop down so JJ can trap the rest of them up here. I know it all sounds a little Raiders of the Lost Ark, but I can't think of any other way, and the clock is ticking."

"But how will you get over the roaches to get to it?" Zach gulped.

"I think I'm gonna have to go through them spud. There's no other way."

Kane just graduated to a whole new level of hero in Zach's eyes as step by step he disappeared into the loft. Within a matter of seconds his hands reappeared and gestured for the ladder.

"It's ok, I've got a bit of room here before I get to the bugs. Pass me the ladder and let's get this over with."

Zach and Meridia responded, folding the ladder until it was ready to be pulled back up.

"Right, you guys need to put your hoods up if you've got them. These things are faster than they look, and I don't know how many are going to break out before we manage to close the hatch."

"We're ready down here mate," JJ called from the opposite side of the opening, stick in hand, ready to push the hatch door closed once Kane was safely out. "Izzy's keeping an eye on Peter, so let's get this done guys."

"I'll be right back," Kane joked, winking at his brother before disappearing again into the dark.

33

KANE STOOD ON THE EDGE OF THE LOFT OPENING, unsure if he was more concerned about the cockroaches or the nine-foot drop he needed to face to escape them. The sound of hundreds of roaches hissing and chirping made his flesh creep, but there was something about their movement he found strangely hypnotic, soothing even.

Tiptoeing to the brink of their perpetual parade, he tried to get a better look at the object they were guarding. His flashlight caught the edge of a creamy mass of soft angles that reminded him of a candle at first glance. It was nested in a more intricate structure made from dried out twigs bound together by something elastic that glistened beneath the glare of his light. The roaches remained undeterred by Kane's presence, maintaining a safe perimeter around the mysterious shape while he debated if he should carry out a smash and grab, or exercise a little more caution.

"Mate, are you ok? JJ's voice startled Kane and turned the loft into a pop-up nightclub as the flashlight jumped and bobbled in his hands whilst he wrestled to keep hold of it.

"I'm fine!" he snapped back, annoyed he'd been so easily flustered. "Just about to grab it, so get ready guys." And with that, Kane decided on his approach and darted towards the centre of the room.

Crunch! Squelch! Crunch!

The sound of shells cracking and entrails erupting rang out around him as he skated and skidded his way across the slimy carpet of screaming bugs. Kane retched as each new crackle underfoot vibrated its way up through the soles of his sneakers and tickled his ankles.

"Gotcha," he boasted, swooping down to snatch the peculiar object.

It felt far lighter in his hand than he'd imagined; fragile even. It was roughly the size of a dinner plate, and up close resembled a creepy handmade Christmas decoration. The floorboard where it had been resting was rotten to its core, stained black and green from the spread of mould.

"Shit!"

The cockroaches all responded in unison to their idol being taken, shifting formation, as they began climbing and scuttling over one another in pursuit of Kane.

"Argh!"

He screamed as hundreds of spiny, prickly legs scurried over his feet and up his jeans. He had to move fast.

"Get ready!" he shrieked, as he charged towards the loft hatch.

Behind him, the swell of roaches rose from the floor like an oily, germ-infested tidal wave of filth. The stifled air turned sour as it weaved its way through Meridia's scarf, filling Kane's lungs with a musty odour, as he fled the angry hissing mob. He could already feel them working their way up the back of his neck and into his hair as he reached the opening.

"Here!" he bellowed, dropping the artifact into the waiting hands of his brother beneath him.

Zach caught it without a hitch, cradling it in his arms.

"Now get out of the way!"

It was too late. The roaches maintained their course, spilling out of the loft and onto the upstairs landing, where they continued to wreak havoc.

"ARGH!" Meridia's shrill screams echoed up and down the staircase, as the scars from her nightmarish encounter with Mr Seth resurfaced and drove her to hysteria.

Crunch! Crack!

Shell upon shell was crushed underfoot, smearing the carpet with mucus and entrails, as Meridia squashed as many as she could like she was stamping out a fire.

The commotion pulled Izzy from her post as she and Zach joined in the massacre.

Above them, Kane stepped across the opening of the loft and carefully lowered himself down as a deluge of bugs continued to rain steadily around him.

"I'm out. Close it JJ! Close it now!" Kane landed with a thud in his haste as JJ slammed the hatch firmly shut behind him.

Crunch! Squelch!

Long after Zach and Izzy settled down, Meridia continued on her own personal mission to rid the world of all its roaches, stamping on every last one she could find. Meanwhile, Kane fed her frenzy as he shook off any stragglers that had hitched a ride on his way down. Each one he brushed off met a grisly end, flattened beneath one of Meridia's size fives.

"Brr, I can still feel them all over me. Can still smell them too." Kane regained his composure as the chaos finally subsided. "Wait, who's watching Peter?!" he exclaimed the moment he realized they were all out in the hall.

"Sorry. He wasn't doing anything when I was watching him." JJ darted back into the office to check whilst Izzy continued her apology. "When I heard the screaming, I didn't know what to do, so came out here to help."

"It's ok Izz, things got a little crazy. That thing better be worth it M." Kane was only half-joking with his tone as he wrestled with the urge to fidget and squirm. "What do you think it is? Have you seen it in any of your visions?"

"Er...guys," JJ's voice was close to breaking as he nervously called out from Peter's office. "I think something's wrong."

A chorus of thumps and creaks rang out on the landing as the others bundled in to see what JJ was gawking at.

"Look!"

Peter's waxen skin was peppered with beads of sweat as he mechanically rocked back and forth in his chair. A strange melodic drone permeated the confusion in the room, battling to break free from beneath his gag as he hummed and chanted inaudibly.

"His eyes, what the fuck is happening to his eyes?" Kane gasped as black preorbital veins began sprouting like weeds from the depths of Peter's sockets, strangling his eyeballs with their sinewy grip and then slowly dragging them back into his skull. "Look! The chair...it's lifting off the floor. M, what do we do?"

Meridia watched on in horror as Peter rocked and wobbled himself off the floor, levitating in front of them as if possessed by some invisible presence.

CRASH!

All five children flinched as the windows behind him violently blew inward, shattering against the blackout curtains, as a windstorm burst into the room and whipped up a ferocious cyclone of broken glass. The debris rattled against the bookcases and scratched at their faces as they all stood is shock at Peter's ghoulish appearance.

"It's got to be that!" Kane shouted above the howling wind, pointing at the macabre object in Zach's hands. All the while Peter slipped further and further away from them and deeper into his deathly trance.

"Smash it! We've got to destroy it!" Meridia snatched it from Zach's hands and threw it to the floor, but the soft pencil-grey carpet absorbed the impact, somehow preserving its fragile structure.

As it lay at her feet, Meridia recognized the arrangement of twigs staring back up at her. The five-pointed star looked like it had been bound together with putrefied animal intestines.

Meridia raised her foot above the waxy object at the centre, she noticed its creamy consistency was clouded by something darker housed within. Glancing at Peter as he teetered precariously in his chair, caught in a deadly web of witchcraft, she knew exactly what she needed to do and swiftly obliged, delivering a crushing blow.

Squelch!

A cocktail of blackened, congealed blood and bone exploded from either side of Meridia's shoe as twigs cracked and snapped underfoot. The foetid smell of rotten eggs wafted up from the floor, as if she'd just smashed an elaborate stink bomb.

THUD!

Peter came crashing down, landing awkwardly on his ribs as the wind dropped and all was still. Sticky traces of the broken vessel's innards streaked across the carpet as

Meridia stepped back from the mess she'd created, still unsure of what actual damage she might have done.

"Hurk. Kaff…kaff."

"He's choking." Izzy was the first to rush to Peter's aid as he convulsed, wide eyed amongst the broken glass sewn into the carpet.

She instinctively ripped the tape off his mouth just as another cough exploded from the depths of his gut. Black, tar like fluid that reeked of bile and vomit spattered across her face, smearing her glasses, and tainting her lips with its acidic taste.

"Argh!" Izzy's composure crumbled as she finally let go of the scream she'd been holding inside for months.

All the trauma, the horror, and unfathomable things she had witnessed rang out of her tiny frame at once, as tears of frustration and resignation poured down her cheeks. While she filled the room with her high-pitched wail, Peter continued to retch and gag on the floor.

Unable to catch his breath, he began spewing out a pool of thick, glossy black goo onto the carpet in front of them.

Meridia had seen this in her vision that night when he came to visit. She'd seen the same pain and anguish in his eyes as he'd tried desperately to warn her, but this was different. This was real. Now he was wheezing on the floor, unable to breathe as he lay tied to a chair in his office. Pale blue blotches gathered around his lips and cheeks as his eyes became puffy and swollen.

Was this Peter's plan all along?

Had he elected to sacrifice himself in his last message and her actions had just signed his death warrant?

Meridia's head spun as she tried to process nights of cryptic premonitions in the hope they would yield an answer. Something, anything, to save her friend's life.

Time seemed to slow around her as JJ ambled over to Peter and began patting his back, hoping to dislodge whatever abhorrent substance blocked his airway. The same substance slowly dripped from Izzy's glasses as she shook her head in dismay, whilst Kane and Zach both looked on from the other side of the room, frozen to the spot in horror.

"He's dying! We've killed him!"

34

"Gack...Blargh!" Peter's body made a snaking motion as whatever growled in the pit of his stomach forced its way up his esophagus. The build-up of pressure made his jugular throb as his throat began to swell and pulsate. Whatever had been starving him of oxygen was about to make an appearance.

"What the f..." JJ reeled back in shock, yanking his hand away from Peter's back as he felt something brush his palm from beneath his sweater.

"Blargh!" Again Peter retched and heaved, but this time what came up was far more than thick, murky vomit.

Consumed by guilt, Meridia could do nothing but sob as a bulbous and slimy globule, the size of a tennis ball, began to slowly push its way out from between his sallow lips.

CRACK!

The hollow sound of Peter's jaw stretching beyond its limits jolted everyone in the room, sparking a chorus of screams as a dark, snake-like creature with an accordion of protruding ribs, jerked and twitched its way from out his mouth and then slithered onto the carpet.

Its head resembled an unborn fetus, a malleable skull contoured with underdeveloped features. Hissing and snarling at the horrified children surrounding it, the embryonic creature continued to wriggle and worm its way free of its unwitting host. Scrawny, fibrous limbs sprung out just below its head and clawed at the carpet, pulling the rest of its trunk from Peter's throat with a nauseating rattle.

One final push saw the gory mess of gristle and slime flop onto the floor in all its glory as Peter coughed up the last vestiges of whatever was left in his stomach.

"What the fuck is that?!" Exclaimed JJ as he backed away from the abomination Peter had just given birth to.

Hiss!

Coiling its emaciated body to face the group, the creature scowled at them through raven eyes, black as night. Its cavernous mouth was teeming with decayed, thorny teeth, whilst an insidious slug-like tongue, slathered in gloopy yellow mucus, languidly probed and lapped at the carpet.

JJ continued to retreat, joining the rest of the group on the other side of the room whilst a cacophony of dislocating joints and twisting ligaments reverberated around them with every move of the creature's bony torso.

Meridia had heard the sickening sound before, transporting her mind back to the bloody scenes of death and devastation she had prophesied at the hospital.

They needed to run.

"It's getting bigger!" Zach cried, pointing to the monster's hands as it pressed its palms against the floor, tensing and flexing its fingers until they resembled those of a young adult.

To its rear, flesh began to rip and tear as legs broke through beneath its narrow frame and hoisted it up onto all fours like a wild animal. Weaving itself whole from unseen spools of tissue and cartilage, the hideous monstrosity filled out to a grotesque soundtrack of bones snapping and slime being slurped through a straw.

"Stop....*kaff*...*kaff*...stop her..." Peter coughed wearily from the floor. "You must...*kaff*...stop her."

But the monster had already reached a formidable size. Time was running out, and their advantage was slipping away.

Kane stepped up and kicked the creature onto its side, giving him enough space to pull Peter's chair upright. JJ joined him as they both set about unravelling the duct tape holding their friend captive.

"We need to get out of here!" Kane yelled as the beast continued to writhe on the floor, its spine cracking with each new jarring contraction.

"I can't...*kaff kaff*...too weak." Kane and JJ scooped Peter up from his chair and dragged him across to the safety of the landing.

"C'mon guys," he bellowed at the others, waking them from their daze.

Zach sprang into action, kicking the creature again, having seen it had returned to a crawling stance.

Once more, it capsized, screaming as it crashed into the bookcase. Patches of pale human skin had congealed, covering its underbelly as the grisly transformation neared completion.

"It's her!" Meridia shrieked, staring into the witch's inky black eyes as Izzy pulled her away, towards the exit. "We need to kill her while she's weak. I know it. If we leave now, she'll only get stronger."

"The knife!" Kane blurted.

"It's in the bedroom," Zach responded, fetching the weapon like an obedient puppy. The bloodied blade appeared larger in his awkward grip as he dithered in the doorway.

"I'll do it!" Meridia snatched the knife and marched back into the office. Her crimson cheeks were ablaze as rage took over. This was her chance to end it, and she leant into the anger she'd suppressed for so long, using it as a crutch to do whatever was needed.

"No wai..." Zach's plea evaporated into the air Meridia left in her wake as she charged off, back into the lion's den.

She arrived to find the witch almost fully formed and on her knees. Lank, brown hair stuck to her viscous face as she glanced up to greet her would-be executioner.

Meridia hesitated, tightening her grip on the knife's smooth wooden handle, before taking another step forward. Her fury had lost none of its venom, but now faced with her intended victim, she wondered if this was a line too far to cross.

The witch staggered up to her feet, punch-drunk from her violent birth, and glared at the weapon in Meridia's hand. Her face twisted into a snarl as she stumbled backwards, connecting with the windowsill before tumbling into the long, dark curtains and out through the empty window frame.

"Noo!" Meridia exclaimed as she rushed to the window's edge, but as she looked down onto the garden, some twenty feet below, there was no sign of her anywhere.

It was as if she'd vanished.

Zach and Izzy came rushing into the room, followed by Kane and JJ, but they were all too late.

The witch had escaped, and Meridia had failed.

35

"I kn...I know where she is..." Peter's voice was weak and crackled through the deafening silence of defeat that now suffocated the room.

Staggering forward, he slumped against the doorframe and then slid down onto one knee. "I'm...s...sorry. *Kaff kaff*... I couldn't stop...her."

"We need to get you to a hospital." Kane was the first to rush to Peter's aid. Despite what he'd witnessed, the guilt of hurting him still weighed heavily, as it did for Meridia, who was next to console him.

"No...no hospital." Peter gripped Kane's arm to make his point.

There was still some strength in him yet, regardless of how awful he looked.

"Water...I need water." JJ was quick to oblige, stepping over Peter and bounding downstairs.

"I thought we'd lost you." Kane teared up as the magnitude of their ordeal caught up with him.

"You did...for a while...*kaff kaff*...." Peter flashed a weary half-smile just as JJ returned with a glass of cold water. He took a huge gulp and continued, "We must stop her...she's there now...at the house. She'll grow stronger by the day... *kaff*...unless we do something."

"How do you know?" Izzy cut straight to the point, eager to understand as Peter took another glug from his glass.

"I was there...the whole time. A prisoner inside my body...watching her do those horrific things. I tried to warn you dear...but she was just too strong. She locked me away in a room...*kaff*...inside my mind. She won't stop, not until we stop her...or..." His mind wandered away from the children huddled round him as he stumbled through a patchwork of unfamiliar memories filled with fire and brimstone, all stitched together in blood.

Exhausted, he was still unsure where his thoughts ended, and the witch's began. It all seemed so real. The encounter at Crooked House in the dead of night, the witch hunter and his men. He could still smell their burning flesh as if he'd been there, but that was impossible.

"You need rest Peter. You need a hospital." Kane pressed again, cutting through his daydream, but Peter shook his head, resolute.

"No hospitals!" he snapped. "The witch isn't working alone...there are others...I...I don't know who else we can trust."

"We can't just sit here while she gets stronger." Meridia blurted impatiently. "I should've killed her when I had the chance...I just froze. My dad...I...I'm sorry. I've just made everything worse."

"We need a plan, and I need to get my strength back. We can't go in half-cocked and ill prepared. Forewarned is forearmed, as they say." Peter pushed himself upright again, wobbling as he rose to his feet.

As the colour slowly returned to his cheeks, painful red blotches clung to his jawline. Every word he uttered sent violent shooting pains up towards his temples and he wondered about the full extent of his injuries.

Kane was right He needed the hospital, but the risk was too great.

"Can someone fetch me some more water, please? My head...it's pounding." JJ again volunteered, as Peter continued, "Thank you. In the cupboard to the right of the cooker, you'll find a first aid box on the top shelf. Can you bring it up with you, please? Kane, could you help me to my room? I'm not sure if I can walk yet."

Kane and Zach both gathered around him as Peter ambled to the next room.

He found his legs were surprisingly stronger than expected, and in hindsight, he probably could have made the journey on his own. Perched on the edge of the bed, he swung both legs up and onto it in one smooth motion.

"Aah, that's better." He let out a deep sigh of relief as the pressure eased from his bruised ribs, then he gently lay his hand on top of Zach's. "I'm so sorry Zach. I couldn't stop her...the things I said...the things I did...it wasn't me. I hope you can forgive me."

"I know Peter. We're cool. We all saw that thing come out of you... What are we going to do now?" Zach held the weight of the entire world in his gaze.

Such a heavy burden for such young shoulders, Peter thought, and one he had only worsened by acting like a maniac and betraying his trust. He needed to find the resolve to end this, and quickly, but there could be no witch hunt today.

"We only have a couple more hours of daylight left, and we know what happens in that place when night falls...I think the best thing to do is regroup in the morning. In fact, I think it's the only thing we can do."

"But what if she comes back? For you, or any of us?! How are we meant to get through the night now she's out there?" Zach was coming apart at the seams with worry as a dozen different scenarios played out in his mind all at once, with none of them ending well.

"Zach's right, what if the guy in the hood comes back? What then? You're in no fit state to fend anyone off, so you'll be a sitting duck if you spend the night here." There was a touch of panic in Kane's voice as he unwittingly wandered into some of his brother's scenarios.

"It's ok, I'll just book myself into a hotel for the night. If you can help me pack some things, I'll arrange a taxi to drop you all off home after."

"I know a B&B that has plenty of room." JJ smirked, unable to resist as he handed Peter another glass of water and the first aid box he'd asked for.

"Ha, thank you. I think I'll stick to a Holiday Inn tonight though. Probably safer." Peter opened the box and pulled out a packet of paracetamol, then a white sachet, which he emptied into his glass.

The powder fizzed as it infused itself with the water, turning it murky purple.

"Rehydration powder," he said, sensing the curiosity brewing around him. He popped a couple of tablets and downed the drink with a grimace. "Not exactly my idea of blackcurrant, but it works." He added, placing the empty glass down beside him.

Peter allowed his eyes to close, and another torrent of unlived memories invaded his mind, transporting him back to a distant time where a young boy, consumed by spite, pelted him with stones.

His scornful words stung every bit as much as the rocks that struck him, with each vile obscenity slinking its way beneath his skin. Soon he felt numb to the pain, as if he'd felt it countless times before, and the barrage of words became nothing more than a hum, fading into obscurity, as they made way for another voice somewhere deep within.

This whispery voice was sly and insidious as it gently rapped at the door to his soul, begging to be let in.

'*I can stop this,*' it said. '*I can end all this hurt. Just let me in.*'

It was a promise that he understood came with a catch, but he was so tired of the pain, tired of the torment, so he yielded, and the darkness waltzed right in.

"Peter? Are you ok?"

Peter opened his eyes again to Meridia looming over him.

"We need to get a move on if we all want to be home before dark."

"Yes...of course dear. Kane, can you grab my overnight bag for me please, it should be in the cupboard under the stairs. It doesn't look like there's a door there, but if you give the panel a shove, you'll find it springs open. Girls, can you pick out some clothes for tomorrow? Just a jumper and some jeans will be fine. JJ, can you grab my toiletry bag from the bathroom and pop my toothbrush in there, please? I'll call the hotel and book a taxi."

"What about the windows?" Zach asked.

"I'll contact the landlord when I get to the hotel. There isn't much we can do now as it's the start of the weekend. If you can grab my laptop for me and just move the screens onto the floor for now, the curtains should be enough to stop any rain damage if the weather turns."

And with that, all five children set about their tasks, leaving Peter alone in his room.

He was certain the dark visions invading his thoughts were coming from somewhere other than his imagination, and he remembered hearing the strangely compelling voice once before. Traces of the witch were still crawling around in his mind, and he knew tonight's self-imposed quarantine was as much for the group's benefit as his own. He needed to be absolutely certain he wasn't a threat to the children.

36

In the taxi ride to the hotel every bump and turn in the road rattled Peter's ribs, but he was optimistic there was no long-term damage from his run-in with the witch, although his jaw had developed a discerning clicking noise whenever he yawned. Glancing into the passenger wing mirror, he observed Zach lost in thought while gazing out of the window behind him. The journey had been one of stilted small talk given their eavesdropping driver, but it had given Peter time to organize his thoughts, assuming they were still his to organize.

"Holiday Inn sir." The seven-seater taxi pulled into a horseshoe drive, stopping just outside the main entrance, and the driver got out to retrieve Peter's bag from the back. A rotund, middle-aged black man, he was at least a foot shorter than his passenger when he handed him his bag in exchange for the full fare.

"That should more than cover it," Peter said, and then approached the window where Zach was sitting. "So, I'll see you all here bright and early at 8:30am for breakfast. In the meantime, make sure you all get some rest. I have a feeling tomorrow could be a long day. Oh, and remember what I said, my phone will be next to me all night so if you need to reach me, you know where I am."

Zach nodded as Kane replied from over his shoulder.

"I hope you manage to get some sleep and I'll text you when we're all home."

"Thanks guys. Take care." Peter was walking a little easier now and somehow found the strength to hoist his bag over his shoulder before waving the children off.

As he watched their troubled faces disappear into the distance, he could see the toll the day had taken on them, and his heart sank. He sometimes forgot they were merely children, embroiled in a war they had neither asked for nor started. Now they found themselves faced with yet another formidable adversary baying for their blood.

The last time they visited Crooked House, they had barely escaped with their lives, and Peter knew if they were to stand any chance of defeating the witch tomorrow, then they would need more than luck on their side.

Stepping into the deserted hotel, Peter checked in via the touch screen at the front desk and ordered a large double espresso from the vending machine while he waited for the lift to arrive. He figured with the help of some caffeine, he would still have a few more hours of research and planning in him before bed.

When the lift arrived it was empty, just like the rest of the hotel, and he rode it all the way up to the fifth floor without any interruption.

He'd booked a deluxe double room purely for the added benefit of a desk, and as soon as he entered, he set his coffee down and opened his laptop. The chintzy mahogany chair let out a loud creak as he sat down, and for a moment he wondered if the sound had come from his weary bones.

Breathing in the steamy aroma of his drink, he questioned if he had the stomach for it, but then took a sip anyway. Every inch of his red-raw throat cringed in pain as the piping hot liquid made its way down towards his hollow stomach.

Welcoming the discomfort, he justified another sip by imaging the hot brew burning away any lingering traces of the witch that might still be taking refuge within him. Content that he was not about to vomit it all back up again, he popped another couple of painkillers and took one more sip to wash them down.

He waited for his laptop to connect to the hotel Wi-Fi, rummaging around in his overnight bag and retrieved a black lever arch folder which he placed on his lap. Peter thumbed through the sheets of handwritten notes until he arrived at the page he was looking for marked 'Children of the Shadows' and then he went to work.

37

When the taxi arrived outside JJ's house, it was a little after 2:30 PM, and the sun had returned from its exile.

Despite having spent the best part of an hour crammed in the back of a cab, unable to speak, the group had agreed to forgo any further scheming that afternoon. Instead, they decided it would be best to spend some quality time with their families and get a much-needed early night. Peter had left them under no illusion it might well be their last opportunity.

"Thanks mate." JJ clambered out of the car and waved the driver on to his next job.

A light breeze rattled the front gate as he stood looking at his empty house in contemplation. The whole discussion about how best to spend their last night before their anticipated showdown with the witch triggered him multiple times, and now here he was, alone as usual.

JJ longed to see his mum waving from the living room window or find his dad working out front. But he knew it was just a pipe dream, so he kept walking. He walked past the end of his street and then kept going. Past Jubilee Park and along the dual carriageway until he reached the old worn-out sign for 'Cold Christmas Lane'.

From there, he followed the winding dirt-track until he could just about see the clearing outside Crooked House ahead of him, and that's when he finally came to a halt. No sooner had he stopped did the wind whip around him, nudging him closer as it always did whenever JJ visited.

Staring the house down from the safety of the path, he wondered if the witch knew he was there, loitering on the edge of her turf, or if she had any inkling of what they had planned for her the next day.

Crack!

A branch snapped up ahead, yanking JJ out of his temporary daze and thrusting him back into the very real and dangerous territory he'd foolishly wandered into.

CRACK!

Another branch broke, this time closer, and JJ felt the gravel give way underfoot as he retreated. Backing away, he could feel the malevolent wind poke and prod at his back as it tried to keep him there.

CRACK!

Something was behind him now and JJ spun around to meet his would-be assailant.

"What are you doing here young man?"

The crisp, commanding voice startled JJ and sent him tumbling backwards in surprise.

"Whoa! Easy there, you'll do yourself an injury out here. I didn't mean to make you jump." The middle-aged man held both hands out in front of him, palms up, so as not to appear threatening, whilst JJ sized him up from the ground.

The first thing JJ noticed was his collar, a priest of some sort, dressed smartly in black, with a matching trench coat that came down to his knees. His hair was once dark, although now peppered with grey, and he wore a pair of round clear-framed glasses that complemented his square jawline. There was a genuine look of concern etched across his face as he reached down to help JJ to his feet.

"I'm Father Alexander," he said behind his outstretched hand. "What are you doing here? This is no place for a boy your age to be hanging around alone."

JJ gripped his hand and was surprised by the man's strength as he hoisted him back up to his feet. Up close, the priest was clean cut and handsome, in a rugged way, and he allowed himself a half-smile once he could see JJ was unharmed.

"I was just passing," JJ replied. "I'm leaving now and think you should probably do the same."

"Just passing, eh? You pass this place pretty often from what I have seen. Are you local?" Father Alexander's face softened as his smile expanded to the other corner of his lips, but that didn't stop JJ's guard from going up.

"What are you doing here?" he asked bluntly. Father Alexander's smile faded as a more solemn look crept across his face.

"I'm looking for someone. A boy from my parish who went missing some time ago. Here, I have a picture... perhaps you've seen him?" Father Alexander reached into his pocket and pulled out his phone, then searched for an image to show JJ. "I'd say he's around your age actually. His name is Archie...have you seen him?"

JJ's blood ran cold when he saw the boy's picture and his reaction gave him away.

"You recognize him, don't you? He's been missing for months now, and his family is distraught. Do you have any idea where I might find him?"

Father Alexander's tone remained calm, but JJ was wriggling on the hook now and it was obvious the priest would not back down until he got some answers.

"I don't know him...but I...I..." JJ floundered, thrown off-guard by the image of Archie posing on an old BMX that looked a little on the small side for him. He looked no different to Kane or anyone else in their year at school, and the knowledge of his death suddenly became very real.

"I know of him..." JJ blurted, knowing he'd now made a rod for his own back. All he wanted to do was flee, to run away from the difficult conversation, but something inside nagged at him.

Archie's family was distraught. They still thought he might be out there somewhere, still alive.

A dozen lies rattled around in JJ's brain as he thought of his next sentence, but he couldn't bring himself to utter a word. Instead, he stood there, frozen and looking more suspicious with each second of awkward silence that passed between them. He glanced back at Crooked House, wondering if Archie knew they were here.

"I need to go...this place...this place isn't safe," JJ said.

The father's appearance was like truth serum, and JJ cursed his loose lips, but the more he let slip, the more he wanted to. He could feel the dam of self-control buckling under the pressure of all the secrets he was harbouring inside, begging him to let it all go.

"Not safe? Not safe how? And how do you know of Archie?" Father Alexander's words pressed the dam even further.

JJ couldn't resist releasing the darkness inside him. It was too tempting. The things he'd witnessed that day, along with his solitude, made it even harder. However, when

Archie's family and their pain were brought up, it completely broke him.

"Not here...they can hear us." As soon as the words left his mouth, he realized how crazy he might sound, but Father Alexander didn't blink at JJ's paranoia and skirted over the odd comment.

"Where are you from?" he asked. "My church is St Peter's in Thundridge...that's where Archie is from too. I'm guessing you're not from Cold Christmas, as you're too young. Shawbrook perhaps? Listen, I know you have no reason to trust me, but I mean no harm. I'm just looking for Archie. Anything you know...that might help...I'll happily meet you somewhere else...anywhere you feel safe, a public place you're familiar with perhaps? I'm just looking for answers."

There was a sincerity in the priest's voice, mixed in with a healthy dose of desperation, but JJ had a feeling he could trust him that went far beyond the collar he was wearing.

"Jubilee Park, do you know it?" Rightly or wrongly, JJ doubled down on his gut, he just knew he had to get away from Crooked House.

"I'll find it." Father Alexander waved his phone for reassurance. "I can meet you there anytime."

"Good, because I was thinking now...or in about ten minutes. There's a café inside the park, next to the basketball courts. It stays open till five on a Sunday, so I'll meet you there."

"Thank you...err...?"

"James...but people call me JJ. I'll see you there." And with that, JJ adjusted his cap and rushed away.

38

When JJ reached the Jubilee Park Café, Father Alexander had already secured a quiet table for two in the furthest corner, away from the shop counter.

The place was empty apart from the owner, and an elderly couple sat by the window enjoying a pot of tea and scones. The warm smell of coffee and freshly baked pastries welcomed JJ in as he entered through the double glass doors overlooking the deserted park playground.

Meredith, the owner, flashed her usual friendly smile from over the glass counter as he walked in and ogled the remaining cakes on display. Despite all the horrors he'd witnessed at Peter's that day, he was amazed he had any kind of appetite, but the sight of his favourite cherry and almond slice made his mouth water.

"Where's the rest of the gang?" Meredith quizzed.

She was a petite brunette in her fifties who was as sweet natured as her baked goods and had a soft spot for the group due to how well they behaved whenever they stopped by. Originally from Australia, she had married an investment banker in the early nineties and started the café when both their children flew the nest.

The group visited often in the summer months, but since their run-in with Crooked House, it had provided an occasional change of scenery at the weekend, and Peter always treated them to a can of drink and a cake whenever he joined them.

"Just me today I'm afraid Mrs Hutson." JJ waved to Father Alexander in the corner who rose to greet him.

"Nice choice of venue. I've just ordered a coffee. Can I get you anything? A drink or a cake, maybe?" JJ mulled over the priest's offer whilst years of listening to teachers banging on about 'stranger danger' echoed in his brain.

"I'm good, thanks," he said grudgingly as he pulled up the chair opposite and sat down.

"Well, if you change your mind, then just let me know. I really appreciate you taking the time to talk to me." Father Alexander removed his coat and folded it neatly over the back of his chair before sitting down again.

Within a matter of seconds, Meredith placed a large cappuccino down between them, followed by two cherry and almond slices.

"These are on the house. I know they're your favourite hun, and they'd only go to waste otherwise." She gave JJ a wink as she placed two forks down and a couple of paper napkins.

"Thanks Mrs Hutson."

"Yes, thank you. That's very kind. They're one of my favourites too." The priest gave Meredith a warm smile of his own and divvied out the cakes whilst she wandered back over to the shop counter.

JJ hoovered the cake up in under a minute without so

much as touching his fork, and Father Alexander couldn't help but chuckle to himself.

"Hungry?" he joked, whilst taking the first forkful of his own. "There was a time I used to have an appetite like that, but these days I only have to look at something sweet and I can hear my belt creak."

JJ gave a polite smile as he wiped the jam from his lips and then got down to business.

"What were you doing at Crooked House?" he whispered. "I mean, why were you looking for Archie there?"

Father Alexander took a sip of his coffee in contemplation and then looked JJ square in the eye.

"If I'm honest, it's nothing more than a hunch really. Archie has been missing for several months now and everyone else has given up looking...everyone except me. The police seem to think he ran away, that things just got too difficult after his mum passed and he wanted to escape it all...start over somewhere new. They've even convinced his dad of it now with all their teenage statistics, but they're wrong, I know it. Archie would never leave, no matter how hard things were at home. He loves his family and would do anything for them. He had...has, this inner strength, you see. In many ways he was the glue holding them all together, looking after his sister while his dad wrestled with his grief. I knew the second I got the call that something must have happened to him, something bad."

"But what lead you to Crooked House?" JJ pressed, continuing to keep his cards close to his chest as he encouraged Father Alexander to go on.

"It was a book of all things that led me there. I'd been handing out flyers with Archie's photo for months and must've walked past that book stall a hundred times, but I never once saw anyone there. It wasn't until I was looking for something new to read myself that I discovered the stall had an owner who spent her days hidden away behind the boxes of books she sold, reading her wares. I didn't even have a flyer with me at the time, but I had the photo on my phone... the one I showed you, and she recognized him instantly. She told me she'd seen him around the time he went missing and that he'd bought a book. Archie was an avid reader, and a rather gifted poet, but she remembered him because he bought the complete works of Poe, which was unusual for a boy his age. Sadly, she had no further insight to offer, but then as I was about to walk away, she mentioned a second book she'd gifted him. This one was all about haunted hotels, and she remembered Archie's excitement when he learned that one of the featured hotels was in a neighbouring village."

"Crooked House," JJ confirmed, and Father Alexander nodded.

"I asked Archie's father if I could stop by and take a look around in his room for anything that might help track him down, and that's when I found it. Next to *The Complete Works of Poe*, just as the stall owner had said, was a book written by Peter Higginsworth. It was the first ray of hope I'd had in months...I mean, what boy your age wouldn't be tempted to investigate a haunted house? Anyway, I picked the book up and as I began flicking through the pages, a bookmark fell out. I eventually found Crooked House on page fifty-seven and skimmed through the extract. I was convinced it was a lead, but I saw no reason to alert the police at that point. When I bent down to retrieve the bookmark, I noticed a pad underneath the bed, so I pulled it out, and that's when I discovered the true extent of Archie's interest in the place." Father Alexander swiped through the photos on his phone and then slid it across the table so JJ could see.

"That looks like something from a detective show." JJ's eyes widened as he tried to take in as much detail as he could.

The mind map looked like a work of art, with dozens of interlinked connections weaving their way around the page, but the scale was too small for JJ to make out any of its detail. The only labels clear enough to read were 'Crooked House' and 'Cold Christmas', and both sat at the very heart of the image.

"What is it?" JJ quizzed as he wrestled with the urge to zoom in.

"I'm not entirely sure what all of it means, to be honest. Parts of it read like a timeline of events, including a number of people who have either been reported missing or presumed dead. Other parts read like the wild ramblings of a conspiracy theorist, tracing all kinds of tragedy back to the same place: Crooked House. Then there is Peter Higginsworth, the book's author. His name was also scribbled down at the top of the page with a question mark. I reached out to his publisher, but I've yet to hear back. From what I can tell, he spends most of his time gallivanting around the world, exposing fraudsters and spinning half-cocked theories about the supernatural."

JJ noticed a sudden rush of blood to Father Alexander's cheeks as he spoke of Peter and detected some animosity lurking behind his amiable expression.

"He's a teacher at our school," JJ blurted, and then squirmed in his chair. "I think he teaches history to the sixth form."

"Really? That can't be a coincidence. He picked this area to teach in..." Father Alexander lost himself in thought at JJ's revelation, then returned to the topic of Archie.

"Back at the house, you said it wasn't safe. What did you mean by that?"

JJ glanced down at the image that was still open in front of him as he mulled over his response. Father Alexander seemed like a decent man on the face of things, but JJ knew all too well that appearances could be deceiving. Although his gut was telling him he could be trusted, he didn't have Meridia's talent for seeing the future, and so decided to bluff his way through the question.

"It's haunted...or cursed. Maybe both. Most people around here know about it...especially since the last owner mysteriously vanished."

"So why were you there again today? Since I found Archie's notes, I've been there every day this past week, after my afternoon service. This is the third time I've seen you now, just staring at the house from that old dirt track. Why do you keep going back if it's so dangerous?"

Father Alexander ramped up the pressure a little as he swiped back through the images on his phone to find the one of Archie again and left it open in front of JJ.

"Is that where you saw Archie? Is he in some kind of trouble? Are you? Whatever you tell me is in the strictest confidence, I assure you. I'm a man of God and you have my word on that."

JJ knew he had been busted, and after he'd swallowed his initial instinct to deny the priest's claims, he allowed the warm feeling of relief to wash over him. The truth was he didn't have the first idea why he kept going back to that god-awful place. His best guess was some form of guilt for getting them all into this mess in the first place.

So many times he'd thought about lighting a match to it,

but that would have required him to venture beyond the safety of the path, and he just didn't have the stomach for that. He often wondered if he'd bump into any of the others during his secret visits. If any of them shared his morbid fascination with the place, but it seemed the only other person interested in going anywhere near it was Father Alexander.

Still, he couldn't tell him the truth about Archie. Not here at least, and not without the blessing of the others. The last thing he needed was for any of them to be implicated in Archie's murder, as he was pretty sure even church confidentiality had its limits.

He looked at the image again.

Archie seemed so happy in the photograph, as if the old BMX he was sitting on was his pride and joy.

JJ's mind drifted to Archie's family and imagined what they must be going through. As fractured as his own family was, he couldn't imagine losing his mum, and although she and his dad couldn't seem to make time for each other, he knew deep down they were still very much in love.

"You mentioned he had a sister?" JJ kicked himself for referring to Archie in the past tense and hoped the priest didn't pick up on it.

"Yes, he has a younger sister, Katie. Archie is her world, and she misses him terribly. Please JJ, if you know anything that could help us find him...no matter how small..." Father Alexander's eyes became glossy as he struggled to keep his emotions in check.

"Crooked House took him. That's what it does...what they do. They take people." JJ couldn't hold the truth in any longer.

He was so tired of the secrets, of the guilt that had been gnawing away at him ever since they first stepped foot in its lousy halls. The mounting pressure that came with each new dark turn of events, the misery and torment his friends had been forced to endure, it all came pouring out at once.

A stream of consciousness so dark and so far-fetched it could have been lifted straight from the pages of Poe, but JJ let it out regardless and damned the consequences.

"People think that place is haunted...and it is...kind of... but it's much more than that. It's much worse. That place is evil. There are monsters hiding in the shadows. I've seen them! One of them tried to kill me...tried to kill my friends."

Tears streamed down JJ's face as his voice shattered into a thousand pieces from all the pain he'd been carrying.

"There are ghosts too. I can show you. We have pictures of them all...*sniff*...the little girl...the owner...and him!"

JJ pointed at the priest's phone as he cuffed his tears away.

"I know how it all sounds, but it's the truth...I swear! Archie is never coming back."

39

Father Alexander felt shaken by what he'd just heard, and his mind immediately leapt into overdrive. He'd been privy to enough confessions during his twenty-plus years as a priest to recognize conviction when he saw it, and the boy in front of him now genuinely believed there were monsters in Crooked House.

Perhaps more devastating, however, was his assertion that Archie was never coming back. Father Alexander's heart sank like a stone the moment those words reached his ears, as it validated what his instincts had been telling him all along, despite the unbelievable nature of JJ's claims.

He wondered what role Peter Higginsworth had played in all this fantasy. Had he been brainwashing these children into thinking his ghost stories were true? And what were the photos JJ had mentioned? That was a worry in itself.

He gently placed his hand on JJ's wrist to reassure him whilst trying to ignore the myriad of conclusions crowding his mind.

"It's ok. Everything is going to be ok. What monsters JJ? Who tried to hurt you?" Father Alexander braced himself for the answer, hoping JJ had been talking metaphorically, and that any monsters he spoke of were flesh and blood, but something about his words said otherwise, as did the fear in his eyes.

"Everything is not ok. Everything is the opposite of ok! The monsters in that house are here for all of us. Peter called them horsemen. They're here because the world is about to end and there are at least three of them hiding in that place. I've seen them with my own eyes. The stupid thing is, they're not even our biggest problem right now. Right now, there's a witch on the loose and she's trying to kill us too! Do you know how crazy this all sounds? I mean, do you have any idea? Ha ha...Even for me? You're sitting there, listening to me talk about monsters and witches and the end of the world and yet you're politely nodding and sipping your coffee like this stuff happens to you every day. Why is that?" JJ's clear agitation didn't stop him from keeping his voice low to avoid causing a scene.

"It's just what I do JJ, I listen." Father Alexander shuffled in his chair and then leaned onto his elbows to close the gap between them both.

"Most of what I do is listen. My old mentor used to say, 'nobody ever learns anything while talking' and there's a lot of truth in that. Whatever's going on, I'm here to help, not judge. I'm not here to lecture either you'll be pleased to know. Just help me understand what's going on and I promise I'll do whatever I can to keep you safe."

JJ removed his hat and let out a tremendous sigh whilst staring at his feet beneath the table.

"What else was in that photo you showed me...the one of Archie's sketch pad? What did it all say? And what's the deal with you and Archie? Why is he so important to you?" He asked.

"There was a lot of information on that pad of his. Some of it I was familiar with, and some not so much. I don't tend to watch the news, so I wasn't aware of the owners of Crooked House going missing until I did some digging of my own. The girl I vaguely remember though as I think it was mentioned at one of the schools I was working at. I provide pastoral care to the local catholic schools you see. That's how I met Archie. When his mum first fell ill, we'd meet once a week. He'd talk, and I'd listen; much like we're doing here. His dad was coping much better then, but when his mum's condition worsened, I saw him more often, carrying out the odd house visit to check on them all, or he and his sister would come to the church and help me in the garden. He had little family beyond his dad and sister, not locally at least. There wasn't anyone else for him to turn to for help. I became quite close to them all as a result. Such a lovely family, torn apart by tragedy. I could relate to their struggles. Cancer took my wife when she was just in her twenties, and I could see a lot of myself in Archie's father. The feeling of complete and utter loss, but then to lose his son too. That's why I've not given up on him like the others. I kept thinking about all the scenarios that would prevent him reaching out and every single one of them spelled trouble. So, when I found the book and his notes, I had to see where it led me. Even if there was the slightest chance of getting some answers, then I had to try. And it's a good thing I did, as it's led me to you. Sorry, I'm babbling...this is why I prefer to listen. So, in answer to your first question, there was a great deal of information in Archie's notes. I even managed to fill in some of the gaps with records we keep at the church. One way or another I was able to verify everything in that pad of his. Tragedies spanning centuries, and all of them some way or another, linked to that house.

Believe it or not, there was even a mention of a witch...or rather, a witch hunter. Now in my line of work you come to realize there is no such thing as a coincidence, so whilst I'm not sure if I believe in monsters or things that go bump in the night, I most certainly believe in the evil of man, and if any harm has come to Archie, God forbid, then I want to find those responsible and make sure they are held accountable." Father Alexander's voice almost broke as he finished his impromptu monologue, and his hands were shaking. He took another sip of his coffee whilst he regained his composure and whispered softly, "Sorry, I didn't mean to turn that into a sermon...I'm just looking for answers."

"I don't have all the answers," JJ conceded. "I can only tell you what I know."

40

The first thing Kane did when he arrived home was race upstairs and lock himself in the bathroom. He'd told Zach he was going for a quick shower and a change of clothes to rid himself of the stench of roaches, but that was only half the story.

Kane lifted his jumper away from his ribs and winced as the fabric tugged at the wound he'd been hiding since Peter had lunged at him with a carving knife. Although the damage was superficial, it been enough to draw blood, and he didn't want to make Peter feel any worse than he already did. Kane raised his left arm over his head and studied his war wound in the mirror while the shower warmed up. Not quite a gash, but long enough to warrant an explanation if noticed. He figured he'd cross that bridge if he came to it, as he had more pressing excuses to come up with; namely, why Zach would be staying at home for tomorrow's showdown at Crooked House. He braced himself for the inevitable sting the shower would incite and bravely stepped into the cubical.

When Kane came back downstairs, he found everyone

in the living room laughing together. Zach had commandeered the TV and was cycling through YouTube shorts of various mischievous cats up to no good. The innocent chuckles provided the perfect tonic for their diabolical day.

Kane stood in the doorway, preserving the moment as he soaked it up. His parents were cozied together on one of the plush blue sofas with their signature brews beside them, a black coffee for his mum, and a cup of earl grey for his dad.

Despite eighteen years of marriage and two teenage children, they both looked happy and in love when compared to other people their age. In their mid-forties now, his dad was showing some signs of age, with a greying beard and temples that framed his narrow jawline, but aside from that, he still looked pretty youthful. He had the much-envied Jackson full head of hair, that was wild and wavy, although he wore it much shorter these days. He looked perfectly relaxed with his feet up on the matching pouf whist Kane's mum nuzzled into him with her legs taking up the rest of the cushions on the three-seater. She was a couple of years older than his dad, but looked at least five years younger, even without her makeup. Although he had his dad's hair, everyone said Kane and Zach were the image of their mum. Her elfin features made her an attractive woman, as if she belonged on a catwalk. She swept her dusty blonde bob behind one ear so she could see the TV screen, and Kane wished he'd brought his phone down with him so he could take a picture. They looked like the perfect poster family, sitting there in their show-home styled living room.

A sharp twinge in his ribs reminded him that this might very well be his last chance to enjoy such a moment and so he wandered in with a beaming smile and sat down on the floor beside his brother.

"What are you so happy about? You look like the cat who got the cream." His dad's attempt at a cat pun would normally result in a dramatic groan from Kane, but he decided to let this one slide.

"Nothing. Just nice to be home."

"You can say that again," Zach exclaimed as he stretched his wiry frame out on the thick cream carpet. "What's for dinner mum? I'm starving!"

"Well, I thought I'd treat us all to takeout and a movie tonight, seeing as it's a Saturday and we've got nothing else on. What do you think boys? Pizza or Chinese?"

"Pizza please!" Zach didn't waste a second staking his claim on dinner, so Kane and his dad conceded, as they often did.

"Ok, I'll order our usual while you guys pick a movie. No horrors though, Kane!" His mum shot him a mock scowl from the sofa, but a horror movie was the last thing Kane wanted to watch that night.

Whilst their parents were busy in the kitchen sorting out plates and various condiments to go with their impending feast, Kane figured it would be the ideal opportunity to broach the subject of Crooked House.

"I need to talk to you about tomorrow spud," he whispered under the cover of the TV.

"I know what you're going to say, I heard you and Peter talking when everyone was busy getting his things together for the hotel. I'm not coming, am I?" Zach's tone was one of resignation and Kane hoped he'd just been spared a difficult conversation.

"We just can't risk it mate. You're too important in all this. The witch is going to be tough enough, but if the creatures show up again...we won't be able to guarantee our own safety, let alone yours."

"Do you think they will come back? The monsters, I mean. Meridia said the other me told her they were coming, but now she doesn't know what it meant. What if the monsters are gone but there are other things in that house, like the witch, or worse? You could all be walking into a trap!" Kane could see the fear projected in his brother's eyes from the twisted picture show playing in his mind.

"We just don't know. For all we know, we might have killed those monsters when we exposed them to the sun that day. Maybe they're like vampires and they can't come back from that. Maybe that's why the witch has suddenly shown up in their place. Even Peter can't be sure. This is all new territory as technically we should all be dead...and if it wasn't for Meridia, we would be. Peter said all we can do is fight what's in front of us, and right now, that's the witch. We won't know what else comes out of that place until we get there tomorrow, but none of us are going to enter Crooked House, ok? We're not stupid...well not completely anyway."

Kane gave his brother a wink and a playful nudge with his shoulder.

"Peter's putting a plan together as we speak. He thinks something happened when the witch was inside him that gives us an advantage, but he's not going to tell us until tomorrow. The last thing we need is for her to get to any of us in our dreams and give the game away, so we've just got to trust him."

"Do you think she can still do that? What if she comes for me like she did Peter?" Kane's poor choice of words struck fear into his brother's heart, so he quickly backtracked.

"Peter doesn't think she'll be able to do that kind of thing anymore now she's in the physical world. We're just being careful, that's all. Besides, I'll be right next door the whole time. You'll be fine tonight, I promise." It wasn't Kane's finest work as far as reassurance was concerned, but it had to do as he could hear the crockery clattering in the kitchen which signalled his parents' return. "Are we good mate? Hopefully, we'll all be back in time for lunch."

"Yeah, we're good. I want to be there, but I get it. We're good."

"What's good? Have you picked out a film yet?" his mum interrupted, carrying a stack of plates whilst his dad followed her in with a set of lap-trays piled high with various oils and sauces.

"It's Zach's choice tonight. I chose the last one." Kane passed the baton to his brother, who knew exactly what he wanted to watch.

"Marvel it is then."

41

Peter had hit the wall. Wave upon wave of unrelenting tiredness crept up on him as he sat hunched over his laptop. One minute he'd be typing up his findings, and the next his screen would be awash with the letter 'k' or 'a' depending on which hand had fallen asleep first. He decided to break the cycle with another coffee, so he put the kettle on and wandered around the room in an attempt to get his blood flowing again. His body still ached from his ordeal, but it felt good to stretch his legs and look at something other than a glaring screen.

When researching, he would always be very regimented about his screen time, making sure he built in breaks for a walk or trip to the local shop, but right now those were luxuries he couldn't afford. He'd already spent far too much time looking for a secret organization rumoured to have originated in Cold Christmas during the 17th Century, only to discover they took their secrecy very seriously. What he wouldn't give to pay the village library a visit and trawl through their archives. However, he suspected the real Children of the Shadows had long since disbanded, leaving a gap in the market for a handful of easily manipulated fanatics to don some hoods and pick up where they had left off perhaps.

His research on witches, or more specifically, how to kill one, had been even less fruitful, with hundreds of conflicting accounts muddying his own understanding of the subject. Witchcraft has such a wide variety of meanings across different cultures and religions it was nigh on impossible to get a clear view of what they were dealing with so far, let alone understand how to defeat her.

Their witch exhibited several supernatural abilities which pulled on ancient African and European mythologies in equal measure. From what he could gather, she had been using a technique known as 'dream walking' in order to infiltrate Meridia's dreams, using her as a gateway into the wider group, which must be how she'd got inside his body. Thankfully, that window into Meridia's consciousness opened both ways and allowed her to find him occasionally, the real him that was. Although the witch's power was so strong it prevented him from being of much use. Yet, her apparent rebirth was something entirely different and lacked any explanation.

Having drawn a blank, Peter turned his attention to the object found in his attic to see if that offered any clues. Whilst he'd erred on the side of caution and left it at his house, he took a few pictures of it before leaving for the hotel. Again, he hadn't found any exact match, but it had components of witchcraft and voodoo which, when put together, kind of made sense.

The overall structure bore close resemblance to something called a 'ghirlanda' which was traditionally placed under the bed of a witch's intended victim to either incapacitate or kill them. This one had been found directly above Peter's office and his bedroom, so perhaps the witch was simply hedging her bets. The animal intestines binding it together sailed closely to a witch's knot, designed to control the movement of another person, which might explain how she controlled him from within.

This left only the centrepiece to explain, which Peter assumed represented the witch herself. The fragments of bone and blood found in the wax mould had to belong to her and was far more in keeping with a conventional voodoo doll, but how the strange concoction of dark magic had found its way into his house he had no clue.

His best guess was the witch had help, and perhaps the hooded intruder Kane stumbled upon was, in fact, breaking in to plant something rather than to steal it. If his theory was true, and he could find no logical alternative, then it meant they might face more than just the witch tomorrow.

Click! the kettle boiled, and Peter slowly stirred his coffee whilst mulling over his final findings.

Unsurprisingly, there was no Wiki-guide for killing a witch, so his research was largely dominated by ducking stools and being burned at the stake. Other than the ramblings of crackpot bloggers who had clearly watched one-too-many horror movies, the only remotely bona fide alternative was to catch her spirit in a bottle.

Although Peter wasn't a betting man, it seemed fire was the only horse worth backing. Now he just needed to figure out how they would use it.

42

Father Alexander's chair creaked softly as he leant back in contemplation. It had been about an hour and another large cappuccino since JJ had told his tall tales of Crooked House, and Father Alexander had listened intently throughout. He hadn't even registered the old couple in the window settle their bill and leave, any more than he had noticed Mrs Hutson patiently waiting on them to clear out so she could shut up shop and return home to her husband.

"You think I'm mad, don't you? Or that I'm making all this up. I know how it all sounds, but it's the truth." JJ looked deflated by Father Alexander's somewhat underwhelming reaction.

"I think...I think we need to take this conversation outside now so Mrs Hutson can close up for the day." He looked at his watch and signalled for the bill. "How would you feel about sitting in the park perhaps? We still have a bit of daylight left and then I can drop you off at home? Or not, if you'd prefer."

JJ looked out the window and weighed up Father Alexander's offer.

"Ok, but I'll walk from here. I'm not far."

"Here you go dear, was everything ok?" Mrs Hutson eagerly responded with their bill, and Father Alexander was equally fast to settle with cash.

"It was perfect Mrs Hutson, and please keep the change. Sorry we kept you here so long."

"Thank you, that's very kind of you. No need to apologize, this one's never any trouble." She patted JJ on his shoulder, stirring him from his thoughts.

"Thanks Mrs Huston, I'll see you soon."

They both stood up and made their way out into the empty park. The sun was on its way down, taking any semblance of warmth with it as it hovered precariously above the toddler's play park in the distance.

Father Alexander popped his collar up in response to the sudden drop in temperature, whilst JJ buried in hands in the pockets of his puffer jacket and gestured with his head towards the open field. "There's a bench just there by the path."

"Great. I promise not to keep you as I know you want to be home before dark, and I understand why, given everything you've told me." They both wandered over to the bench while Father Alexander considered his response.

"It's ok. I don't even know what I was expecting you to say." JJ pre-empted, filling the awkward silence while they walked. "Everything I've told you is true though. The monsters, the files on each room, Archie and now the witch...it's all true. I think maybe I just needed to tell someone on the outside. Get it all out of my head, so I'm not looking for answers...or anything really. No offence."

"None taken. I get it, as much as I can, at least. It's a lot to take in though, as you can imagine. Just putting the paranormal stuff aside for the moment though, what exactly are you all intending to do when you come face to face with this witch tomorrow?" Father Alexander remained heavily torn.

Despite the far-fetched and disturbing nature of everything he'd just heard, he couldn't ignore the huge overlap between what JJ had told him and what he had uncovered with his own investigation. Along with Crooked House, Peter Higginsworth was the only other common denominator between JJ's group and Archie, which meant either he was a master manipulator, hoodwinking children into thinking his ghost stories were real, or there really was something sinister going on in Cold Christmas. Regardless of the reasons, he couldn't ignore the fact this meeting had been a cry for help, and that someone could be in genuine danger tomorrow.

"I don't know what the plan is. Peter's working on it tonight, so I guess we'll all find out in the morning." JJ appeared to be honest in his response, but Father Alexander had an underlying sense he might be on the brink of losing him, based on his lukewarm response. "I think I should get going now actually. They'll be locking the gates soon and my mum will wonder where I am."

"What if you're walking into a trap tomorrow? What then?" Father Alexander's question was enough to tug at JJ's sleeve and stop him from leaving. "What if you've missed something? Something important. You said yourself you don't have all the answers. What happens if you go in there tomorrow and things don't go your way? What happens to Zach then? Or any of us for that matter? If the stakes are as high as you say, then surely you can't afford to leave any stone unturned before you waltz in there tomorrow, guns blazing."

"But the longer we leave it, the stronger she'll get. Then we'll lose for sure. You haven't seen what she's capable of... what she's done."

"All I'm asking is that you hold fire for an hour or so tomorrow. I can bring mine and Archie's research and we can see if that changes anything. What have you got to lose? Surely another hour is neither here nor there in the grand scheme of things. What do you say?" Father Alexander's only real chance of averting a tragedy was to stall, so that's exactly what he proposed.

Deciding he wouldn't break his oath of confidentiality and involve the authorities just yet. He was sure he could come up with a better strategy between now and the morning. He just needed more time, and the opportunity to meet with the others, specifically Peter, offered the promise of greater clarity, and with that clarity would surely come answers.

"I don't know...it makes sense to see what you have. We've been spending all our lunchtimes researching and bouncing theories...I'd have to ask the others first though..." JJ slipped his baseball cap off and rubbed his brow in consideration.

"Then you should know I have access to local records, archives that are unique to the church. We're both looking for answers. Maybe by comparing notes we can get some. You see, my church was originally based in Cold Christmas, but by the turn of the eighteenth century, the village had become completely corrupt. Overrun by various outlaws and criminals who had muscled their way in and seized control of the land. That's actually where Crooked House gets its name from. Unoccupied, it was adopted by the underworld and used as a safe-house of sorts for thieves and murderers travelling across country. Its reputation became so renowned that no lawman in the county would go near it, so the presiding Bishop at the time made the difficult decision to relocate St Peter's for the sake of its flock. Brick by brick, it was moved to the neighbouring village of Thundridge, all except the east turret, which the original village kept as its own place of worship, despite it being renounced by the church. That turret still stands there today, although derelict now, it's accompanied by the graves of those villagers who stayed. They saw the church's relocation as a final act of condemnation."

"What do you mean by final condemnation?" JJ was eating up every word now.

"They saw the church's decision to move as an act of abandonment, leaving them at the mercy of Cold Christmas and its lawless streets. It was an impossible situation, the perfect storm in many ways. The country had a new and united parliament but was still finding its feet, so whilst that was going on, clergy couldn't be expected to stand up to the violence that was rife by that time."

"But why there? I mean, why Cold Christmas of all places? It's in the middle of nowhere." JJ almost answered his own question.

"The land looked very different back then JJ, and the location had good through-roads, making it a perfect base of operations for criminals. What you see there now is the legacy of that activity as reputations get passed down from generation to generation. When the church moved, Thundridge became a haven for many, a beacon of hope. As a result, its local economy thrived, whereas Cold Christmas' perished." JJ nodded as he allowed the new insight to sink in and then glanced at his phone.

"I need to get going Father..."

"Please, call me Martin," he reached into his pocket and pulled out a business card. "I meant what I said JJ, I want answers the same as you. Please, speak to the others and let me know if you'd all like to meet. I'd hate for anything bad to happen tomorrow...to any of you."

"I will, Fa...err Martin. Thanks." JJ took the card and shook hands before hurrying away towards the park gate.

As he disappeared into the distance, the streetlight behind Father Alexander came to life, illuminating the path and casting his long shadow towards the open field. The soothing amber haze signalled the end of another day, and he became aware once more of the chill the evening air carried on its breath. He hoped his efforts were enough to get a foot in the door.

As he walked to his car, he pondered JJ's story and its possible truth. Recounting his own findings in some strange way had only added more weight to the unbelievable stories he'd heard in the café, and he reminded himself there was never any smoke without fire.

Regardless of what was going on with JJ and his friends, he wasn't prepared to let anything stand in the way of his quest to find Archie, and currently all signs pointed to Crooked House.

<h1 style="text-align:center">43</h1>

Izzy was stuffed by the time she ambled upstairs to her room. Approaching dinner as if it was her last meal, she'd gorged on everything she could get her hands on. The rich, creamy chicken and mushroom risotto that failed to touch the sides, the delicious herb-infused French bread she'd used to mop up the leftover sauce, all topped off with a large slab of New York cheesecake her mum had bought from the local bakery.

It was a feast fit for a queen, and whilst both her parents were amazed by the amount of carbs their waif-like daughter had consumed, they were essentially a family of feeders, so took great satisfaction from every mouthful she packed away.

After spending an hour in the snug, allowing her substantial meal to digest, she left them to enjoy a bottle of Châteauneuf-du-Pape while listening to Michael Bublé's greatest hits.

It had been a lovely evening, liberating even, as for a mere couple of hours she had allowed herself to relax and enjoy the moment with her family.

However, as she returned to the twilight of her room, the darkness of the day's events slithered its way back into the forefront of her mind. She lingered in the doorway for a moment and studied the incalculable number of shadows as they conspired to cast unfamiliar patterns in her room and claim it as their own. Staring into the gloom, Izzy sensed the hairs on the back of her neck rise to attention and wondered if she'd ever feel safe alone at night again.

Click!

With a flick of a light switch, she banished their murky presence from her sight and warily stepped inside. On paper her room was the largest in the Di Salvo house, but its L-shaped layout wasn't so appealing to her parents when they bought the place, so it ended up going to Izzy. In her eyes the room was perfect, providing her with a separate study area to house her desk and MacBook Pro, that also doubled up as a dresser from time to time.

The décor was in keeping with her overall style, neutral, with a multitude of Ikea inspired shades of white and grey. Breaking up the room with the only visible splash of colour was a large print of Van Gough's '*The Starry Night*', which her mum had insisted on hanging on the wall facing her luxurious double bed. Despite the allure of her fresh cotton bedsheets, she could feel her brain shifting through the gears as she replayed the day she'd endured.

Things had escalated way beyond the realms of logic, which left Izzy feeling like an astronaut who'd become detached from their spacecraft and was now hopelessly adrift in space. At times that day she had been nothing more than a dumbstruck observer as the chaos unfolded around her. It was a feeling she neither welcomed nor enjoyed, yet despite the nigh on crippling sensation it left her with, she still believed logic had its part to play in tackling the witch.

Izzy recognized they had been riding their luck of late, and she wondered where they would all be without Meridia's gift, but the way things had escalated at Peter's was the final wake-up call. Without an adult's guidance, they had exposed themselves, walking straight into a trap, and with the stakes so high they couldn't afford to keep learning on the job. Tomorrow the stakes would be higher than ever, and although they would have Peter's help this time around, the witch had already beaten him once.

Ping!

Izzy looked at her phone to find a message from JJ in the group chat.

```
I know it's a bit late in the
day but is there any way we
can jump on a quick call? It's
kind of urgent.
```

Izzy watched curiously as the thumbs-up count rose to three before adding her own. She knew whatever it was, it had to be important and didn't have to speculate for long when the phone rang after a matter of seconds.

Izzy put her Airpods in and tapped accept. The entire group was online except for Meridia, which wasn't unusual at this time of the evening, as she often ate later than everyone else.

"Hey, what's up mate?" Kane was the first to speak. A lengthy pause followed his cheery greeting before JJ replied in a shaky voice.

"Ok, so I'll get straight to it as I know this is all a bit last minute, but I met someone today...a priest."

"Mate, I know tomorrow could go either way, but it's a bit late to be pledging your allegiance to god isn't it?" Kane's attempt at humour missed its mark and JJ continued.

"He was looking for Archie. His name is Father Alexander, and he comes from the church in Archie's village."

"Thundridge?" Peter asked.

"Yeah. I checked him out online and he seems legit..."

"Where did you meet him?" Peter interrupted.

"That's the thing...so don't get annoyed, but I walked up to Crooked House today after the cab dropped me off..."

"WHAT?!" a chorus of exasperation boomed in Izzy's ears as she sat waiting patiently for JJ to explain himself.

"I know, I know. Look, I got home to an empty house and still had plenty of daylight left, so I just started walking. The next thing I knew, I was there. But it's ok, I didn't go right up to the house, I stayed at arm's length and didn't stray from the path. I guess I was thinking I'd scope it out for tomorrow, and that was when I saw him."

"You're lucky nobody else saw you!" Kane's agitation was evident.

"Oh, they saw him." Peter added, "I have no doubt. But it changes nothing, so no point dwelling on it now. You are home now, I assume? You're safe?"

"Yeah, I went to the park on my way back and got home before the sun went down. I'm fine."

"So, what was the priest doing there at the same time as you?" Kane pressed.

"Dunno. Coincidence I guess. He was just looking for Archie. He said everyone else had given up except him; he'd been trying for months and found out about Crooked House a few days ago. He showed me a board he'd found under Archie's bed, and no joke, it looked like one of the murder boards from *It's Behind You!* Archie obviously did a lot more research than we did before going there, and

Father Alexander has done some of his own. Guys, he knows tons of stuff we don't. He said he had records at his church that could help us." Izzy picked up on JJ's last comment and couldn't contain herself.

"Help us what James? What did you tell him?" The line went silent again whilst the others caught up and then waited for JJ's answer.

"Er...so here's the thing. I kind of told him everything..."

"WHAT?!" Kane and Izzy snapped in unison.

"I met him at Mrs Hutson's place to talk, and when he told me what he knew, and what Archie's family had been through, I...I just couldn't stop myself. I'm sorry guys, I know we agreed not to tell anyone about any of this, but...I just had this feeling about him. I think he can help us get some answers." Izzy's mind started racing at JJ's confession.

"What if he calls the police James? Or worse, what if he's in on it? Peter said someone on the outside is helping the witch, remember?"

"Let's all take a beat." Peter intervened with authority, "Looking at Father Alexander online, he appears to be an upstanding member of his community. He was assigned to St Peter's in 2011 and provides ad hoc pastoral support to the Catholic schools in the area by all accounts."

"That's how he said he'd met Archie," JJ leapt back in to make his case. "His mum got sick, and Father Alexander got to know him through the school...Guys, we can trust him, I know it! He said St Peter's started out in Cold Christmas, and then the church ordered it to be moved to Thundridge when things got too dangerous. He has records dating back from that time...it's got to be worth looking at, right? And besides, he said anything I told him was confidential, that the Church didn't allow him to share it with anyone."

"The seal of confession," Peter confirmed. "Although I'm not sure how that extends to hunting witches and demons. Especially if you told him everything in Mrs Hutson's café...It's hardly hallowed ground. I'm assuming he'd like to meet us then. In the morning before we set off?"

"Yeah, he said all he was asking for was an hour...hang on, how do you know he asked that?" JJ sounded miffed.

"Because that's exactly what I would do in his position. Depending on how much detail you went into, I expect he was caught off-guard by what you said, given his position. My best guess is he's looking to stall us until he can figure out what truth there is in anything you told him. What did you say about Archie when he asked?"

"I told him everything..."

"JAMES!" Again, Izzy couldn't prevent her dismay from leaking out.

She'd wanted nothing more than to tell someone else about Crooked House, namely her parents, and she knew Meridia felt the same. All these dark secrets had been eating them both from within for weeks, and meanwhile JJ spilt the beans to the first person he comes across just because he was wearing a white collar.

"I know...I said sorry. You weren't there Izz. He showed me a picture of Archie and told me about his family. He left behind a little sister and a dad who'd already lost his wife. If it was you that had been taken by that place, wouldn't you want your parents to know the truth? I know I would."

JJ made a pretty good point, and it was one that Izzy had given more thought to recently, particularly that evening, whilst letting her food go down. Still, it irked her he'd blabbed to the first person who asked.

"JJ, I understand why you did it." Peter stepped in again to mediate. "It was risky, that's for sure, and I guess we won't know how risky until tomorrow. Father Alexander appears fine on paper, but who's to say he isn't more involved than he's letting on? Regardless, what's done is done and we must move forward. Izzy, I understand why you're upset too. This is so much for all of us to carry and it's easy to lose sight of how much of a burden that is every day. I don't have a family. I go home of an evening, and I read or research, or on the rare occasion watch some tv. I don't have to hide things the same way all of you do. I can't even imagine how hard that must be. So, let's just agree that if we feel the urge to talk to anyone outside the group from now on, we take a vote first. If just one of us talks to the wrong person, it could put everyone in danger."

"Like we're not already in enough danger as it is," Kane quipped. "Peter's right though, at least Zach and I have each other to talk to outside of school. We all need to be here for each other. Mate, I'm sorry you went back to an empty house. If that ever happens again and you need company, just come here. You know you're always welcome."

"Thanks mate. I will. So, what do I tell Father Alexander then?" JJ threw it back out to the group.

"Let's vote on it," Peter reiterated. "I say we meet him. He knows about us now anyway, so we may as well find out who we're dealing with, and who knows, he may well have some information that helps us."

"I'm with Peter."

"Me too."

Both Kane and Zach gave their seal of approval, which just left Izzy. Like Peter, she could see the appeal of obtaining more information on Crooked House, for even if, by some miracle, they beat the witch tomorrow, they would not be out of the woods by any means.

God only knew what other abominations were waiting

to take the witch's place should she fall, and that was without factoring in the horsemen themselves, who remained conspicuous by their absence.

"Let's do it!" she declared.

44

JJ breathed an enormous sigh of relief as he ended the group call. Once the vote had been cast, he'd felt an immediate sense of calm, although he was disappointed that Meridia wasn't online to share any of her impressions of Father Alexander.

Part of him hoped that fate had brought the two of them together, and the priest's last-minute insight would somehow tip the scales in their favour. He figured a bit of good luck might help alleviate his guilt.

They would soon find out, and with that, JJ took to his phone again to let Father Alexander know. For a moment, he considered calling him to invest a little more time in sussing him out, but eventually rose above any lingering doubts and sent him a simple text. The day had finally caught up with JJ, and despite the empty house and uncertain future surrounding him, he felt like he might actually get a good night's rest.

Hi Martin, this is JJ. I've
spoken to the others and we're
all happy to meet in the
morning and compare notes.

We'll be at the Shawbrook
Holiday Inn at 9:30am.

JJ hit send and then checked the alarm on his phone before setting it down to charge for the night. Electing to forego getting undressed, he shuffled his way down the bed until his head could reach the pillow, laid back and closed his weary eyes.

The soft sting of tiredness gently seared the insides of his eyelids, and within minutes JJ had drifted into a deep sleep. So deep, in fact, he didn't even hear the sharp beep announcing Father Alexander's reply.

45

Father Alexander set his phone aside on the mahogany coffee table, leant back into his emerald-green leather armchair, and gazed at the ceiling.

The impromptu plan worked, buying him an extra hour in the morning to talk the group down, if necessary. As he stared at the hairline cracks in the aging paintwork above him, he wondered if there could be any semblance of truth in what JJ had told him.

Archie was more than intelligent, he was also street-smart and therefore nobody's fool. The more he let that simple truth percolate, the less likely it seemed Peter Higginsworth could be the instigator of all this. Whatever 'all this' was. As the cool leather of the chair's headrest creaked beneath his neck, his brain see-sawed back and forth, trying to reconcile the supernatural stories he'd heard with the cold, hard facts both he and Archie had uncovered. Something wasn't sitting quite right with him, yet he still couldn't put his finger on what.

"Could it be?" he muttered to himself as he continued to search the ceiling for answers, and then he remembered.

Gripping each arm of his chair, he launched himself up onto his feet and, with renewed purpose, made his way towards the study.

The faint yellow haze radiating from the antique brass lamp that sat perched on his desk served as the only source of light to brighten up the glorified cupboard where he had been spending most of his evenings lately.

He thumbed through the stack of papers that were smeared across the polished wooden surface until he landed on a page that was larger than the rest.

"There you are!" he blurted triumphantly, pulling it out from the pile and placing it under the lamp's bleary eye.

He thought he'd done a pretty good job of evolving Archie's sketchpad and he pondered over it in appreciation, as if it was one of the many works of art he's admired during his trip to the Vatican Museum. Although he lacked artistic flare, he made up for it with his unwavering attention to detail. As he traced the many names and dates that were meticulously woven together, he paused on the name Molly Harding.

He'd stumbled upon her in the church archives when trying to track down the original owner of Crooked House. In the months leading up to, and after, the relocation of St Peter's, there had been a strong emphasis on record keeping to ensure a smooth transition from Cold Christmas. As a result, far more information was documented in relation to the regular registries of births, deaths, and marriages during that period.

One such entry had struck Father Alexander as strange, detailing the mysterious purchase of an empty plot and gravestone in the year 1727. The residing priest at the time was informed it was to memorialize a missing villager from Thundridge, who had wandered into the woods one day, never to return. Whoever paid for it had insisted their name be kept from any ledger. Naturally, the church obliged without question, as it often did back then when donations were few and far between.

A couple of months prior to that, the body of a teenage boy, also from Thundridge, was found skinned alive and nailed to a large oak tree. It was a hideous crime, but one that Father Alexander had gathered no further information on. Sadly, the legal system was not quite so diligent in their record keeping back then, but it wasn't the boy that interested him now.

It was Molly, or more to the point, her absence.

Looking at the names that JJ had linked to Crooked House, they all had one very distinct thing in common, each and every one of them had disappeared from the face of the earth. Jessica Adams, Jonathan and Helen Ashfield, then more recently Archie Faulkner, had all mysteriously vanished.

What if Molly wasn't just another tragic victim of Cold Christmas? What if she was more than that?

Crack!

Father Alexander's entire body flinched at the sharp, sudden noise beyond his study window. His eyes darted to what he thought was the source and came face to face with a man staring at him from the shadows.

Appearing startled, the intruder fled the window toward the front of the house and Father Alexander took up chase, bounding out of the study and down the narrow hallway towards the front door. His heart was pounding as he fumbled with the latch to catch the prowler before he disappeared into the night, but by the time he eventually broke out of his own home, the trespasser was long gone.

Crash!

The street door slammed behind him as he flew down the garden path like a bat out of hell, shattering the serenity of St Peter's Road and setting a neighbour's dog off in the process.

The evening air carried more than just a chill as the drizzling rain lightly saturated his brow whilst he scanned his surroundings, but all he could see was the gravity defying flurry of wet mist as it danced in the breeze beneath the streetlights. The barking soon subsided, leaving behind it a deafening silence that rang in Father Alexander's ears like a distant fire alarm.

Creeaak!

The wrought-iron gate at the foot of the path gently drifted ajar in the breeze, but there was no-one there. How could he have gotten away so quickly? He had to be somewhere nearby, hiding in a neighbouring garden perhaps, but he wasn't about to go searching.

Instead, he took in a deep breath of the earthy, damp scent the rain had served up and slowly backed away towards the house. Father Alexander didn't believe in coincidence, and the fact his unwelcome visitor had been wearing a hood only strengthened JJ's wild claims.

"No smoke without fire," he muttered as he anchored the deadbolt on his door and returned to his study.

46

Lurking behind the soggy wooden fence, Silas Grady felt a sudden flush of anger swell in the pit of his throat as he watched the pathetic excuse for a priest retreat inside. All this waiting had him craving violence and bloodshed.

If he'd had his way, he would have waited beside the street door and slit the meddler's throat the second he set foot in his garden. They were all about to die soon anyway, so what was the harm in offing this one a day early? Still, it was not for him to question the dogma of his masters. His job was to watch silently from the shadows, for now at least.

Despite his orders, he continued to wrestle with his urges, doing all he could to stop himself from marching across the street, kicking the priest's door down and dragging him out by his hair to slaughter in front of his precious flock.

"Soon," he whispered under his breath, studying the priest's window opposite with steely blue eyes to ensure the watcher had not become the watched.

Content that he hadn't been spotted, Silas continued to

bemoan the priest inaudibly, turning the air around him blue as he shimmied along the fence towards the rear of the garden he was crouched in. He could feel the growing weight of his hood and cloak as they soaked up the clandestine rain like a hungry sponge.

It was time to leave.

Satisfied the priest would offer no hidden surprises, he now had to return to Shawbrook if he were to make his date with the seer on time.

Nimbly scaling the wall at the rear of his hidey-hole, he vaulted over the top and landed with the agility of a cat in the adjoining Marsh Street. The streetlight overhead was out of commission, just as his masters had told him it would be, and he indulged himself with a smug half-smile before continuing on to the cul-de-sac Rivers Close. From there, he could get back to his car under the cover of darkness and no-one would be any the wiser.

"Idiots," he muttered, shaking his head before wittering angrily to himself as he crept along the unlit alleyway to where he was parked.

In a matter of minutes, he emerged on Exeter Road and broke cover as he advanced to his gun-metal transit van. The layer of rain it had collected in his absence sparkled beneath the dusty moonlight, and the familiar waft of black cherry air freshener soothed him as he opened the passenger door and slipped inside.

"Run into any trouble Silas?" Meredith Hutson asked as she turned the key in the ignition.

"Everything happened just the way they said it would." He assured his driver calmly.

"Good. Time to pay the little bitch and her mum a visit then." And with that, they set off for Nightingale Lane.

47

It was a little after 9pm and the only sound in the Wilson house was the distant drone of an electric toothbrush. It had been a gruelling day that Meridia was keen to put behind her, and although she'd salvaged some enjoyment, courtesy of a cheesy rom-com and carpet-picnic with her mum, it was now time for bed.

Trudging out of the bathroom and across the hall to her room, Meridia was completely dead on her feet. Her eyelids weighed a ton, and despite the powerful sense of foreboding she was harbouring, her memory foam pillow and marshmallow duvet had never looked so appealing. For once, her mum was ahead of her and already in her bed, nursing a migraine she'd been struggling with all afternoon.

"Night mum," she whispered as she softly closed her bedroom door and wandered across to pull the curtains.

Gripping the plush yellow fabric, she glanced out onto the street below just in time to notice the headlights dip on a grey transit van as it pulled up out front. With a quick yank, she blocked out the rest of the world and switched her bedside light on. Its amber glow used to have such a calming influence on her, getting her through so many turbulent nights when she didn't know if her dad was going to show up again drunk and angry. Now, it had lost its shine, and she wondered if the toll of Crooked House was gradually forcing her to outgrow it.

She looked at the soft toys decorating her shelf and struggled to relate to any of them anymore. The classic teddy bear her nan had bought her before she passed with its plump golden fur and ruby red collar, the floppy white rabbit that she'd had ever since she was a baby; they all seemed so childish now as she prepared to face down yet another monster. Turning the main light off, the shadows softened around her, and her eyelids responded, shutting down for just a second to two.

Her knees buckled, jarring her awake, as she almost nodded off on the spot. Meridia could barely contain her excitement when she finally climbed into bed and felt the instant relief only cool, clean bedsheets can deliver. She thought about checking her phone for messages as it had been on charge all evening, but that's as far as she got before the gentle embrace of her duvet put her softly to sleep.

"*Wake up Meridia...*" the whispery voice sounded familiar as it fluttered into her ear with the delicacy of a butterfly, and she smiled, a lazy half-smile that let slip a drowsy mumble.

"*Meridia!*"

It came again, this time stirring her from her slumber, and she sat up with a start. Her eyes were a blur, still full of sleep, and the kaleidoscope of brown and orange hues dominating her room all merged into one as she struggled to come to.

"He...hello?" she muttered into the hazy abyss. Despite the recent slew of unwanted nighttime visitors infiltrating her dreams, her gut told her this was different, she felt calm and unafraid.

At the foot of her bed, she could see a vague outline, a person standing over her, yet still she felt unthreatened. With each blink, the shadow sharpened until she could make out his features clearly. "You're Archie, aren't you?" she asked innocently.

"*I am.*" He replied.

He was taller than she'd imagined, likely giving Kane a run for his money, and his wiry blond hair looked matted and dirty, as did his face. Wearing an old grey hoody and ripped blue jeans, he was covered in the same ash the others were, but it was a look he seemed to carry off somehow. In fact, if it wasn't for his haunting blacked-out eyes that glistened unnaturally in the dark, he would have looked like any other boy his age; just grubby from playing football at the park.

"Am I dreaming?" Meridia wondered aloud. Her mouth dried as she spoke, feeling her nerves creeping in. However, she didn't feel scared as she had grown so accustomed to these days. This felt more like meeting a celebrity. She and the others had spent such a long time talking about Archie with Peter, it felt as if she already knew him, a feeling that was reinforced when he spoke again.

"*Yep, afraid so. I've been waiting for a chance to speak to you again. You've been pretty busy lately though.*" He gave a wry smile, revealing dimples under the soft amber lighting of her room.

"It was you, wasn't it? Before, in my dream. I recognize your voice. It was you I could hear telling me where to go..." Meridia's bright blue eyes widened as the penny dropped.

"*I've helped a couple of you now...wish I could've done more, but I've got to be careful. There are things in that house even I don't understand."* He shook his head and let out a deep sigh, *"Sorry about my eyes by the way...I know they must be creepy."*

Meridia wasn't sure if she'd become desensitized over recent weeks, but as she looked at him without the fear of god in her, she realized they were quite beautiful, shining in the dimly lit room like twinkling Christmas lights.

"It's ok...I'm getting used to it now. How are you here? In my dream, I mean..." Meridia's brain fog had all but evaporated and she was much more alert now.

"I'm not sure yet. I don't know if it's your gift or the old woman's. Dreams are funny that way aren't they...often not making any sense until they do."

"Old woman? What old woman?" Meridia probed in her pursuit of answers.

"You saw her, remember? She saw you too. She's different to the rest of us...I don't know why...she just is." Archie leaned in a little closer as he continued. *"Like I said, there's still a lot I don't understand, but she knows you. You have to be careful. They know you are coming."*

His eyes flashed to the bedroom door as if he could see something she couldn't, and a surge of panic rippled its way through her body, leaving a warm tingling sensation in its wake.

"What is it?!" she blurted, sensing something was wrong.

"Someone is coming! I don't have much time. You need to look below Meridia...the answers you're looking for, that's where you'll find them. It's where you'll find me too..."

And with that, the glimmer in his eyes bled out into the room, engulfing Meridia in a dazzling, brilliant white light that crackled around her like static on the radio.

Shielding her eyes from its rays, the noise swiftly

subsided, and her bedroom returned to its familiar orange haze. When she lowered her arms again, Archie was gone.

Creak!

Meridia's eyes caught sight of a shadow as it drifted past the gap beneath her door. Archie was right, someone was outside. Another wave of panic washed over her, turning her knuckles white as she clutched the hem of the duvet in fear.

Scrape...

The handle slowly turned, and the door gradually opened.

Gripped by terror, her body seized up beneath the bedcovers, and she could do nothing but watch anxiously as a thin band of light from the outside hall crept across her soft cream carpet and struck her bedside table.

"Are you ok M?" her mum peered around the gap, blinking heavily as if half asleep, "I thought I heard voices."

"Sorry mum...just a dream." Meridia felt an immediate rush of relief as her angst loosened its grip and allowed her to sink back into her mattress.

"Ok hun...well, try to get some sleep now, its late."

As the door closed, Meridia blurted back, "Love you mum!"

The door paused a moment and a soft reply slipped through the gap before closing completely.

"Love you too M."

48

WHEN HER ALARM SOUNDED THE NEXT MORNING, Meridia had no recollection of falling back to sleep, nor having any more dreams for that matter. It seemed as if she'd blacked out immediately after her mum had checked in on her.

Her body had been crying out for a good night's rest, but even with the hundreds of questions that still lingered from the horrific events at Peter's, all she could think about was her brief encounter with Archie. His appearance was totally unexpected and made a refreshing change from ghouls hellbent on either abducting or killing her.

Still, it irked her that any help she got these days was always tied up in riddles. Meridia concluded she would be hard-pressed to come up with any answers on an empty stomach, so she left the comfort of her bed, grabbed her phone, and wandered downstairs.

The house was uncharacteristically quiet as she made her way through it. By now her mum would usually be awake, but the door to her bedroom remained closed on her way down. Meridia figured she might still be resting her head, besides 7am was a little early for a Sunday, even by Meridia's standards.

When she entered the kitchen, she made a beeline for the breakfast cupboard, pulling out a cereal bowl and the family sized box of Coco Pops she was halfway through demolishing. Chocolate was Meridia's passion, and the sound of pouring Coco Pops never lost its charm. Creating a tiny mountain of crispy chocolaty goodness that sat way above the rim of her bowl, she added a smidgeon of milk so as not to rob them of their crunch and then sat down at the rustic-looking pine dining table.

"Now let's see what I missed." She muttered before taking a huge spoonful of cereal. A frown gathered on her freckled brow as she read through last night's messages.

Naturally, she felt gutted she had missed the call, but grateful for Izzy's succinct summary of the conversation via text. In response, she sent her trademark yellow heart emoji.

The introduction of Father Alexander intrigued her. Perhaps he could provide them with some fresh answers, and god knew they needed some. His connection to Archie was also interesting, given his impromptu visit from beyond the grave, and she wondered if the priest's emergence had anything to do with Archie's decision to show himself. If she'd learned anything from her gift, it was that everything had a meaning, even if it didn't always reveal itself immediately.

Meridia recalled Archie's message in her mind, struggling to perceive her own thoughts over the rambunctious crunching clattering inside her skull as she polished off the rest of her breakfast.

What did he mean by 'look below' she wondered. Below what? And what exactly was it they were meant to be looking for? She could feel her frustration simmer, and parked the matter until she met up with the others. The last thing she wanted to do was leave the house in a huff again.

Glancing at the mint-green numbers of the tiny digital oven clock, Meridia realized she'd better jump in the shower. She hurriedly rinsed her bowl and downed a glass of water before returning to her room. Her mum's bedroom door was still firmly closed when she walked past, and it kick-started a quandary of what to do if there was still no sign of her when JJ and Izzy knocked. It was unlike her to be in bed so late, but Meridia had heard migraines could be super painful.

She gently touched the white painted wood and pressed her ear against it in an attempt to hear any sound, but the room on the other side remained utterly quiet. Sighing, Meridia continued along the hall to her room, chucking her phone onto the bed en route to the bathroom before disappearing inside.

By the time Meridia was dressed, it was already 7:56am, leaving her with only a couple of minutes before her escort was due to arrive. A cluster of worry congealed in Meridia's stomach when she saw her mum's door was still closed, and for a moment she contemplated entering.

What if none of them lived to return from Crooked House today? The thought triggered a sudden, sharp pang of anguish that made her skin tingle, and she reached out for the door handle. Although her mum knew she'd be heading out earlier than usual, it was unlike either of them not to say goodbye in person.

Ding dong!

Meridia jumped, rattling the handle as she let go. She waited, expecting the noise to wake her mum, but there was only silence.

"Love you mum," she whispered through the wood and tiptoed down to answer the front door.

Quietly twisting the latch, she opened it to find Izzy and JJ patiently waiting for her on the doorstep. "Hey guys. Just give me a sec, my mum is still asleep so I just want to leave her a note."

JJ gave her a silent thumbs up as Meridia retreated inside. "Be positive M. We're going to make it back."

She grabbed the notepad beside the fridge and wrote:

Off to see the others.
Hope your head is feeling better when you wake up,
and I'll be back this afternoon.
Love you! M xx

Meridia's pen lingered over the pad for a moment as she contemplated what lay ahead, then she added a big heart at the bottom of the page before setting the pad down on the kitchen table next to her mum's favourite mug.

"We're going to make it back," she repeated to herself, this time with more conviction, as she tenaciously stomped her way back towards the front door and the three of them set off to meet Kane.

49

"Remember what we agreed spud. You've got a bad belly, so you're going to stay home." Zach nodded as he slumped, dejected, on the edge of his bed. "It's going to be ok mate. I promise."

"What happens if it's not? What happens then?" tears had gathered in the corners of Zach's big brown eyes as he looked up solemnly at his brother.

"If something bad happens...which it won't...then you tell mum and dad everything like we agreed. You tell them to call the police and send someone out to Crooked House, ok?" Kane placed his hands firmly on his brother's shoulders. "Ok!" Zach nodded again as he battled to contain a sob. "It's not going to come to that though. We're going to stop her. All this shit ends today!"

Ding dong!

"They're here. I'd better get going. I'll text you when we're leaving the hotel, ok?" Kane gave Zach a rare hug and smoothed away some of his brother's tears on his cheek. "We'll be back soon, I promise." And with that, he walked downstairs to join the others.

"Hey mate, how's Zach?" JJ asked as Kane stepped out into the garden.

"He's upset, but he'll be ok. He knows why he can't come, but that doesn't make it any easier." Kane closed the door and ushered everyone out onto the street. "Peter said there would be a cab waiting for us all on the corner to take us to his hotel. Did Father Alexander confirm?"

"Yep." JJ affirmed as they walked. "He's going to join us at 9:30. Thanks again for understanding guys...I know I didn't exactly go about it the right way, but I really do have a good feeling about him. Are you sure you don't mind M?"

"It's ok, honestly. Besides, I wasn't going to tell you this until we reached Peter, but I saw Archie last night." Meridia waved off any questions before Izzy could blurt one out and continued, "I'll tell you what he said when we're together, but I don't think it was a coincidence he showed up at the same time as Father Alexander."

"We'll see what Peter thinks when we meet him. Judging from what JJ told us last night he clearly knows things we don't... I think that's our cab." Kane pointed to the silver seven-seater marked A1 Taxis parked by the side of the road, and then led the others towards it.

"Cab for Kane?" he asked once the driver had rolled his window down.

Nodding, the unshaven man behind the wheel fastened his seatbelt and started the engine. He looked as though he'd rolled straight out of bed and into his car, and the taxi stunk of body odour when Kane climbed in the passenger side.

"Holiday Inn, right?" he grumbled whilst unwrapping a boiled sweet he'd plucked from the cup holder between them.

"Yes, that's right," Kane responded politely and the cab

abruptly took off like a rocket, thrusting everyone backwards into their seats as it raced away.

It was only a fifteen-minute car ride from Kane's house to Peter's hotel, yet somehow their driver had achieved it in ten. When they came to a halt outside the entrance of the Holiday Inn, all four passengers clambered out, looking drained of all their colour, and the taxi sped away without so much as a word.

The hotel lobby was deserted. Too early for most of its guests, who were likely still recovering from a Saturday night on the town, Not that Shawbrook had much of a nightlife to offer. The Sunday morning sky was chock-full of dense grey clouds, reflecting its dismal haze on the streets below.

"Jeez, I feel sick after that." JJ wheezed as he hunched over the edge of the curb.

"I don't know what was worse, his driving or the smell. It was like riding a rollercoaster full of onions." Kane moaned. He felt genuinely queasy as he gathered himself at the hotel entrance. Filling his lungs with a deep breath of crisp morning air, he then got back to business. "Peter said he'd meet us in the restaurant, but I'm not sure I can face a fry-up after that journey."

"I'll have yours mate," JJ quipped, despite looking green himself.

"There he is!" Meridia waved at the large glass window to the left of the entrance.

Inside, Peter was sitting waiting at a large round table, beckoning them to join him. One by one, they entered the glass revolving door and disappeared inside.

50

Peter took a sip of his coffee as he watched the group pour in. His throat was still sore as the hot liquid trickled its way down to his stomach, but he needed the caffeine. Despite managing an early night by his standards, he was still understandably weary from his brush with the witch and needed all the help he could get if he was going to be any use to anyone that day.

"Wow, that bruise looks bad." Kane was the first to point out the purple and green patches that had formed around Peter's jaw.

"You should see the other guy..." he replied with a painful smile as the children all took a seat around him. "Miraculously, it looks far worse than it feels. Do help yourselves to breakfast. It's a buffet, so the plates are behind me, and the drinks are just tucked around the corner there."

Peter had spent half his adult life in hotels whilst investigating various hauntings around the world, and so to him, this might have been any other Sunday. "Don't be shy guys...take as much as you want, just don't make yourselves sick. We have a big day ahead of us."

A chorus of chairs scraping along the grey-tiled floor erupted in the empty dining room as all four children raced to where the food was. Whilst they were off looting the buffet cart, Peter removed his black lever arch from his bag and placed it beside him on the table. Looking around at the somewhat dated décor of the dining room, it seemed odd for the hotel to be so empty during peak breakfast time, but he wasn't complaining. Perhaps the flimsy looking MDF tables and soiled green tablecloths had put people off, but his scrambled eggs and beans had been perfectly adequate, even if he'd only chosen them to avoid the pain of chewing.

When the group returned, Peter couldn't help but chuckle to himself at some of the peculiar breakfast concoctions that surrounded him. JJ had stacked his plate high, but only opted for hashbrowns and sausages accompanied by a river of ketchup. Meridia, also known for her appetite, had taken a more balanced approach, aside from the pain au chocolat swimming in baked beans. Kane had surprisingly gone light and opted for jam on toast, whereas Izzy rounded off the eclectic feast with a modest bowl of chocolate hoops.

"Why are the glasses always so small in hotels?" JJ complained as he downed his glass of apple juice.

"One of life's great mysteries I'm afraid JJ," Peter conceded. "Why don't you grab the jug and bring it to the table, seeing as we're the only ones in here."

"Apple or orange guys?" JJ asked as he stood up. The group unanimously chose apple, and within a matter of seconds, everyone settled at the table and started eating their breakfast.

"As we only have a short while before Father Alexander joins us, I thought I'd run through what I came up with last night, unless anyone has anything new to share?" Peter announced, opening his folder and watching as everyone immediately looked at Meridia.

Gulping down a thimble of apple juice, she explained. "I had another visitor last night in my sleep. It was Archie."

Peter felt himself choke up as the mention of his name caught him off guard. "What happened?" he asked, trying to hold his fragile voice together.

"He didn't stay long as my mum interrupted him. She came into my room saying she could hear voices, which is odd now I think about it because Archie told me I was dreaming...unless I've started talking in my sleep? Anyway, I just told her it must have been me that she'd heard. Before that though, Archie said he'd been trying to help us as much as he could, that he'd helped a couple of us already, but he didn't say how. He mentioned an old woman too...that she was different from the others, but he didn't know why. He said she has a gift too, and that we'd seen each other in one of my dreams. I think I remember her, and him now I've heard his voice, but every new dream I have seems to take something away from the last. It's as if they fade quicker."

"Did he mention anything about Father Alexander?" JJ jumped in.

"No, he didn't. He just mentioned the old woman, and said we needed to be careful...that they knew we were coming. Then he told me we needed to look below for answers."

"Below what?" Izzy spoke for the first time all morning.

"He didn't have time to say...he just vanished and then my mum came barging in. All he said was we need to look below for answers, and that he would be there too...no, sorry his exact words were that we need to look below and that's where we'd find the answers we're looking for...and that's where we'd find him too. Why are all my dreams so bloody annoying? Why can't ghosts just get to the point and say what they mean in plain English? It drives me nuts!"

Peter could see that the more of her dream Meridia relayed, the more frustrated she became. He jotted down the key points of her story next to the plan he was about to run through and then glanced at his watch.

"Try not to put yourself under so much pressure M." He tried to pacify her. "We're all in this together, remember?"

"I know...it just leaves me feeling dumb, you know? When I can't figure out what they're trying to tell me, I just feel like it's my fault if something bad happens after, but it's so hard." Meridia's bottom lip quivered as she spoke, and Peter could see the weight she was carrying.

"Try to let go of that feeling if you can dear, or perhaps try looking at things from a different perspective. The gift you have is new and you're still finding your feet. I've interviewed hundreds of people claiming to have similar abilities and it took each of them years to get to grips with it. I've already lost count of how many times you've used your gift to save the lives of those around this table, so whenever you feel like you're struggling, share it with us. We're all here for each other, no matter what, and just remember we aren't all born walking and talking...it takes time to learn. Give yourself that time. The more you force things, the harder it will feel, and trust me, there is never any pressure on you to have the answers. We're a team."

Tears rolled down Meridia's cheeks as she looked down at her half-eaten breakfast.

"If anyone needs to have a good cry, or rant...or anything for that matter, then we're all here for that too, okay guys?"

The group all nodded as Izzy placed a reassuring hand on Meridia's shoulder and piped up.

"Peter's right. We can't force anything. So far, things have always come together just at the right time, so maybe Archie's message is meant for Father Alexander…I mean, maybe he'll know what it means."

Peter raised his eyebrows in recognition of Izzy's wisdom. It never ceased to amaze him how smart she was.

"You may be right there Izzy. Perhaps the key to all this is letting go and trusting the answers will come when we need them. I feel like we have a jigsaw puzzle to solve, but don't quite have all the pieces yet. I think I may have found some more pieces last night, and maybe Father Alexander is another piece too."

"I really hope so," JJ added. "I guess we'll find out soon enough."

"Exactly." Peter glanced at his watch again and pulled his lever arch closer. "There are two things I need to run through before our guest arrives, but they shouldn't take very long."

JJ topped up the glasses dotted around the table as Peter continued.

"First off, it should come as no surprise there isn't a great deal of reliable information on how to kill a witch, and my research into the object you retrieved from my attic seemed to borrow from a number of different cultures. As a result, I ended up going down numerous rabbit holes last night in my search for information that could help us. Witches aren't my area of specialism, and of course all this is based on the assumption that we are in fact dealing with a witch and not some other form of monster. That said, each culture had certain points they agreed on, or at least overlapped with each other. So, the big takeaway was that witches are not indestructible. They are just regular people with access to powers most of us could only dream of. This may make our life a little more straightforward as the body she occupies now is flesh and blood. That said, the most common weapon used against those accused of witchcraft was fire, which makes me wonder if any other approach might be less reliable. I did come across a technique which traps the demon's spirit in a bottle but it seemed way too risky so I discounted it."

"So, can't we just burn Crooked House down in that case? Won't that solve all our problems?" Kane quizzed.

"Well, I think that might be a little extreme, given the surrounding woodland. The last thing we need on our conscience is a raging fire that wipes out the village of Cold Christmas." Peter turned the page in front of him and traced his notes with his finger before continuing.

"I have a feeling the witch has a score to settle with us all following our last encounter. We can use this to our advantage and lure her out into the open...that is, if she's not already waiting to greet us when we arrive. Let's not forget Archie's warning. Anyway, in simple terms, the aim is to burn her."

"But what if she doesn't come out? Or if she's not even there?" Meridia doubted.

"Oh, she'll be there. It's the only place she has left to hide. If there is no sign of her, or she doesn't come out, then and only then do we consider burning the house. I'm reasonably confident the recent rainfall should limit the spread of any fire. I just don't want to risk it if we don't need to."

A sudden hush swept its way around the table as the children all paused from eating to process Peter's plan.

"I know this might all sound extreme, but we've seen

what we're dealing with...what she's capable of. She is more than a shadow lurking in the dark, or a ghostly apparition. She is a different kind of monster, a formidable one made of flesh and blood, who will have no qualms attacking us in broad daylight if we give her the chance." It was only in sharing his plan aloud had Peter realized how drastic and absurd it all sounded.

He'd been so engrossed in his research, so hung up on stopping the witch at any cost, he hadn't stopped to think about the cost it carried for the uncertain faces that now surrounded him. They were children, none of them more the fifteen years old, and here he was telling them they would burn someone alive later that day.

Peter wondered if he'd lost his mind, but in all his soul-searching, he couldn't find any other way. Since his ordeal, he had been plagued by memories that weren't his own, but he was reluctant to share that piece of information. He couldn't tell them he knew the witch would be at Crooked House because he still saw her, just like he couldn't tell them about her vile plans to kill them all. They would never trust him if they thought she still had some kind of hold over him. But she didn't, and of that Peter was certain. Although the tie that once bound them had now been severed, his mind had been permanently seared by hers, and was now riddled with centuries of torment.

"So, how are we going to do it? Burn her, I mean..." JJ's question jogged Peter from his thoughts and he returned to the tawny florescent lighting of the hotel's dining room.

"Super soakers!" He blurted, trying to lighten the mood. "I ordered some online yesterday, and they are due here within the hour."

"Wait, what?!" Kane replied in shock.

"I know it sounds ridiculous, but please bear with me.

Actually Kane, you'll be pleased to know I took the idea from an old eighties vampire movie. Once I'd landed on fire being our weapon of choice, that only really gave us a handful of options. My first thought was petrol bombs, as I wanted something that we could use from a safe distance, and that's when it occurred to me. Super soakers full of petrol! If we are all armed with them, we'll be able to hit her from up to thirty feet away...according to the website, anyway. Once she has enough petrol on her, I can light her up, as they say in the movies." Again, Peter questioned his own sanity as he heard his words hang in the air, but to his surprise, the children all seemed to welcome his plan with open arms.

"That's awesome!" Kane beamed. "We can use the triangle attack like we do in Fortnite!"

"Defo! There will be plenty of cover from the trees too, just like in the game. She won't know what's hit her," JJ chimed in. "M, you were a great shot when we had that water fight in Kane's back garden last summer."

Meridia chuckled through her tears at everyone's newfound enthusiasm, and her laughter was infectious, quickly spreading to Izzy.

"I remember James. You and Kane looked like you'd both wet yourselves by the time she was finished." She gave a little snigger under the cover of her hand. "I don't think anyone could believe how accurate she was, hitting such a small target."

Both boys laughed at the unintended joke and Peter couldn't help himself but join in, despite how much it made his jaw ache.

"Guys...guys! This isn't a game...or a joke." Meridia assumed a more solemn tone that sobered the rest of the group. "This isn't a water fight. I've seen her...in my dreams...she's evil...she's deadly! She's not going to sit there and let us soak her with petrol. And what if she's got help? The shadow creatures...the killer in room 4...the man in the hood? Archie said they know we're coming. They! It's not going to be as simple as a game of Fortnite. This is real. Zach...our parents...everyone is depending on us. I'm sorry... it just doesn't feel right that we're joking around, that's all."

"I know M, honest I do." Kane sat up in his chair, his voice more assertive.

"We're not treating this like a game. We're just trying to find a way through it all. It's been so long since I've heard any of us laugh...but here we are staring down an evil witch with super soakers full of petrol and...c'mon, even saying that out loud is pretty funny, you've got to admit. That bloody house has taken so much from us already...I'm sick of it! I want to go back to being fourteen again! I want to have water fights in my back garden while my mum tells my dad off for cremating the burgers on the barbecue. Today is massive...this is our chance to get some of our lives back...so why not do it our way? Who's to say we've not been practicing for this moment our entire lives? All those hours of gaming, the horror films, the water fights...who's to say it's not been for this? We must be here for a reason. Super soakers guys, I mean, what are the chances? We've got this, I can feel it...between us we've got this!" Kane's voice broke, and JJ gave him a reassuring pat on the shoulder as he sat back in his chair.

"You're both right." Peter matched Kane's tone to rally them all. "I believe we are all here for a reason. Like it or not, we are embroiled in a secret war, and it is a war we must win. Laugh or cry, it doesn't change what we're up against, so I can only ask that you enter this on your own terms. If I could do it alone and spare you, I would in a heartbeat, but I can't. That's something I'm learning to deal with every day. The fact is, I wouldn't be here if it wasn't for all of you. There is a strength in that. Yes, we're still finding our way, and we won't get everything right, but we must keep fighting. Today we have a job to do, and a plan to do it, but Kane's right, I can feel it too. Between us, we have got this."

"So let's do it then!" JJ was bouncing in his chair from Peter's call to arms.

"Peter, you said you had two things to tell us. What was the other?" In true Izzy fashion, she pulled the group back to the original agenda, forcing a wry smile from Peter as he got himself back on track.

"Yes Izzy, you're quite right. Thank you. The second thing I have learned recently is of a secret organization called The Children of the Shadows. They once operated in this area and I have a theory someone might be trying to resurrect them. There is sparse information about them, but I have a theory that the man in the hood, whom some of you have seen, may be connected to them."

"I've seen him too it seems." The stranger's voice made Peter jump as a priest emerged from behind the group. "Sorry, I got here a little early and couldn't help but overhear what you said. I'm Father Alexander..."

<h1 style="text-align:center">51</h1>

Father Alexander offered Peter his hand as he approached and was shocked by his height as he stood to accept it.

"You're taller than you look on TV." He exclaimed as the two men shook hands. Noticing the bruising around Peter's jaw and neck, he winced, adding, "Is that as painful as it looks?"

"Thankfully no, at least not right now, but I expect it might be tomorrow. Thank you for joining us this morning. JJ told us a lot about you. Please, sit. If you're hungry, help yourself to food. I believe breakfast is served until eleven today." Peter gestured to the empty seat opposite him, and Father Alexander obligingly took it, placing his black leather satchel at his feet as he sat down.

"Thank you for inviting me, and for the offer of breakfast, it's very kind. Alas, I've already had mine, although if I'd known there was a cooked breakfast in the mix, I'd have skipped my daily porridge."

"You said you've seen him too?" Peter got straight to business, skipping any further formalities. "Seen who?"

As Father Alexander looked around the table, he was taken aback by the youthful appearance of some of the children. He'd figured they were all the same age as JJ when they'd spoken, but clearly the two girls to his left were a few years younger. They looked tired, haggard even, as did his host, the famous author.

"I had a surprise visit last night. I saw him at the window. He ran, of course, and disappeared into the night. I didn't get a particularly good look at him as it all happened so fast, but I can say for sure that it was a man, probably in his late twenties, and he was wearing a hood. I took up chase, but he was gone by the time I got to the front of the house. I must say I was a little surprised by the timing of it all given our meeting today. I've not had an intruder in the twelve years since I moved here."

Father Alexander studied the shocked faces surrounding him as he delivered his revelation and was satisfied that their astonishment was genuine.

"I initially came here looking to talk you out of whatever it is you're about to do today. When I first met JJ and he told me about Crooked House, I couldn't believe it. Witches go way beyond my beliefs, and that of the church. But something was niggling me...something I couldn't put my finger on it until last night. After I'd chased away our friend in the hood, I revisited my research into Archie's disappearance, but this time I overlayed your story. At first, I thought I was trying to find holes...flaws in everything you'd told me, but the more I went over things, the more actually fell into place. I was up half the night in the end. Maybe the intruder gave me the shot of adrenalin I needed in order to see things differently...maybe deep down JJ knew all along there was more to this place. Now I make no secret of the fact I don't believe in coincidences, and yet here I am, surrounded by them. Too many to ignore in fact! So, forgive me if I come straight to the point. I know time is precious and we only have an hour, but I need to know, does the name Molly Harding mean anything to any of you?"

52

Peter felt the colour drain from his cheeks and his stomach churn as the name Molly Harding rattled around inside his head.

A cold sweat ensued, leaking from his brow and neck, then sticking to his collar as he wrestled with the urge to vomit. Then came the burning smell, but not the nostalgic aroma of Sunday bonfires at his parent's farm. This carried something putrid with it, the rotten smell of spoiled meat sizzling on an open fire.

Looking up at the priest, he felt the room begin to swirl and whirl around him as if he was on a fairground waltzer. Around and around, everything raced past as his eyes struggled to keep pace, and so he gripped onto the edge of the table to steady himself. All the while, the name Molly Harding echoed within him, building momentum like the menacing chant of an angry mob.

"Are you ok Mr Higginsworth? You look like you've just seen a ghost." Father Alexander rose from his seat and gestured to JJ. "Quick, fetch him some water. He looks like he's going to pass out!"

His words floated in and out of Peter's awareness, languid, as he struggled to keep his breakfast down.

"Here!"

The next thing he knew, JJ had thrust a glass of water under his nose and he took it, gulping down the ice-cold liquid to drown out whatever had stirred within him. Each gulp triggered a dull ache in his jaw, but he welcomed the pain as it brought him back to his senses, slowing the room's rotation.

"I'm...ok..." he stuttered, flummoxed by the sudden bout of vertigo. "It's her, isn't it? Molly Harding is the witch."

53

Peter's reaction was all the validation Father Alexander needed. This was real. He reached down into his satchel and retrieved a handkerchief which he meticulously laid out in front of him and then pulled out a plastic zip-lock sandwich bag and a pair of white cotton gloves.

Slipping the gloves on, he opened the sandwich bag and removed an old leather-bound notebook while his audience sat mesmerized, as if he was a table magician about to dazzle them all with a trick. Battered and frayed around its edges, the tiny handmade black book would have looked at home in any museum.

"This is Father John's journal. He was the residing priest when my church moved from Cold Christmas to Thundridge. As you can probably gather, it's very old. It really shouldn't leave the church grounds, but I needed to show you so you would believe me."

He chuckled at the irony of what he'd just said.

"Something struck me after our chat JJ. It took a while to sink in, but it jogged my memory of something unusual I'd seen in the private records held at the church. It was a grave, but not just any grave: an empty plot, bought and paid for by an anonymous patron back in the early 18th century."

"Molly Harding?" Meridia asked.

"Yes. Meridia, isn't it? I'm sorry I skipped formal introductions when I arrived. You must think I'm very rude, but I was so eager to share my findings I got a little carried away. I'm Father Alexander, but you can all call me Martin if you prefer. I noticed one of you is missing today. Zach?"

"Yeah, my brother. He's at home. We needed to keep him out of this...JJ probably already told you why."

"He did. So that means you must be Kane...which just leaves you...Izzy?"

Kane and Izzy nodded in unison as Father Alexander continued his story.

"It's a pleasure to meet you all. So, I found this matter of an empty grave a little odd, particularly given the time. It was extremely uncommon for anyone to spend money on such a thing back then, and this was made even more strange by the fact the church had only recently moved to the area. The records didn't tell me much at first, only that whoever purchased the plot insisted on remaining anonymous. A dead end, or so it seemed. That led me to this."

Father Alexander framed the notebook with his hands as if he was presenting it as a gift to the rest of the group.

"In this journal, I believe I may have found some of the missing pieces to whatever puzzle we are all faced with. You see Father John's entries straddle both locations, giving us unique commentary around the time I believe this all started. Now, don't get me wrong, this isn't a handbook on Crooked House that ties all the answers up for us in a tidy little bow, but it does suggest that maybe

Molly was one of the first to fall victim to whatever forces are at play here."

Father Alexander gently opened the journal where it was bookmarked by a single strand of leather. He could almost feel the historian in Peter spring to life as he revealed two full pages of calligraphy inside.

"Molly is the second, from what we can tell. We have a working theory that the rooms run in order, which means someone came before her, but so far, we have drawn a blank with who that might be. We have images though."

Peter riffled through his file and produced a set of stills, then passed the one marked 'Room 2' across the table. "This is her. We've just never had a name to go on until now."

Father Alexander studied the image of a young servant girl perched on the edge of a bed, cradling her head in her hands. "Fascinating!" he exclaimed, wide-eyed. "The reflection behind her...it represents the witch?"

"We're not sure. Perhaps. I also spent a great deal of time researching last night, and the common consensus online is that witches...real witches that is, are possessed by demons of some kind. My best guess is this picture shows both the woman and the demon inside her, but I'm only speculating of course. Witchcraft isn't exactly my area of expertise." Peter came over sheepishly as he took another sip of his water, which allowed Father Alexander to continue.

"I see. It's not mine either, although a demon might be more in my wheelhouse I suppose. Just fascinating." He slowly shook his head as he processed the image. "Does this mean you also have a picture of Archie?"

Peter nodded solemnly as he closed his file, nixing the chance of seeing any more.

"I see...Sorry, where was I...yes, the journal. Although

there is a smattering of detail within the book, it was this entry that stood out the most, having now read it front to back last night. Although I must warn you it's not for the feint hearted." He traced down the page with his finger and read aloud.

October 10th, 1727.

Yesterday, they found a boy in the woods, strung up and skinned like the spoils of a hunt. It took five villagers to bring his bloodless corpse down from the tree he had been nailed to, and although his mutilated remains were unrecognizable, it is now confirmed to be the body of Ralph Venning. A local boy who had not been seen for several days this week.

His remains currently rest in the chapel, waiting for arrangements to be made, and I must say if it were not for the nails crucifying him to the old oak, I would think it was the work of an animal. In all my years I have never seen such savagery, not even on the streets of Cold Christmas.

A girl is also missing, a loner named Molly Harding. It is not yet known if she is another victim or indeed the culprit. I do not know how a relative simpleton so slight of build could be responsible for such an atrocity, but she had many a run-in with the dead child and rumours of witchcraft are now beginning to spread. It is true I heard her conversing with herself on numerous occasions when passing on my rounds, and it has been suggested she often preferred to mingle with livestock over villagers her own age.

This does not bode well, as despite the witch hunts concluding some years ago now, they still cast a long shadow over us all. The truth will out, I am sure.

Father Alexander raised his head a moment to address the group who were hanging on his every word. "There are a couple more mundane entries which are of little importance until we reach October 12th." He delicately turned the page and resumed his narration.

There is still no sign of the Harding girl, and a search party has now been gathered, although I suspect they are in fact baying for her blood rather than her rescue. It seems the Venning family has rallied together a small mob, even adding a former witch hunter to their ranks. I have a bad feeling about this and will pray for them during today's service. We are still but an hour's walk from Cold Christmas, and God only knows what terrors may wait for them out there in the woods.

It has been six hours since the group embarked on their search and there has been no word since. Darkness has now fallen and even the people of Thundridge know to stay away from the woods at night for fear of straying onto the wrong path. Their absence has sparked further talk of witchcraft amongst the village and Lucy Venning attended my afternoon service, lighting three candles before leaving. I share in her fears for her remaining sons and pray for their safe return, but if they are not back by morning, we will have no choice but to prepare ourselves for the worst.

October 14th, 1727.

Two whole days have passed since the Venning brothers left to avenge their youngest sibling and we can only assume they have met a similar fate to poor Ralph. Word has reached us of a fire on the border of Cold Christmas, and Crooked House is said to have perished. This cannot be coincidence, and whilst I am glad that cursed place has finally fallen, I cannot help but wonder what price we will all pay for its demise. One thing is certain, the long, dark shadow cast by Cold Christmas will continue to sully our streets, even more so in the absence of our best men. God give us strength.

"Sorry to interrupt Father, but why would someone purchase the grave in Molly's name?" Izzy waded in as soon as she sensed a natural pause. "I mean, it doesn't sound like she had anyone looking out for her when she went missing, and I know the identity of whoever arranged it was a secret, but what was the point? I don't get it."

"That's an excellent question Izzy, and one that troubled me too. It brings me nicely to the final extract I intended to share with you all."

Father Alexander gripped a slither of paper that he'd used as a makeshift bookmark further into the journal and delicately turned to the corresponding page.

"It was actually a good month or so after that last entry that Molly's plot was purchased, and although no official record of the buyer was permitted at the time, there was nothing stopping Father John from making a note of it in here. It seems The Children of the Shadows have been operating for a very long time in these parts and are referenced several times within this book. Mostly anecdotal, Father John mentions sightings of their members on the old church grounds in Cold Christmas, with one entry alluding to a secret passage as the only plausible explanation for their presence. From what I can tell, they were the reason a solitary turret of the original church was left behind when it relocated. But it is this excerpt that is arguably the most telling." Once again, Father Alexander traced down the page with a white cotton finger and narrated.

A stranger visited the chapel this evening under the cover of dusk. He forwent any introductions but was stately in his appearance and well educated. His cloak, however, was perhaps more telling as it featured an unmistakable brooch I had seen on numerous occasions during my time in Cold Christmas, and I recognized its unholy star instantly. He was a self-proclaimed child of the shadows, a new order who are rumoured to have claimed the remains of St Peter's for their own place of worship.

As a man of God, it is not for me to judge, nor turn anyone away, regardless of their beliefs, and so I granted him entry. He had travelled alone, and our conversation was brief, albeit intriguing. He purchased an empty plot for Molly Harding, the girl implicated in the brutal murder of Ralph Venning and who herself vanished without trace a little over a month ago. Since her disappearance, she has been branded a witch and credited with another five murders of those who sought to bring her to justice.

That aside, his commission remains most unusual, particularly as he insisted on the church omitting his name from our records. But who am I to turn away money during such times of hardship, especially when he offered to pay over and above the plot's worth? Six pounds, to be exact, although I expect much of that was to buy my silence.

He requested nothing more than a modest stone and simple inscription before departing in haste. The Harding girl had only an aunt in the village who appeared not to mourn her absence and has remained withdrawn since the discovery of the Venning boy.

This has left me to ponder the man's motives for such a peculiar commission, and I wonder if The Children of the

Shadows now boast a witch within their ranks. If they do, then it would make sense for them to keep her a secret, and what better cover to use than that of her own death?

Time will tell as it always does, but the sect's presence here does not bode well for the future of our new home. We came here to escape their reign of tyranny and violence, yet upon today's evidence, it seems they may have followed us.

Father Alexander softly closed the journal. "There are other insights buried within this book, but what I've read here today was enough to convince me there are indeed sinister forces at play in Cold Christmas, and as my search for Archie has already told me. All roads lead to Crooked House."

"I still don't know why they bought a grave?" Meridia looked puzzled as she leant over her half-eaten breakfast to reach for the apple juice. "Why bother?"

"Misdirection maybe." Peter perked up again from across the table, his green eyes ablaze with thoughts.

"A coverup, as Father John suggests in his journal. There could be several reasons they did it. Let's not forget the creatures behind all this have been playing the long game. Perhaps Molly's murder of the boy was unplanned and so was that of the villagers sent to find her. Molly's grave glosses over the fact she was never found, and beyond those who were there to witness events her very existence would have simply faded out over time. There's a saying that the greatest trick the devil ever played was convincing the world that he did not exist. This witch has been undetected for three-hundred years."

"But why reveal herself now?" Father Alexander was thinking aloud as he mulled over Peter's hypothesis.

"Because of Meridia." Peter replied instantly. "Her gift

disrupted the order of everything. Since then, the witch has targeted her at every opportunity, and it seems the cult has now resurfaced to watch us all from the shadows. But where are the horsemen during all this? We have not seen hide nor hair of them since our last visit to Crooked House."

"Maybe we just beat them last time?" JJ speculated.

"And now the lunatics have taken over the asylum? I doubt it sadly." Peter looked at his watch again and took another sip of water. "Wherever they are, it doesn't change what we have to do today I'm afraid. We need to be on our way soon."

A nervous energy swept across the table, and Father Alexander detected a spike of apprehension among the children.

"I know that time is running out. Now, I have no idea what you are planning today, but whatever it is, I want in. For Archie, if nothing else. This place has witnessed centuries of tragedy, and if I can help put an end to that cycle, or at least avert another, then it is my duty before God to do so. Plus, it won't hurt your cause to have the big man upstairs in your corner when you face whatever is waiting for you all at Crooked House." Father Alexander flashed the briefest of smiles as he gave the group time to process his request.

"I want to thank you for coming here today. JJ was right to open up to you." Peter was the first to speak. "I must say, initially I thought you'd come to talk us down, or failing that have us all arrested."

"The thought had crossed my mind. I must say...that was until last night's events. But as the great Sherlock Holmes often says: when you have eliminated all which is impossible, then whatever remains, however improbable, must be the truth. And so, here I am, offering my help."

"And we're grateful for that, really we are, but there is a big difference between being open to the existence of all this and having the stomach to face it head-on. Today will not be pleasant Father, and I have no idea what lengths we may need to go to in order to save the lives of those we love. We are prepared to do whatever it takes. I guess what I'm asking is: are you?" There was grit in Peter's tone which Father Alexander hadn't been expecting, but he had raised a valid question.

"From what I've heard, I cannot imagine the burden you have all been carrying these past months, and yes, you are quite right; there is a gap I need to overcome in order to justify my seat at the table. Perhaps there is still a part of me looking to prove I'm not mad for entertaining all this. I don't think I am. Can I safely say I can do what's needed? I'd like to think so, but this is so far beyond the realm of anything I could imagine that I'm afraid I cannot make any guarantees. I'm definitely no coward, but until I'm faced with whatever horrors that might be in store, I suppose it's impossible to know for sure. I thought about this long and hard last night, and again on the journey here this morning, and I believe the only guarantee I can offer is that I will give it my best."

54

The insipid smell of cold baked beans was making Meridia feel queasy as she watched the two men play verbal tennis across the breakfast table. Enlightening as Father Alexander's revelations had been, the time for idle chit-chat was over now.

In her eyes, he'd proven his worth by stating his intentions, and now surely all that was needed was to accept his request to tag along and get on with the task at hand. At the very least they had a witch to kill, and now there was the distinct possibility she would be accompanied by a gang of hooded maniacs.

"Why don't we just vote on it?" The words blurted out unfiltered, cutting both men off at the knees. Meridia noticed a smile form in the corner of Peter's mouth, which swiftly turned into a grimace as the pain kicked in.

"Quite right M, we're in danger of wasting precious time here. Father, you have my vote. JJ?"

"Defo!" JJ looked to his left and Kane nodded in agreement.

"Same. Does that mean we need to order an extra super-soaker?" Meridia watched as Father Alexander's expression see-sawed between amusement and bewilderment before stepping in to have her say.

"I agree."

"Me too!" Izzy added abruptly, which signalled to Meridia her impatience was brewing too.

"Shall we get going then?" Meridia asked, rising from her chair to escape the whiff of her leftovers.

Peter rose in response, packing his folder away and then checking his phone briefly. "My parcel is in reception so I'll arrange for a taxi big enough to take us all if that's ok with you Father? We can fill up the super-soakers en route."

Father Alexander looked bewildered again, swept up in the urgency of everyone leaping to their feet in anticipation of the mammoth task ahead of them. "Er...yes, that's fine. I can get my car after. What do we need water pistols for?"

"Don't worry Father," Kane quipped. "We'll tell you on the way."

55

As they approached the exit for Cold Christmas, Peter signalled for the driver to pull over so they could travel the rest of the way on foot.

Once she had clambered out of the back seat, Meridia felt a cool breeze rush to greet her, tingling the back of her neck as it gently brushed by. To her rear, Peter lugged the box of super-soakers out of the boot and placed it on the ground with a thud before gesturing for the taxi to leave. All the while, the breeze continued to size them up, snaking its way around the group and glancing the lid of the box, which obligingly flapped open to release the sweet woody aroma of petrol. Its intoxicating fumes instantly transported Meridia back to the deserted petrol station they had stopped at along the way, and a part of her longed to be back there perusing the sweet section in the safety of its kiosk.

Truth was, she'd rather be anywhere than here, standing in the cold, preparing to face her deadly nemesis. A cloak of silence surreptitiously draped itself over them all, broken only by the sound of gravel grinding against rubber as the car pulled away. Marooned, and less than a stone's throw from Crooked House, there was no turning back now.

"Now remember, the second you hit the witch with your gun, I want you to toss it to ground and stay as far away from it as possible. These are highly flammable, and we don't want any accidents." Peter was stern with his advice as he handed out bright blue and white plastic rifles to each of the children.

The fumes were even stronger now the guns were out in the open and Meridia wondered if the witch could already smell them coming.

"When it comes to lighting her up, I'll be the one who does it, and only me. If anything goes wrong, then Father Alexander will be on hand to make sure you all get away as far as you can, and as quickly as you can. Are we all clear?"

The group nodded nervously in agreement with Peter, although Meridia couldn't help but notice the look of worry on Father Alexander's face.

"Are we sure there's no other way Peter?" he asked. "I mean, we're talking about burning a person here. What if we've got all this wrong?"

"We haven't Father," Meridia took it upon herself to answer. "You'll see that when the witch shows herself."

There was a calmness and maturity in her response that took even her by surprise, but what she couldn't fathom was how she knew the witch would appear. She could feel her nearby, the same way she had sensed her in her dreams, and then her mind instantly gravitated to Zach. She wondered what he was doing whilst they were out here on the battlefield. At least he was safe, she thought, even if the rest of them weren't.

"Meridia's right Father." Kane added whilst getting to

grips with the weight of his toy rifle and testing its sights. "This is the only way."

And with that, he began marching toward the house. Meridia wondered how much of Kane's bravery was bravado, as he seemed unwavering in his conviction, whereas others, even Peter, were showing signs of worry. He must love his brother very much, she thought as she followed his lead.

The closer they got, the angrier the knot of dread tugged at Meridia's throat. It had been months since her last visit, and on that day, the 'other' Zach had followed her all the way home to warn her of more horrors to come. Now here she was, the roof of Crooked House coming into sight through the gaps in the trees ahead, and she hated every minute. The smell of petrol still hung heavy in the air as she walked, but somewhere below it hid the damp musty scent of wet leaves in winter.

"Wait," Kane whispered, coming to an urgent stop. "Someone is there, standing outside the front door."

He crouched and sidestepped to his right to get a better look at the grey silhouette which cut through a layer of mist surrounding the house. "It's...her...she's just standing there."

For the first time that day he sounded anxious and Meridia felt a strange sense of relief.

"*Come out, come out wherever you are...*" The woman's crackly voice was unmistakable as it echoed around them, carving its way through the trees they were all hiding behind. "*I've been waiting for you.*"

56

Everyone froze, trapped like rabbits in the headlights as the witch stood her ground, bold as brass in the middle of the clearing where, not too long ago, Meridia had watched her friends perish at the hands of death.

Meridia stayed low and moved to a better viewpoint, passing Kane until she reached the large oak where Zach had once been murdered. As she felt the rough bark pressed against her palm, an icy shiver rushed up her spine, pinching her shoulders together, as the traumatic scenes from that fateful day all came flooding back. She'd spent weeks trying to forget the helpless expression etched on Zach's face as the creature mercilessly slit his throat.

"Stay out of the shadows!" she blurted, remembering the creature had only required a sliver of shade to attack them that day.

"*Ah, there you are!*" The witch snorted with glee, but she did not pounce. Instead, she remained statuesque for all and sundry to see.

Meridia peered around the oak to get a clear line of sight and almost gagged the moment she saw her.

The witch was a bag of bones, barefoot and draped in a dirty, rag-like poncho that looked as if it was cut from a heavily soiled bedsheet. Her scrawny, elongated arms hung lifelessly beside her, wildly out of proportion with the rest of her body, as her gnarled, pointy elbows protruded just below her waistline. Skeletal fingers dangled limply below her grubby knees, resembling the claws of a sloth, with thick, overgrown nails that curled at their ends. She looked feral, standing there in the dirt, but it was her face that made Meridia retch. Clumps of dark, matted hair framed her balding misshapen head, while her wilted and drooped features resembled a melted candle. Her nose was raw and exposed like a skull's nasal cavity, flanked by black raven eyes that seemed to slither down her cheeks. A lopsided mouth completed the horrifying spectacle, down-turned to the left and devoid of any teeth as she licked her absent lips with a slug-like tongue.

"*Look at me Peter,*" she taunted. Her voice took on a fragile tone like cracked glass. "*Looookkkk how preeetttttyyyyy I am!*"

She raised her arms as if she was about to perform a plié and they bowed as if they might break under their own weight.

"*You did this to me! You and those bastard children! Destroying my hex! You'll suffer for this...that you will. You will all burn in hell! Hahaha...*"

But before the witch could threaten them anymore, Kane took his chance and broke cover, pumping his super-soaker furiously in her direction as he ran to the next tree. In a matter of seconds, he had emptied his gun and tossed it to the ground at her feet.

Shellshocked, the witch tried to empty her mouth of

petrol, coughing and spluttering as her eyes danced around to catch up with what had just happened.

"Light her up!" Kane shouted.

Peter sprang into action and reached for the zippo he'd bought at the petrol station. From there, it all happened so fast.

As the witch continued to flounder, JJ followed Kane's lead and gave her another barrage, dousing her face and hair, before darting back under cover. Meridia remained spellbound behind the oak, a mere spectator, as if she was watching a movie play out in front of her. Surely it couldn't be this easy, she thought, as Peter launched the zippo with pinpoint accuracy, striking the witch's rags and instantly igniting them.

Amber flames flickered and corkscrewed around the witch's emaciated body, engulfing her in fire and smoke as she crumpled to the ground in a heap.

"*Aaargh!*" her blood-curdling screams shook the birds from their trees as she broadcast her agony throughout the woods.

Meridia shuddered from her trance, doing her best not to breathe in the rancid smell of burning flesh and bone.

"*Aaargh!*"

Another shrill scream rang out as the inferno reached its peak, turning the air black with smoke that stung Meridia's eyes and lungs.

Suddenly, she felt a hand grasp her elbow and pull her away. Father Alexander had his mouth covered with his sleeve and guided her back to a safe distance whilst the others gathered around them.

"We need to get out of here!" Father Alexander pleaded, overwhelmed and panicked by what he was witnessing.

Over his shoulder, Meridia could see the witch thrashing around in the dirt, wailing as the fire continued to devour her sallow flesh.

"Wait!" Meridia exclaimed, digging her heels in as she snatched her arm free. "We need to be sure." Her own nagging voice replayed over and over in her mind. *This is too easy...this is all too easy.*

But easy it was, and the witch's struggles were soon reduced to lethargy as the fire began to falter and burn itself out before all was eventually still. Her steaming corpse glistened under the grey winter sky as the suffocating smell of burnt flesh and petrol fumes filled the surrounding air.

"We must be sure!" Meridia maintained staunchly, and then took a hesitant step forward, towards where the witch had fallen.

"I'll do it!"

She heard Peter volunteer behind her, but she needed to know for herself. There could be no doubt, and so she continued. One by one, the group joined her as she trudged out of the woods and onto the ashen path of Crooked House.

Snap!

As she drew nearer, she could hear a faint crackling, like the slow popping of bubble wrap, and she stuttered for a moment, half expecting the witch to leap to her feet and charge at her.

"It's just the effect of the fire," Peter reassured. "Her body is still burning even though the flames have died down."

"The way coals crackle on a barbecue," Izzy added, almost as if she was talking to herself.

"I'm not leaving here until I know she's dead!" Meridia bleated as she resumed walking. She could feel her cheeks getting warmer with each step as she approached the pile of charred remains that had scorched the earth ahead of them.

When they reached her resting place, all that remained of the witch was a smouldering heap of sharply angled bones with traces of raw, blistered skin.

Meridia could taste the sweet, sickly leathery smell of burnt flesh and felt herself slowly surrender to the vomit that was brewing in her stomach. Hunched over at the witch's side, a slither of bile rose to the pit of her throat, and she tried desperately to swallow it back down, but the putrid smell continued its relentless attack on her senses.

Snap!

The sudden sound of bones cracking sent Meridia reeling backwards, almost stumbling over JJ's feet, as the witch made a grab for her ankle. She was relentless, like a machete-wielding maniac from an 80's slasher movie.

No matter what they did to stop her, the witch just kept on coming.

57

Panic ensued as everyone scrambled to step away from the witch's hideously burned carcass as she clambered to her feet.

Crack...crack!

One at a time, her spindly, charcoal limbs jerked and snapped back into motion as she awkwardly rose from the ashes until reaching all fours. There she sat, a mass of elbows and knees, coiled like a spider waiting to pounce, as the group formed a semicircle and slowly backed away.

"You came here to kill me? Me!..." Her raspy voice crackled and fizzed at them as they all watched dumbstruck and on the back foot.

"Fools, you came here to die!" The witch snarled, cracking the remnants of seared flesh that gripped her skeletal face.

Her saggy, deformed face had been stripped clean to her skull, exposing a hideous, hate-filled expression that instantly struck fear in Meridia's heart as she gawked in horror. The witch's angular face looked like it had been carved from onyx by a hand consumed by hate. Jagged and twisted, she bore the look of the devil with her painfully sharpened features and eyes that sparkled from deep within their cavernous sockets.

Meridia glanced at Peter to her right, and then at Father Alexander to her left. Both appeared to be in a stupor, battling to break free from shock.

"Run!" Kane shouted. His voice croaked under the strain of the monster they were now faced with.

JJ and Izzy bolted for the woods, almost sweeping Meridia up with them in their sea of hysteria.

The witch now appeared larger than life, as if her long limbs had always been destined for this form. She locked eyes with Meridia and scuttled an inch or two toward her before pausing.

"*You'll be the first to die, seer!*" and with that, the chase was on.

<h1 style="text-align:center">58</h1>

PETER COULD DO NOTHING BUT WATCH AS THE SPIDER-like witch scampered off at speed in Meridia's direction.

The others had all fled, scattering to the four winds and each assuming the other was beside them. He and Father Alexander had failed to protect anyone as they both stood idle like dummies while the children ran for their lives.

His ill-conceived plan had descended into utter chaos, revealing him to be nothing more than a rank amateur. But, as the screams of his pupils rang out in the desolate woods around him, he heard another, muffled and unfamiliar. The unexpected sound woke him from his temporary slumber as it pulled his ear back towards Crooked House. Someone else was screaming from the inside.

"*Help!*" sobbed the muted voice. "*Please help!*"

Peter strained to make it out, but it remained too faint. His mind raced to Zach.

Could it be they had got to him somehow?

"Martin!" he grabbed the priest by both arms and shook him out of his trance. "You need to help the children.

There's someone else here...someone inside the house. I think it might be Zach."

Father Alexander met him with a lost and vacant expression before blinking his way out of it. He took a deep breath as he nodded and sped off in pursuit of Meridia and the witch. He proved to be quicker and more athletic than Peter had given him credit for, and in a matter of seconds, he vanished.

Kane, JJ, and Izzy soon converged toward him from either side as they all rushed to save their friend, leaving Peter behind to face the horrors of Crooked House alone.

59

Emily Wilson screamed.

She screamed until her lungs ached as she sat helplessly bound to a chair, but nobody came. Still woozy from whatever drug had been used to put her to sleep, she had no idea where she was or how she'd got there. The vague recollection of screams coming from outside lingered, prompting her to awaken, but now the silence that enveloped her, left her wondering if it had merely been a fragment of a nightmare.

She remembered hearing voices back at the house, and then checking in on Meridia before going downstairs for some water. As she reached the kitchen, she'd heard it again, a man's voice, angry and arguing with himself. Emily could still feel remnants of dread, coursing through her body at the thought of Gregor Wilson coming back for revenge, but the intruder's accent was different, local. Whoever it was, he sounded furious, muttering obscenities in the night.

She remembered turning around to flee, and that was when everything went dark. Now she found herself bound to a creaking windsor armchair, in a chintzy living room full of cobwebs, with god knows how many creepy crawlies lurking in the shadows. The tiny triangular window in front of her was grubby, smeared with dust and grime, as it bled light into the dingy room, but all she could see beyond it was an assortment of treetops. Beneath the window, an open flight of stairs led down somewhere, but she wasn't close enough to see where. With eaves framing the room, this had clearly been an attic at one point or another, now converted into living quarters with identical closed doors to her left and right, which she presumed were additional rooms.

"Help! Please!" She cried again, but there was no reply. All she could think of was her beloved Meridia: her world. She had to find a way back to her.

60

Up close, Crooked House looked even more decrepit than Peter's previous visit. Its paintwork had all but crumbled away, leaving flakes of raw plaster and brickwork in its place. An old weather-beaten rocking chair was tipped over on its side, splintered, and gathering mould, whilst fragments of broken glass peppered the large paving slab where a welcome mat had once laid.

The cool breeze that had danced around him in the woods had now picked up pace, and Peter could feel it pushing him away as he continued his approach. Reaching the broken porch door, he heard the cry for help again, although this time he was sure it was a woman's voice.

For a moment he hesitated, grinding broken glass underfoot as he wondered if the call might be a trap. He gazed into the dimly lit entrance hall, now filled with leaves and debris from the surrounding woods, questioning his strength to venture inside. He knew all too well the dangers that lurked within, although he was sure the opaque light streaming in over his shoulder would be enough to ward off any of the horsemen.

"Please! Somebody!"

The muffled cry came again as Peter dithered in the doorway, trying to rediscover his nerve. His indecision infuriated him, still preoccupied with thoughts of the witch, but this time he was sure the voice was above him. The old owners had lived upstairs when they were alive, and he was sure the stairwell was just to his left, beyond the porch. He could be up there in a matter of seconds.

Crunch!

Peter crushed more shards of glass as he took a few steps back to survey the tiny window above. The glass was filthy, but unobstructed, which meant he would at least have some light up there.

"C'mon Peter, we don't have time for this," he berated himself.

Snap!

He stomped down hard on the rocking chair, breaking its frame, and then pulled the largest spindle he could get his hands on. Holding it like a knife, he took a breath to steady himself and then charged inside.

61

Meridia heard the relentless snapping of twigs in the distance behind her as she fled her arachnid assailant.

She was sweating now and felt the cold winter air biting at her flushed cheeks and stinging her lungs as she ran. A light mist gathered, closing in on her as it ensnared the trees with its hazy web, and she wondered if it might be the witch's handiwork. Thick, impenetrable branches strangled the bright grey sky above, leaving Meridia lost and alone in the murky woods below. Needing to take a beat and catch her breath, she ducked behind a gnarled and twisted alder tree to get her bearings. Looking out into the foggy abyss, all she could see were a few trees ahead of her in either direction.

"This has to be some kind of spell," she thought, squinting into the gloom.

Vaporous shadows continued to drift around her, dancing on the current of the air as it whisked its way in and out of the trees. An eerie silence ensued, ominous and suffocating, as Meridia battled to suppress the sound of her own heavy breathing.

Either the witch was still, biding her time as she watched from beneath the blanket of fog, or Meridia had given her the slip. She wondered where the others were and how they would ever find her now she had ventured deeper into the woods. The witch was cunning and strong, brushing off the fire as if it were nothing. Meridia needed to find a way out, back to the road. Perhaps that's where the others had gone and were now waiting for her to join them?

Slowly backing away, Meridia fixed her gaze on the direction she'd just run from. The witch was still out there somewhere.

Snap!

As Meridia shifted her weight to her back foot, the ground beneath her suddenly gave way. Stunned and with nothing to cling onto or break her fall, gravity took over and Meridia tumbled full tilt down a deep, dark hole.

62

Father Alexander signalled for the others to stop. The mist ahead of them was now too dense to go blindly running into at full speed.

"Where is she?" Kane whispered anxiously.

"She ran off in this direction. The mist would have slowed her down too, so all we can do is fan out and tread carefully. I don't want anyone drifting out of sight though. The witch is here too remember, and she could be close." Father Alexander gestured for everyone to space out and form a line so they could comb the woods in search of Meridia.

As they began plodding forward, Father Alexander's mind was cast back to Archie's disappearance and the short-lived search party that followed. A mix of anger and frustration flowed through him, tightening his jaw as he cautiously trudged onward. He would be damned if he'd let another child disappear on his watch.

"What are we going to do guys?" JJ murmured. "I mean, if we see the witch...what are we going to do? All the fire seemed to do was piss her off. Sorry father."

"It's fine JJ, given the circumstances." Father Alexander gripped the silver crucifix around his neck as he scrambled to come up with a plan.

He often rubbed its smooth metal base between his thumb and forefinger when in need of inspiration, and over the years it had become more than a symbol of the church, it had become a way of channelling his thoughts. When he'd set off in search of Meridia, he'd given little thought to anything apart from finding her before the witch did.

"If we see the witch, then I want you to all get behind me. I'll try to buy you enough time to get back to the road and away from this retched place so you can go get help."

The children fell silent in their response, continuing the slow methodical search, as Father Alexander's mind frantically rallied to ready himself for what might happen if they found the witch first, or worse still, she found them.

63

Emily braced herself as she heard someone thundering up the stairs. Had her cries for help merely angered her abductor? She'd never been a fan of horror movies. Often rolling her eyes at the hapless victims they portrayed, but now she was the one tied to a chair, wondering if she'd just made a colossal blunder by making such a racket.

Thud thud thud!

Came the footsteps until a man emerged clutching a jagged piece of wood.

"Please don't hurt me," Emily pleaded, wincing as she grappled with her restraints.

"Huh?"

The man turned to face her, and she recognized him instantly. It was Peter Higginsworth, the famous author who was lecturing at Meridia's school. She'd seen his face plenty of times in the local press and, at one point, had even considered going back to school just so she could meet him. He was far taller in real life. Athletic and strikingly handsome, but his brooding expression softened the moment they locked eyes.

"What are you doing here?!" he asked, puzzled as he quickly set to work, loosening the rope she'd been bound with. Whilst up close, she drew in a waft of his scent, and it was a welcome relief from the dust-filled prison she'd been trapped in.

"I...I woke up here. A man...he took me... Where are we?" Peter paused from untying her for a moment and gripped the lump of wood he'd placed down beside her.

"Man? What man? Is he still here?" his voice dropped to a whisper as his eyes darted back and forth between the doors on either side of them.

"No...at least I don't think so. I've been shouting for ages and you're the first person I've seen since I came to. Please, just untie me so we can get out of here. My daughter...I need to know she's ok." It suddenly dawned on her that Meridia might be behind either door, unconscious or worse.

Emily began to wriggle and writhe again in a panic, which seemed to kick Peter back into action. He set his make-shift weapon down and went back to work on the ropes that were now beginning to burn Emily's wrists.

"Hold still, so I can untie you," he said, as he focussed on freeing her right arm. "My name is Peter. I'm a lecturer at your daughter's school Mrs Wilson. I'm not going to lie, she is in great danger so we must hurry, and I'll explain more as soon as I can."

Emily felt her heart rise to her throat and as his words sank in, the tears she had been holding in were finally set free.

"Danger?! Wh...why? What's going on?" Her composure eroded and she fell limp in the chair.

"She's outside...in the woods. We must hurry!" There

was a slight tremor in his voice and Emily couldn't discern if it was fear or concern, but after a few seconds she felt the rope loosen and fall to the floor.

"Get started on your ankle if you can reach, while I free up your other hand," he urged, taking his piece of wood with him as he switched sides.

Tugging blindly at the knot on her ankle, she felt the slightest of movement before Peter had freed her left wrist and moved down to finish the job.

"Where is Meridia? Why is she in the woods?" She begged, kicking the last piece of the rope from her legs as she stood up.

The room spun, and Emily felt her knees wobble as she teetered on the brink of passing out. Floundering, her head pulsated as the room's dim light suddenly grew dimmer, reducing everything around her to a grey, hazy blur, before disappearing altogether.

The next thing Emily felt was a cool breeze on her face as she gently swayed back and forth as if she was in a hammock being rocked to sleep. Opening her eyes, the bright grey of the winter sky was blinding at first, but as she adjusted, she could see the trees waving in front of her. Flinching as she regained consciousness, Emily found herself high in Peter's arms, being carried away from an old run-down house in the middle of what looked like nowhere.

"Meridia!" she shrieked. "Where's my daughter?!"

64

"MERIDIA...WAKE UP," THE BOY'S WHISPERY VOICE FELT familiar as it drifted into Meridia's awareness.

Taking a deep breath, she could smell damp wood and soil in the air, but everything was beyond dark.

"*Open your eyes Meridia.*" The gentle voice nudged at her again as she did as instructed.

Standing over her was Archie, in the same garb as he was the last time she saw him. The sight of him made her recoil at first, as his eyes seemed more luminous down here in the dark.

"*It's ok. You've had a fall. You need to get out of here and find the others,*" he explained as she gingerly rose to her feet.

Her ankle felt tender the moment she put weight on it, making her wince a little in pain. She must've fallen heavy, she thought, but it was nothing she couldn't cope with.

"Where am I?" she asked, looking around through bleary eyes.

At first glance, it looked like a cave of some sort, with rounded walls made from jagged brown rocks. To either side of her was a sprinkling of old-fashioned dormant lanterns, each row nailed to the rocks and illuminating the darkness ahead. A thin shaft of light trickled in from the hole above, revealing a makeshift ladder that someone had fixed to the only solid wall, one rung at a time.

"What is this place?" she asked again.

"*It's a tunnel. It leads back the way you came...to Crooked House. It's where they keep us all.*" Archie retreated a little, putting himself between Meridia and the tunnel's entrance. "*It's not safe down here Meridia. You need to leave.*"

Meridia felt her temper flare. She'd had a gut-full of cryptic messages and wanted answers..

"Why? Please, just tell me what's going on Archie...All I keep getting from anyone is riddles. How can we stop that bloody witch and put an end to all this?" Meridia's voice echoed away from them down the tunnel, and Archie followed it nervously with his ghostly eyes.

"*I don't know...I'm sorry. Things are vague here, like a dream.*" He looked frustrated with himself as he tried his best to answer. "*I wish I could tell you everything, but I just don't know...all I know is this is where we all are, and you need to leave.*"

"All of who?" Meridia pressed, unwilling to let Archie off the hook now she had him in front of her.

"*Us.*" He whispered. "*The spirits of those taken.*"

Meridia looked over his shoulder at the lamps lighting the tunnel with their pale orange glow. Had she been here before? All at once it seemed familiar, as if she'd just broken a distant dream of her own.

"Have I been here before?" she blurted.

"*Yes. Once, in a dream. You need to go now!*" he was more assertive this time in his request.

"Bu..."

"Meridia!" she was interrupted by another voice from above. Looking up, she could see Father Alexander leaning over the hole. "Are you hurt?" he whispered. Meridia turned back towards Archie, but he was gone.

"Why does everything have to be so bloody difficult!" she raged and then directed her attention back to the sky. "I'm ok. There's a ladder here. Just give me a sec and I'll try to climb back up."

65

Father Alexander reached down and helped Meridia clamber out of the hole he'd discovered. As she got to her feet, her friends immediately mobbed her, swamping her in an exuberant group hug.

"I nearly ended up down there with you," he admitted. "If it wasn't for the fog slowing us down, I'd never have seen it! Now we need to get back to the house and find Peter so we can all get out of here." He had lost all sense of direction now and could only hope Crooked House lay somewhere beyond the large, twisted alder tree they had passed on their way here. "This way...I think," he gestured to the others. "But stay close this time."

"Wait!" Meridia exclaimed. "We need to mark the tree...so we can find this place again. It could be important."

"No need," Kane replied, pointing at the tree's bark. There, carved into its centre, was a pentagram, and Father Alexander recognized it instantly from Father John's description.

"The children of the shadows..." he muttered. "We need to go."

All five of them set off, trudging through dirt and mushy leaves as they navigated the heavy fog that surrounded them.

"We just need to keep a straight line if we can, and that should take us back to the path." Father Alexander sounded more confident than he actually felt as he tried to guide them all back to safety.

"Where is Peter?" Meridia asked, as she hobbled alongside him.

"At the house. We heard someone calling for help, so had to make a choice. Lucky we chose the way we did or we might never have found you." Father Alexander was trying hard to temper his relief at finding Meridia unscathed, as he knew the witch may still be lurking nearby.

"Maybe we should've just followed the tunnel back to the house, but Archie said it wasn't safe down there." The mention of secret tunnels and Archie in the same sentence was almost too much for Father Alexander to resist, but he held his tongue to keep hundreds of questions from breaking out into the woods. There would be plenty of time for questions later, he hoped.

"Wait! Did you hear that?" Izzy interrupted his thoughts and brought the group to a sudden stop. The mist had seemed to thicken since pulling Meridia from the ground, cocooning them in murk.

Snap!

The harsh sound of twigs breaking underfoot rang out ahead, and Father Alexander instinctively reached for his crucifix. His palms were already sweating, a warm clammy cocktail of physical exertion and fear, causing the metal cross to slip and slide beyond his grip as he fumbled to grab hold of it. An eerie whisper floated dreamily on top of the fog, an inaudible melody frolicking in the gloom, as the vaporous blanket drifted ever closer.

"Get behind me!" Father Alexander trembled, and one by one the children fell back and huddled together as he came nose to nose with the sinister white wall of smoke.

It continued to snake and worm its way toward him as if it were alive, all the while the whispering continued, gathering pace and momentum. This was the ultimate test of faith as he prayed for protection, thrusting his crucifix out in front of him until its modest chain tugged at the back of his neck. The mist briefly dispersed around him, as if it was fleeing from the sign of the cross, before closing in again at speed, gripping his wrist and twisting it back on itself, forcing him onto his knees. Streaks of black smoke rippled away from his buckled hand, cutting through the grey like tiny jet-streams as they weaved their way outward, then formed an all too familiar shape in front of him.

"Argh!" He cried out, unable to mask his pain from the children.

"*Hahahahaha!*" The witch's laughter announced her return as the black smoke congealed in the air and solidified into the same spider-like creature that had stalked Meridia earlier, bringing with her the same sickly stench of freshly roasted flesh.

"*Your cross has no place here, holy man!*" she shrieked, her eyes ablaze as the remnants of the fog evaporated and seeped back into the earth.

"Stop!" Meridia screamed.

The witch continued to twist his hand until he felt a sharp snap just below his wrist. A warm, prickly heat engulfed his body, making him feel queasy, as an abrupt surge of excruciating pain raced to his elbow. His crucifix bounced back to its rightful place around his neck as he let go in agony, but he didn't have the stomach to scream. Instead, he stared down at the dirt whilst trying to stave off the impulse to vomit. Somewhere beyond the whistling pressure in his ears he could hear the children screaming at the shadow looming over him, begging for his release, but her grip was vice-like as she continued to twist.

Snap!

Another sickening break, this time causing his hand to fall limp within hers, and his view of the dirt became hazy, as if the fog had returned. His mind rushed in search of an answer, anything to fight back with, but all he was capable of was prayer.

Steadying himself, he looked up at his vindictive assailant and felt the blood drain from his face as he took in a mouthful of her rancid breath. Eyeball to eyeball, her scorched face twisted into a demented smile, whilst her black eyes burned brightly, consumed by pure hatred, the likes of which he'd never seen. Over her bony shoulder, the trees all spun, swept up in a tornado of pain and confusion that raged inside his head whilst he wrestled to stay conscious. He had to do something, the children needed him. And then he started speaking, unsure of where it even came from. If a prayer was all he had, then a prayer it would be.

"You...you are my refuge and my fortress...my God, in whom I trust." His voice was weary and broken, but he persisted, unable to move in the witch's grasp.

"I ask for your protection... I...I ask for your protection against the perils of this world, both seen and unseen. Cover me with your feathers and shield me with your wings. Though I may face challenges and trials, I will not fear, for you are with me."

All fell silent around him as his voice grew steady in

stature. He couldn't be certain, but he thought he felt the witch's grip loosen slightly. Staring deep into her bright, unearthly eyes, he saw them flicker briefly and with it, he felt her confidence give way to his.

"Your presence gives me comfort and courage. Your angels are encamped around me, protecting me from all harm. I rely on your promises, knowing that no evil shall befall me, and no plague shall come near my dwelling."

He felt the strength to stand, towering over the witch as she cowered in his shadow. His hand was free now, and he felt no pain, only the gentle vibration of his words as they flowed through him loud and unhindered.

"Your angels will bear me up in their hands, so that I will not stumble or fall. I commit my life into your hands, O Lord. Protect me and these innocent children."

The witch wailed, an awful, gut-wrenching wail like a newborn baby in pain, but Father Alexander continued, unwavering until her wail morphed into a high-pitched whistle.

Venomously hissing and spitting at him, her contorted body vibrated until she became translucent against the line of trees behind her. As the whistling became more intense, the ground shook beneath them forcing the children to cover their ears, but Father Alexander remained unperturbed, staring down the witch's gnarled body as it started to splinter and fray in the rising wind.

"Grant us your peace, your strength, and your presence. In the name of Jesus, I pray. Amen."

The moment he concluded his prayer, the witch violently evaporated, immersing them all in a putrid black smoke that stunk of rotten meat, before giving way to the familiar damp, musty aroma of trees in winter.

Father Alexander slumped to his knees, exhausted and overcome with pain as the children rallied to his aid.

"Holy shit, what just happened?!" Kane was the first to break the silence. "Sorry…I mean, what the hell just happened?"

"Father your hand. We need to get you to the hospital." Izzy glossed over Kane's poor choice of words and created a protective barrier between his injury and the group's enthusiasm.

Father Alexander was in a daze, unsure of what had just happened. He looked down at his lifeless hand that laid palm-up on the ground beside him, and if it wasn't for the intense shooting pains that had now made their way up to his shoulder, he would have sworn it belonged to someone else. Turning his attention back to the children standing over him, he suffered another bout of dizziness kick in and his body faded.

As he watched their worried faces flash past on his own private carousel, he thought he noticed an extra child standing amongst the crowd, but before he uttered a word, his brain slowly turned down the dimmer switch and Father Alexander passed out.

66

MERIDIA WASN'T SURE WHAT HAD JUST HAPPENED. HAD God really intervened? Until now, she'd just assumed he had abandoned them all and washed his hands of this world. Until now she wasn't even sure he existed, and yet here they were apparently saved. As Kane and JJ cradled the fallen priest, she looked around at the desolate woodland and wondered if it was really over. Had this unexpected show of divine power somehow banished the witch for good? It didn't take long for Meridia to find the answer she was looking for, as in her dumbstruck scrutiny of their surroundings, she noticed the group's number had mysteriously increased by one.

Standing alone, on the other side of the hubbub that enveloped the hero of the hour, was Zach, or rather the 'other' Zach. It had been weeks since she'd last seen him in this form, and whilst her heart broke at the sight of his ghostly appearance, part of her longed for him to tell her it was all over. They were finally safe. She drifted past the others, floating on a wave of disregard, to see what cryptic message her best friend had brought her from the future.

As before, his eyes were as night, each containing a single star that sparkled in the daylight, and the moment she gazed into them, she knew he wasn't here to deliver good news.

"*It's not over M.*" He whispered in a voice shrouded by static. "*This was a battle, not the war. She will be back for you all...if you let her. You need to go below. Father Alexander will know what to do.*"

"MERIDIA!!" Before she could process any of Zach's message, Meridia was lifted clean off the ground by someone colliding with her at speed. Almost wetting herself at the sudden impact, her entire body went rigid in response to being hoisted up and down in the air like she'd scored the match-winner in a cup final.

"Mum?!" Meridia felt sick to her stomach at the realization her mum was there with them.

Behind her, Peter wearily raised his hand before noticing Father Alexander in a crumpled heap, and rushed past them both.

"Mum, what are you doing here?" She looked over at the patch of mud where Zach had been standing to find it empty and felt her temper flare. The piecemeal nature of her gift, beyond terrible dreams of impending danger, was nothing short of infuriating.

"I was kidnapped! Peter found me tied up in the house and rescued me. He even gave me his coat to stay warm... he's such a lovely man..." Emily let go of her daughter, quickly pouncing on her again for a more traditional hug, speaking this time into Meridia's thick auburn waves. "I was so scared...thank god you're safe! Are you ok? Did anybody hurt you?"

Emily backed away again to make a fuss, cupping her face as she looked her up and down for any signs of injury.

"I'm fine mum, just a sore ankle is all." Overwhelmed by a mix of raw emotions, Meridia didn't know what to say or do next so she just collapsed into her mother's arms and sobbed.

She'd had no idea her mum was even missing and should have listened to her gut that morning before leaving the house. All she could think of was how much Crooked House had already robbed from them, and the fact it had now targeted her mum made Meridia's blood boil. She hated this place, and the fact that Zach had just delivered yet another ominous warning filled her with a newfound rage.

"He's beginning to stir. Give him some air guys." Peter's voice cooled her thoughts as Father Alexander let out a breathy groan. "Try not to move Martin, your arm looks badly broken."

"Ow!" Father Alexander's eyes were now open, and he let out a yelp from the pain before clenching his teeth to regain his composure.

Meridia's concern was met by Kane's grimace as he not-so-subtly pointed at her mum standing behind her.

"How the heck are we going to spin this one?" He whispered under his breath.

"We don't need to spin anything." Peter overheard him, "Once way or another, Emily is part of all this now, so we owe it to her to tell the truth...for her own protection if nothing else. We'll address that in due time though. Right now we need to get Martin on his feet and get as far away from this place as possible before they realize what we've done."

"Who?" Kane asked. "The witch is dead, isn't she?" Before Peter could answer, Meridia cut him off with deadpan authority.

"No, she's not, she's coming back! I've been given another message...this one is definitely for Father Alexander...We need to go below."

67

IT WAS A LONG WALK BACK TO THE SAFETY OF JUBILEE Park, and the light wind at their backs carried with it a delicate drizzle speckling them with rain. Having drawn a blank with the local taxi services, they had to flee the village of Cold Christmas on foot.

Using Peter's scarf as a sling had eased the excruciating pain in Father Alexander's arm a little, but he still had to pace himself as they trudged along the highway. Even the slightest bump in the road, or absent-minded movement, resulted in a bout of hot sweats followed by debilitating nausea.

Despite Emily insisting they call an ambulance, followed by the police, the FBI, and the army, she had eventually conceded it was best to regroup first and then come up with a more sensible plan. The park was an obvious choice given it was familiar to them all, and perhaps more importantly, out in the open.

Crooked House had remained dormant as they skirted past it from within the woods. With no sign of either the witch or Emily's abductor, it didn't take them long to reconnect with the main road where they drew comfort from the odd Sunday driver as they whistled past.

As they brought each other up to speed on their recent exploits along the way, the group pondered Zach's cryptic instruction. Although Father Alexander struggled to concentrate because of the pain, they were all in agreement that 'below' must be referring to the mysterious tunnel Meridia had discovered.

"I thought Archie said it was dangerous down there?" Izzy challenged as they walked.

Despite his brain fog, Father Alexander still found the mention of his name jarring, particularly now he had well and truly crossed the belief barrier during his confrontation with the witch. The thought of Archie moving on from this plane of existence alone filled him with a deep sorrow, not only for a life tragically cut short, but for the impact his death was sure to have on his surviving family. Father Alexander knew he needed time to grieve, but time was a luxury that eluded them for now.

"Tell me a place that isn't dangerous at the moment Izz?" Meridia sighed. "Remember what happened at the hospital? I can't even fall asleep in class! It doesn't matter where we go, the witch always seems to find us. And now we've got some psycho in a hood running around kidnapping parents!"

Meridia was a force of nature, and irrespective of her incredible gift, Father Alexander had never encountered a child quite like her before. Wise beyond her years, she exuded an inner strength that was nothing short of formidable.

"Meridia's right," Peter interjected. "Whatever's down there, we may have no choice but to face it. We've only got a few more hours of daylight left, so it could well be a case of now or never. I know we've yet to see any sign of the horsemen, but we must assume they are still behind all this, and we know only too well what they are capable of in the dark. I know you're hurt Father, and I don't want to add to your pressure, but is there any reason you can think of why Zach might think you'd know what to do?"

Father Alexander had been racking his brain since hearing Meridia's message, but the pain was overwhelming, interrupting his every thought. All he wanted to do was get to the hospital and have something to numb him, but deep down, he knew his work wasn't done.

"I'm trying...I just need a moment to rest and gather myself." But as they reached Mrs Hutson's café they were welcomed by a large red, retro 'Closed' sign hanging in the glass-paned door.

Peter checked his watch, puzzled. "That's odd. It's only just turned one o'clock."

They had hoped they could rest in there whilst waiting for a taxi. The drizzle that had followed them all the way back was now threatening to get heavier, and although there were plenty of trees scattered around the park's grounds, none of them would offer much shelter without their leaves.

"Our house isn't far, if we cut through the park?" Emily spoke up. "We can go there? I have pain killers, tea and coffee, and we can figure out what we do next. To be honest, after last night I don't think I'd feel safe going back there without you all anyway. What do you say? Father, do you think you can walk a little further?"

Father Alexander felt her hand rest gently on his good side and he gave everyone a subtle nod. "Yes," he said wearily. "It isn't any worse since we set off. So long as it's not too far?"

"About another ten minutes I'd say. It's this way." Emily

grabbed hold of Meridia's hand and set off along the winding tarmac path.

In the distance, Father Alexander could see a small green iron gate set between two banks of houses.

"It's just the other side of that road," Emily added, and with that, they all trudged on.

68

When they arrived at 72 Nightingale Lane, both Meridia and her mum hesitated at the garden gate, reluctant to step foot across the threshold.

Despite the problems with her father, they had both worked hard to make this a safe place: a haven. The fact that someone else had been creeping around in there uninvited, and then gone to the terrifying extreme of taking her mum made her sick to her stomach. Looking at the modest plot, Emily set some expectations.

"It may not look like much, but it's...home." Meridia could almost feel the word home stick in her mum's throat as she welcomed everyone in and led them through the front door.

A series of clips and clops, accompanied by the occasional squeak, ensued as they all followed her along the faux-pine laminated flooring towards the rear of the house. The familiar scent of vanilla and fresh cotton provided soothing relief to Meridia as she entered, enabling her to finally release some of the tension she had been carrying on her shoulders. Once they reached the kitchen, Emily pulled a chair out from under the rustic pine dining table and robbed a plump green cushion from one of its neighbouring chairs to give Father Alexander a more comfortable seat.

"We're short of chairs wherever we sit I'm afraid, and I don't want any muddy shoes ruining our living room carpet," she explained, as she hastily raided the first-aid cupboard and filled a glass with water from the draining board.

"Here Father, take your pick. I had a terrible headache last night, and these seemed to work." She waved an open box of ibuprofen in front of him, looking for his approval, and then popped two tiny tablets out onto the table beside him. "I also have some paracetamol that you can take at the same time."

It was still a little surreal for Meridia to see all the people she cared about finally in the same room together, and despite the shock and anger she'd felt that her mum had been dragged into this nightmare, there was a small part of her that was relieved she didn't have to lie to her anymore.

"Thank you Emily," Father Alexander mumbled, grimacing as he adjusted his arm to a more comfortable position.

"I still think we should call an ambulance," she declared, filling the kettle, and pulling three mugs off an ornate rack that sat beside the sink. "M, can you sort your friends out while I put the kettle on?"

Meridia was amazed at how her mum had gone straight into, well, mum-mode, since they had arrived.

Fetching the jug of filtered water from the fridge, Meridia knew today's revelations were bound to catch up with her mum at some point. After all, she had only recently turned a corner, taking them out for pizza the other evening, and Meridia knew they would both be devastated when Crooked House inevitably undid all the progress she'd made. For now, though, she noticed she couldn't seem to take her eyes off Peter and was twiddling with her hair like a school girl as she asked him how he took his coffee.

"Zach's still not replied to my text," Kane announced, distracting her from the growing suspicion her mum had the hots for their teacher. "I sent it when we reached the main road and he's not read it yet."

"It's lunchtime, and you know how your mum gets about phones at the table mate," JJ reassured. "I'm sure everything's fine and he's playing his part like we told him to."

"Maybe...If I've not heard soon though I'll have to try my mum." Meridia could tell Kane was agitated, but given the rollercoaster they'd all been on, it was understandable. It felt wrong leaving Zach out the way they had, but she, more than anyone, knew it was for the best.

"May I Father?" Peter knelt beside a washed-out Father Alexander as he sat silently with his eyes closed. "I've had some first aid training in my time and only want to take a look."

Carefully removing the sling, he helped Father Alexander lower his arm onto the table beside him. Meridia watched as he turned a shade of grey, and sweat poured from his forehead.

"Now I'm just going to raise your sleeve a little so I can see better."

"Argh!" Father Alexander's cry made everyone jump as it vibrated around the cramped kitchen.

The skin around his wrist and all the way up to the tips of his fingers was a patchwork of purple and grey, and it was clear the bones connecting his hand had been completely severed. Meridia felt sick as his arm twitched briefly and exposed how flaccid his hand was. Another cry escaped him, and Peter withdrew.

"It's completely snapped. The only thing we can do right now is make a splint to keep it in place and protected. Emily, do you have anything we can use? Some strong tape perhaps, and a towel?"

"I reckon I might have something better than that. I'm sure I have an old tubular support bandage upstairs somewhere. I'll run up and take a look. It might be too small for his wrist, but maybe we can cut it and tape it back up to fit. I'll be right back."

"Don't say that Mrs Wilson. We never say we'll be right back. Horror 101," JJ quipped as she rushed out into the hall, looking miffed.

"Are you ok Izz?" Meridia asked, noticing she'd been unusually quiet all morning.

"Just thinking..." Izzy had distanced herself from everyone else, opting to linger by the back door as she wistfully sipped her glass of water. "I just feel useless today, like I haven't done anything."

"You've been here. That's more than enough." Meridia wandered over and gave Izzy a reassuring hug. "And besides, the day's not over yet."

"That's what I was thinking about." She shifted her attention to Peter and whispered, "What does the church say about witches?"

"Not much I'm afraid Izzy," Peter sighed. "Unless Father Alexander knows anything different, they don't really acknowledge their existence. Even during the witch trials, the Catholic church remained sceptical of the whole thing from what I could tell during my research."

"Demons..." Father Alexander muttered under his

breath. "We believe in the existence of demons, not witches per se..."

His response pricked everyone's attention just as Emily returned, and with her a waft of freshly sprayed perfume filled the room which Meridia recognized instantly. It was her fancy Chanel perfume, reserved only for special occasions. For a moment, she considered calling her out, but concluded that whatever was happening between her and Peter was diverting her attention from the fact she'd been kidnapped by a madman while the rest of them had battled a 300-year-old witch in the woods.

"Found it!" She said, handing Peter a navy-blue padded support. "What did I miss?"

Upon closer inspection, her mum had also done something to her hair. Dry shampoo, Meridia suspected, although Peter seemed oblivious, getting straight to work making the temporary splint.

"Have you got scissors and some tape? The thicker, the better." Peter asked as he continued to stretch and loosen the tubular bandage. "We were just talking about the church's position on witches, and it seems they only believe in demons."

"What if we've got this all wrong?" Izzy probed again as her analytical brain kicked in. "What if the church is right and witches don't exist? What if Molly is a demon? You said yourself that was the common belief. Witches were people possessed."

The room fell silent as they considered the possibility they had been barking up the wrong tree the entire time. Meridia watched as Kane's mind sprang into action.

"That would explain why the fire didn't work, but then Father Alexander's prayer did..." he said, pacing.

Meridia had seen this look before and knew he was

busy interrogating his mental database of horror movies for anything remotely useful, but this time, JJ beat him to the punch.

"Wouldn't the church just perform an exorcism or something to get rid of a demon? I mean, that's what they do in the movies the second a ghost gets dangerous, right? They call the priest in."

All eyes suddenly switched to Father Alexander, who, for the first time since he'd sat down, looked vaguely comfortable.

Peter on the other hand was anything but and looked as if he'd just seen a ghost himself. Glazed-eyed and drained of colour, his face twitched erratically. After a slight delay, he opened his mouth to speak, but all that came out was a mishmash of gobbledegook.

Meridia had seen this once before, a few years ago, when her nan had suffered a stroke while visiting one weekend. She never fully recovered and eventually died a few months later. It was a memory that had haunted Meridia ever since.

"Peter?" She cried. "Peter, what's wrong?!"

69

PETER COULD SEE MERIDIA'S LIPS MOVING, BUT HER words evaded him, as if she was talking to him from behind soundproof glass. Slowly, the kitchen and everyone in it dwindled away, consumed by misty hues of lacklustre grey that deepened to a murky black, until nothing else existed, only Peter and the darkness.

"*I am with you now,*" came a cacophony of whispery voices, all overlapping with one another like a misfiring choir, dominating his senses as they reverberated inside his mind. "*We are one.*"

"Who are you?!" Peter begged, as an ice-cold chill engulfed him.

His own voice sounded unfamiliar. Distant and echoey, as if it was caught up in the static of an old radio. Looking around, he saw nothing, not even himself, and his body felt beyond numb. It felt absent, as if all he possessed now were his thoughts.

The whispers continued buzzing around him like a swarm of locusts, inaudible, smothering and suffocating him with their relentless chatter. This episode had the hallmarks of something far darker than the others Peter had experienced so far, a plague that was all-consuming, corrupting and crushing whatever resistance he mustered until he could no longer tell where he ended, and the voices began.

In a matter of seconds, his very sanity felt compromised, infiltrated by some unseen entity as it weaved an elusive and enigmatic spell he was unable to fathom. The whispering soon made way for screams and from within the gloom, a crimson river of bodies emerged beneath him, flooding his eyes with torturous, blood-soaked visions of torment as its victims writhed and twitched in the final throes of an agonizing death.

As he choked on the sweet metallic stench of blood, all Peter heard were the deafening cries of a thousand souls trapped below, each staring straight at him, wide-eyed and begging for mercy.

Forced to watch, he witnessed the faces of all those he cared about battle their way to the surface, their bloody outstretched hands looking to him for salvation, while he remained helpless, a useless spectator, powerless to save them.

"Stop!" he screamed in desperation, but the river continued to flow, filling every crevice of his mind with its murderous intent, until everything became awash with bloodshed and gore.

Drowning in a perpetual sea of violence, Peter became numb to the chaos and his screaming vision of hell slowly evaporated before him, making way for the dark once more.

The murmuring horde softly returned, encircling him with its melodic chant, as it whittled its way down to one solitary voice, a voice that Peter recognized instantly as his own.

"*As below, so above...*" it whispered seductively, over and over again. "*As below, so above.*"

70

"Please! Somebody do something. I think he's having a stroke." Meridia's sudden panic infected everyone except for Father Alexander, who reached out with his good hand and rested it on Peter's arm.

"Peter..." He whispered, gently shaking him. "Peter, wake up." Peter's muttering trailed off as he rejoined everyone in the room with a start.

"Wh...what happened? Why are you all looking at me like that?" He quizzed.

"We lost you for a second there. Anything you'd like to share?" Father Alexander's voice was calm and soothing as he did his best to mask the immense pain he was still in. "It's ok Meridia, he's not having a stroke...he was actually speaking in Latin."

A miffed expression drifted across Peter's face, followed by one of contrition, as he cleared his throat to speak.

"Ok, so I wasn't sure if I was going mad until now, but ever since the incident at my house, I've been having visions...or more like flashbacks...I think. I didn't want to mention anything at first as I was still trying to make sense of them myself, but it seems I have these memories rattling around inside my brain that weren't there before and sometimes they get jarred loose, by a trigger of some kind, and come storming to the forefront of my mind…I thought it was all internal until now, but it seems this one has got me speaking Latin. Do you know what I said?" Peter looked at Father Alexander expectantly.

"Ut infra, ut supra…it means as below, so above. What did you see Peter?"

Peter shifted uncomfortably in his seat as the group closed the circle around him in anticipation.

"Hell, Father. I think I was just given the briefest of glimpses directly into hell…" Peter gazed out the kitchen window over Emily's shoulder, disturbed by the horrors he'd just witnessed, and so Father Alexander decided not to press, despite the level of expectation rapidly growing inside the crowded room.

"I think we have an answer to your question Izzy. It seems we've had a demon on our hands the entire time. I also know what needs to be done now." Father Alexander looked solemnly at Peter and grit his teeth in readiness. "I need you to tape my wrist up now. We have work to do."

<h1 style="text-align:center">71</h1>

ZACH ANXIOUSLY WATCHED THE PHONE ON HIS BEDSIDE table, willing the signal to return. He felt useless enough as it was being stuck on the sidelines while the others risked their lives for him.

The last thing he'd needed was the internet going down and cutting him off from them all completely. It wasn't helped by the fact he'd been cooped up in his room all morning too, but he had to convince both parents that his phantom virus was real. His dad was easy enough, always so trusting, but his mum was a much harder nut to crack. Zach only had himself to blame for that after he got caught feigning illness in fifth grade to avoid a math test. He wasn't the best at math but seemed to perform even worse in exam conditions. Something about the forced silence and patrolling teachers with their stern faces flustered him.

Today, however, his mum had taken him at his word, doting on him with regular glasses of water and dry toast to help settle his stomach. Maybe it was a trap, and she was just waiting for him to slip up like he did last time? The bag of cream donuts JJ had left in their fridge that time had been his undoing, but he wouldn't make that same mistake again, despite how much he loathed toast without butter.

Shuffling round on his bed, he peered out of his window and was instantly reminded of what freedom looked like when he saw a group of teenagers bounce past, laughing and juggling a shiny blue leather football on their way to have a kick about. Feeling even more depressed, Zach turned his attention to the half-eaten crust and tepid glass of water beside him, quietly reinforcing his prisoner status, before turning back to his phone.

"C'mon! I need to know what's going on." His impatience boiled over, before the rattling of a car engine outside snapped him out of his strop.

The unfamiliar grey transit van pulled up at the front gate and a man stepped out, dressed in royal-blue overalls with a beige baseball cap that obscured his face from Zach's view. At his side was a dusty grey rucksack which Zach reasoned had to be his tools, and his heart leapt at the prospect of being able to text Meridia. The visitor continued towards the house until disappearing under the cover of the front porch, where he rang the doorbell, sending its raucous chime echoing up the stairs.

"About time!" Zach exclaimed. Help had finally arrived.

<h1 style="text-align:center">72</h1>

St Peter's Church cut a dramatic silhouette against the luminous grey of the afternoon sky as the winter sun fought to make its presence felt. Long and narrow by design, the tall yet unassuming limestone building was located on the crossing of St Peter's Road and Hereford Lane. From there it overlooked a small patch of grass imaginatively called Peter's Green, which was often used as a play area for toddlers and the occasional dog when the weather permitted.

However, today, nobody was on the green or its surrounding roads. With his usual service cancelled because of a last minute 'family emergency', Father Alexander reasoned the locals were holed up in their homes recovering from their Sunday roasts, or enjoying a pint or two at the local pub.

As he entered the tiny courtyard, the sun made one more push to escape the clouds that seemed hellbent on hampering its rays, and its feeble appearance served up a stark reminder of what little daylight they had left.

"I thought it would be bigger," Emily exclaimed, looking

up at the slender tower that sat alone next to the church's main entrance.

Its original large oval door, made from thick oak, looked impenetrable as if it belonged in a castle dungeon, whilst the decorative beige window frames worked tirelessly to add a touch of elegance to the church's otherwise unspectacular aesthetic.

"We're missing a tower from the original design," Father Alexander grunted, still in severe discomfort, as he led everyone to a private entrance partially concealed by an old brick wall and instinctively reached for his keys. "Argh... blast it!" he cursed, wincing in pain.

"Let me help." Peter stepped forward and awkwardly fished out a set of keys from the father's pocket.

"It's the silver chubb first, top and bottom, then use the brass yale for the middle," Father Alexander instructed. "We must move quickly once we're inside, as we don't have much time."

Unable to drive because of his injury, Father Alexander secured a taxi to the church, but now with more group members than a cab could accommodate, Emily was forced to follow on in her car, bringing Meridia and Izzy with her. Despite the great job Peter had done repurposing what looked like an ankle support to secure the break in his wrist, the slightest movement was still agonizing, but somehow, he had to find the strength to see out the day. If his suspicions were correct, he would have plenty of time for a trip to the hospital once they had paid Crooked House one last visit.

"I still can't get an answer from Zach, so I'm going to stay out here and try my mum," Kane announced, hanging back from the rest of the group as they disappeared inside the church. "We should have swung by on the way here and just picked him up. I've got a really bad feeling about all this guys."

"I'm sure he's fine mate. He's most likely safe at home with your parents, and it's the best place for him right now." JJ tried to reassure him again before Emily waited until out of earshot to wade in with her take on things.

"I don't want to be the voice of doom here," she whispered, "but someone took me from my house in the middle of the night, and my only crime was to go downstairs for a couple of painkillers. If Zach's as important as you all say, then maybe we should be worried? It's not too late to call the police...even if all we do is ask them to send someone over to check on them."

"Let's not do anything rash just yet and see if Kane can get a hold of him first. We have enough to contend with at the moment without the police getting involved." Father Alexander tried to pacify Emily, sensing her impatience might be about to get the better of her again.

"Ok, but if you think I'm going to let any of us go out like extras from a crappy Channel 5 horror movie, then you've got another thing coming. I'd rather get in trouble with the police and know everyone is safe than leave anything to chance. Embarrassment is much easier to live with than regret."

Father Alexander appreciated Emily's candour, and it was becoming increasingly apparent where Meridia got her grit and tenacity from. Ushering them all inside the main entrance hall, he gestured for them to take a seat on one of the large wooden pews.

Inside, St Peter's had a far more contemporary feel to it, with spotless magnolia walls that cradled its nave by virtue of a series of striking, symmetrical archways. The contrast of natural oak herringbone flooring and matching sideboards provided the perfect picture frame to a minimalist, yet highly stylized interior, whilst a smattering of stained-glass windows on either side injected a much-needed dash of colour and warmth.

"Just give me two ticks and then we can be on our way." He said as he set off towards his private office.

When Father Alexander gripped the brass door handle, he felt a cold sweat break out across the back of his neck, but this time it wasn't from the pain in his arm. He was about to cross a line, and it was one he could neither see a way around, nor a way back from.

Upon entering, the familiar scent of leather infused with sandalwood tried its best to soothe him, but Father Alexander was inconsolable. Having held himself together for the entire car journey, his stoic facade crumbled and all he wanted to do was lock the door behind him and sob his broken heart out. The moment Peter had slipped into his trance and began his Latin ramblings, he'd known exactly what they were up against, and what would be required of him.

Taking a moment to compose himself, he stepped across to the tiny desk facing the door and delicately traced the cover of his prayer book with his fingertips. Its black goatskin sleeve felt soft and vaguely reassuring, yet cold to the touch, having been neglected all Sunday.

"Give me strength," he muttered, his glance lingering over the picture of his late wife as he picked the book up and tucked it firmly under his arm.

Knock knock!

Father Alexander jumped and then felt another shooting pain tear its way up his arm.

"Sorry Father, I didn't mean to make you jump." Izzy

was standing sheepishly in the doorway behind him. "Peter said the taxi's on its way here. Is there anything I can do?"

"Thank you dear, but I've got what I came here for now and was just on my way." He watched as the dot of a girl before him nodded compliantly and then wandered away to join the rest of the group outside.

The incredible bravery amongst this band of friends was by no means lost on him, and he only hoped he could live up to their lofty standards in the hours to come. This was not how he saw his Sunday afternoon unfolding. Breaking one of the precepts of the church by attempting an unsanctioned exorcism would have serious repercussions if he was ever found out, but given everything that was at stake, he had no other choice.

73

Kane paced up and down the church forecourt with his phone pressed firmly to his ear.

"Someone answer!" he fumed as another call to his mum rang out like all those before it.

"Still no luck?" JJ asked. His usual calm tone had a hint of worry in it now.

"No, none of them are picking up! Something's definitely up mate. Not one of my messages have been read by any of them and I told Zach to keep the act up to make sure they didn't take him anywhere. I've got to go find out what's going on. With that nut-job in the hood on the loose, anything could've happened." The more he thought aloud, the more he worked himself up.

"I dunno mate, your dad isn't exactly small, and don't even get me started on your mum! I've seen her when she loses her shit with Zach and wouldn't want to get on the wrong side of her." JJ did his best to diffuse the situation, but Kane's mind was made up. He had to go home.

"What's going on?" Peter emerged from inside, accompanied by Emily and Meridia.

"I've got to go home. Something bad has happened, I know it...I can't get through to any of them and they wouldn't ignore my call...I don't know what else I can do!" Kane felt his bottom lip tremble so turned away to hide it. Emily was quick to console him, gently squeezing his elbow.

"Let's go round there, shall we? We can be there and back in twenty minutes, or just meet the others at Crooked House when we're done." Kane was torn. He knew how important the next few hours were in the grand scheme of things, and an unscheduled pit-stop in Shawbrook threatened to jeopardize everything. It was an impossible situation.

"I don't know what to do," he lamented. "What if Zach needs me...or my parents? I can't be in two places at once. Maybe I can get a taxi there while the rest of you take down the witch...or whatever she is?"

"I can't let you do that Kane," Peter declared. "Not alone with a maniac still on the loose. We still don't know what his part is in all this, or if there are others like him. If the Children of the Shadows are attempting a comeback, then we must assume he's not working alone."

"I'll go with him," JJ announced. "If we see any sign of trouble, we'll call the police. That way, you guys will still have Peter with you in case things go sideways at Crooked House."

"Erm, excuse me, but I'm here too!" Emily made her feelings known about JJ's sexist remark. "I can look after myself. Thank you!"

"I wasn't saying you can't Mrs Wilson..."

"Miss!" she interrupted, glancing at Peter as JJ continued.

"Sorry. I wasn't saying you can't. It's just that we can't all go check on Zach. Meridia and Father Alexander need to be at Crooked House, and with his hand busted, they're going to need all the protection they can get." JJ adjusted his cap and let out a deep sigh. "I don't see any other way. Like Kane said, we can't all be in two places at once."

"He's right," Father Alexander conceded. "I don't see any other way, as we need to give ourselves the best shot at ending this madness. The only way we can do that is by freeing Molly from the demon's grasp, and I'm not sure I can do that without Meridia's help. For all we know there may be other horrors waiting for us in that tunnel, so we can't afford to enter it lightly. At least this way, Kane and JJ can look out for each other, and more importantly, Zach, without the need to alert the police and cause any undue attention."

Silence befell the group as they each searched for another solution until Peter eventually conceded.

"So, it's decided then. Emily will drive the five of us to Crooked House as planned whilst Kane and JJ use the taxi I booked to take them both back to Shawbrook. But guys, you must be careful. We can't rule out the possibility this is all part of a wider plan to divide and conquer, so the moment you see something out of place, you get out of there and you call the police, ok? There can be no hesitation, and no unnecessary heroics."

"We promise," Kane replied. "I'll text you as soon as we know what's going on and if everything's ok then we'll head straight to Crooked House."

"We must all get going." Father Alexander added, looking up at the overcast sky. "With these clouds, we'll only have a couple of hours at best."

"It's ok, you get going and we'll just wait here for the cab." Kane remained twitchy and on edge but gestured for them to leave all the same. Father Alexander was right, this was their best chance of ending things and saving Zach.

Kane and JJ escorted the rest of the group to Emily's tiny white Fiat Panda, where they exchanged hugs before folding themselves into it.

"Good luck and Godspeed," Father Alexander declared from the front passenger seat. "God be with us all." And with that, they went their separate ways.

74

WHEN THEY ARRIVED IN COLD CHRISTMAS FOR THE second time that day, they had the luxury of bypassing Crooked House altogether.

Packed into the car like sardines, their journey was teeming with angst, and Meridia remained silent throughout the entire way there. Watching the empty streets and lifeless houses flash past along the way was all she could do to block her mum's thinly veiled attempts at flirting with Peter. She hoped it was all just a coping mechanism for whatever lay ahead. A build-up of nervous energy working its way out, but it had still come as an immense relief when Father Alexander had insisted on taking the front seat, despite giving away several inches to Peter in height. Whatever her mum's reasons, those cringe-inducing exchanges should have been the least of Meridia's worries. Despite being warned against it by a dead teenager, they remained determined to venture into a dark tunnel beneath the epicentre of evil. At what point had this all become normal, she wondered, as her mum slowed to a halt and pulled into a layby next to the spooky woods.

She slid out of the back seat and her thoughts shifted to Zach as she checked her phone. She wished she'd brought his pen with her, and maybe she would have been able to tell if he was ok. It was still too early to hear from Kane, with Cold Christmas being a far shorter drive from St Peters than Shawbrook, but she checked all the same. Her own messages to her silent crush remained unread, and it was only adding to the tension building in her neck and shoulders again. A sudden blast of cold air hit her face as she stood up straight on the roadside, and the muscles in her back pinched together in a unified response. This bloody place, she thought, wondering if there would ever come a time she wouldn't have to come back here.

"Now all we have to do is find that tree," Peter announced with a groan as he stretched his tall frame back to its original length.

"It was roughly a hundred metres from the house, and a little to the left." Izzy clarified straight-faced from the other side of the car before walking away in that direction.

Meridia chuckled to herself at Father Alexander's bewildered expression as, one by one, they all followed Izzy into the woods.

In a matter of minutes, sure enough, Izzy had successfully guided them all to the tree in question.

"Remarkable!" Father Alexander muttered under his breath, shaking his head as he gathered everyone around the hole in the ground.

Meanwhile, Meridia studied the strange star-shaped carving once more and then glanced pensively at her mum. It was the same symbol she had seen in her nightmare, emblazoned on the ruins of her street. Looking around, she became acutely aware that the other two people from that terrible dream were standing beside her. The prospect of her most devastating prophecy coming true hit her all at once, and a waterfall of tears followed, gushing from her big blue eyes and warming her rosy windswept cheeks.

"What is it hon?" Her mum noticed her sobbing and stooped to comfort her.

Meridia knew all-too-well that every one of her grim visions had come to fruition so far, and suddenly the shadow of dread hanging over her became too heavy to bear.

"I'm ok." She wept, lying as she searched for the resolve to make this premonition the exception. "I'm just tired of this," she added, cuffing at her tears. "I'm fine."

If there was ever a reason to summon all of her courage, this was it. Her mum, her world, was at her side; a living, breathing reminder of what was at stake. She couldn't let her down now. She couldn't let any of them down.

"Let's do this," she said through gritted teeth, digging deep within herself to muster every ounce of courage needed to enter the lion's den.

75

The rich, salty smell of earth filled his lungs as Father Alexander edged his way down the crudely made ladder, cursing his injury at every rung. Unsure if the pain had eased a little, or if he had become numb to it, the stiffness of his strapping made it difficult to navigate the damp decaying wood as quickly as he would have liked, and he could feel the pressure eating at him.

"Almost there Father...just a couple more steps." Peter encouraged him from below, having volunteered to be the first one down.

Their plan was straightforward. Peter would accompany Father Alexander and Meridia into the cave until it became clear what they needed to do. With so much uncertainty of what to expect, they had landed on the tunnel either being a hiding place for the witch in her new form, or a resting place for the bones of her old body. Whichever way the cookie crumbled, they expected to meet some kind of resistance down there as Archie wouldn't have warned them off without a good reason. Therefore, Peter would provide the muscle, should they need it, and buy enough time for Father Alexander to perform his part in all this. Meridia was there as an insurance policy of sorts in the hope she might detect danger before it presented itself, as she had done so many times before. In the meantime, Emily and Izzy would remain above ground should anything approach them from that end.

"I'm still not happy about being a lookout," Emily whispered down as Father Alexander completed his descent. "You may be bigger and stronger than me, Peter, but I'm no shrinking violet. I can handle myself."

"I have no doubt Emily...sorry, I mean Miss Wilson. But if anything goes wrong, you need to stick to the plan and get the girls out of here." Peter handed Father Alexander his prayer book and then beckoned Meridia down.

"You can call me Emily. Just make sure nothing happens to my daughter. I'm trusting you Peter."

Father Alexander watched in wonder as Meridia nimbly made the journey down in a matter of seconds and activated the flashlight app on her phone. Its brilliant beam flooded the dark hollow, revealing a cavernous structure made from grubby limestone which seemed to be bolstered by handmade bricks and mortar further ahead.

"What can you see Meridia?" He quizzed as she swung her light from left to right, establishing the confines of the passage they were about to venture into.

"Just rocks and bricks," she replied. "The same as you."

"Sorry...I wasn't sure how your gift works." Father Alexander felt himself blush in the gloom as he used his own less sophisticated phone to illuminate the pages of his prayer book.

There was an eerie silence that stifled the mouldy air around them, making it difficult to breathe. He could sense the panic simmering in his chest as the environment tapped into his most primal fears of claustrophobia and suffocation.

"Don't worry, I'll let you know if I see any ghosts," Meridia whispered in jest, administering another healthy dose of embarrassment.

"Shall we then?" Peter said before leading the way forward into the dark.

76

"Where is it?! It should be here by now!" Kane was irate, pacing again as he and JJ continued to wait in the cold for their taxi to arrive. "The others will be there by now and we've not even left yet."

"Mate, I've tried all the other cab firms in the area, and the earliest they can get one out to us is 3:00pm." JJ was equally flustered now, glued to his phone, looking for alternative transport.

"That's another twenty minutes! And what if that one lets us down too? What then? I think we should just start walking. Maybe there's a bus or something we can catch on the way?"

"It's Sunday mate, you know what the buses are like back home. Can't imagine this place is going to be any better."

Kane knew JJ was right. He swept his chocolate brown mop away from his face to cool down. Despite the steady drop in temperature as the sun began its descent, his frustration was getting the better of him and causing him to overheat. Unable to reach anyone at home, he was now certain something terrible had happened to his family.

The longer they both waited, the more horrific scenarios played out in Kane's mind, each one taken directly from his mental movie database of violence and gore. Despite JJ's best efforts to keep him distracted with more optimistic explanations for their silence, there was no escaping the fact it had been hours now since anyone had heard from Zach. Meanwhile, they found themselves marooned in Thundridge, in the middle of nowhere, with no means of getting back.

"It's about a forty-minute walk from here. Maybe if we jog for parts of it, we can get it down to half an hour?" Kane was convinced that any movement towards his house, no matter how slow, would feel like progress.

He had to get to Zach.

"Ok, let's do that. We can keep checking for taxis and buses along the way."

And so, they both set off jogging towards the main road, using JJ's phone to guide them. Their sole intention, chipping away at the 3:24pm ETA as much as humanly possible.

<h1 style="text-align:center">77</h1>

As THEY VENTURED DEEPER INSIDE, THE TUNNEL became increasingly humid. A damp, moldy smell had melded itself with the thick sticky air that clung to Meridia's face as she trudged over the loose, stony ground. It felt stifling, hostile even, as they forged ahead in search of the witch.

Haphazardly bandying their flashlights around, Meridia and Peter tried their best to flush anything out of hiding that might have been lurking in the shadows, waiting for them. Up until now, all they had discovered were the ancient remains of what was once a dungeon or prison. Crumbling, decayed bricks formed a series of open mouths that boasted jagged panels of splintered wood for teeth where doors had once stood. Each depraved cavity contained rusted shackles and ominous stains splattered across their stone walls and floors.

Although the onset of time may have washed away any stench, the congealed traces of torture and murder remained ever-present, and Meridia knew exactly where they were.

"I've seen this place before," she whispered. "In a vision. I was here, but the doors were locked, and people were screaming inside."

"Can you sense anything now M?" Peter asked.

"No, not now, but I was chased when I was here before. It looked different then though...something's missing." She shone her light on the bricks above one of the openings. "There were numbers before...like the rooms inside the house, but they're not here."

"Maybe what you saw happened in the past?" Peter mused. "Who was it that chased you?"

"Men...women too, maybe. They were all in hoods, so I couldn't tell. The ones I could see were angry though, like they wanted to kill me." She turned and looked back at where they had just come from. Half expecting to see the amber glow of her nightlight calling her back to safety, but all she could see was blackness as far as her torch could reach.

In the distance ahead, she made out the vague outline of a stone archway. Silence enveloped the darkness, leaving Meridia isolated from her mum and the rest of civilization. All she could hear was the muffled sounds of her own breathing as her lungs fought against the tunnel's suffocating atmosphere.

"Stay sharp everyone." Father Alexander's whisper echoed its way up the tunnel, startling her as he brought them all back to the task at hand. "This may be the calm before the storm."

78

"It's odd, isn't it...What do you think it means?" Izzy scrutinized the upside-down star carved into the tree trunk as she traced its oblique trenches with her finger.

"For all we know, it could be a medieval sign of danger. I can't believe I've let M go down there...I keep thinking I'm going to wake up and this has all been some horrible nightmare." Emily was keeping a watchful eye on the woods as she paced nervously on the spot.

The temperature had plummeted drastically since they'd arrived, and a whispery wind rattled the branches and thickets surrounding them.

"I used to feel like that...in the beginning. I even used to pinch myself sometimes when no-one was looking, hoping it would snap me out of it. I never used to believe in any of this...whatever this is. Now I suspect everything, even old Mr Richards, who lives around the corner to you."

"Albert? He wouldn't say boo to a goose, bless him. He's been through a terrible time these past couple of years. Why would you suspect him of something?" Izzy's comment pricked Emily's curiosity.

"He keeps looking at me weird, like he hates me. Once outside your house, then again at the hospital. I have a bad feeling about him. He gives me the creeps." Izzy succumbed to the cold and shuddered as the thought of Mr Richards' hateful expression came flooding back to her. "I think we're all scared of our own shadows at the moment," she added flippantly, trying to gloss over her remark, but Mr Richards was the least of their concerns.

Izzy felt a sharp tug on her sleeve from behind as Emily pulled her to the ground.

"Shh..." Emily whispered, placing a trembling finger to her lips. Her bright blue eyes were wide and her pupils dilated, as they darted from left to right.

"Something's coming!"

79

Hiss!

Meridia froze as all flashlights frantically searched for the source of the unsettling sound.

"Rats!" Peter exclaimed, as hundreds of tiny orbs glistened back at them from the shadows beyond the archway.

The tunnel became infested, as an oily sea of hissing and scratching vermin poured out of the darkness and streamed toward them.

Frozen in fear, Meridia watched in horror as the swarm of matted fur and razor-sharp claws rapidly devoured the ground in front of her, desperately scrambling over each other in their frenzied onslaught.

"Don't move!" Father Alexander cried out from behind her, but Meridia wasn't going anywhere.

She'd always been afraid of rats, despite never coming across one until now, and couldn't have moved a muscle even if she'd wanted to. The rampaging scavengers continued to hiss as they swamped her, scuttling over her feet and ankles in their hurry to flee the sudden intrusion of their home. Meridia did her best to swallow the scream that was clawing at her throat to get out, as the stampede died down, leaving a trail of their pungent scent in its wake. The unexpected surge drew to a close as the last remaining stragglers scampered past, and all was still once more.

"We must keep moving." Father Alexander rallied them as he led the way towards the mysterious arch. "She must be close."

Still, Meridia could sense nothing out of the ordinary. The gift that had served them all so well until now seemed to have abandoned her just when she needed it the most. Was this all a wild goose chase? A big distraction designed to separate them all?

Peter illuminated Father Alexander's way while Meridia remained lost in thought, still reeling from her encounter with the rats and wondering if her mum would be safe from them above ground.

"Here! Peter, look!"

Father Alexander's excitement stirred her from her daze, and she responded, jogging over to join the others at the mouth of the archway.

"This is it," she said, taking in the long corridor and dungeonesque cells that lined each of its walls. "This is the place I visited in my dream."

The eye-watering stench of rat droppings and mould was suffocating as she crossed the threshold of the entrance. They had also reached the end of the line. With five doorways on either side of them and a brick wall up ahead, there was nowhere else to go from here. Someone had ripped each heavy wooden door from its hinges and shattered them into pieces, which now lay strewn on the ground like scraps of firewood.

"Look! Numbers...just like you said M." Peter dragged

his light above each doorway to reveal rusted brass numbers ranging one to ten.

"Ten," he muttered, half thinking out loud. "Just like Crooked House..."

Peter shone his light back where they had come from for a moment, and then slowly retraced their steps with the beam.

"This is Crooked House...I'd bet my life on it. We must be directly below it, which means..." He marched over to the door marked '2' and directed his flashlight inside.

Meridia watched Peter's expression turn from one of fortitude to one of sheer horror as a cacophony of tormented, blood-curdling screams rang out, and Peter dropped his phone to the ground.

In a matter of seconds, every light they had to guide them inexplicably flickered and died, but not before Meridia caught a glimpse of what they had found.

There, in the doorways surrounding them, for the briefest of moments, she saw every single spirit ever claimed by that wretched place. A legion of glimmering eyes and ghoulish faces, stared at her from their shadowy mausoleum, as Meridia, and everything around her, was plunged into total darkness.

80

Emily shielded Izzy with her arm as she peered above the hawthorn bush they were both cowering behind.

Snap!

Another twig breaking in two shattered the silence of the woods, making them both jump as they clung onto each other in fear. Emily had to do something. Staying perfectly still, she closed her eyes and waited for another sound, hoping to pinpoint the source this time.

Snap!

Another twig, this time closer, but to their right.

Gesturing for Izzy to stay put, she shuffled her feet around to square her body up to whatever had found them. Leaning onto the balls of her feet in readiness to pounce, she paused, interrupted by the rough bark of a branch brushing against her palm. Emily glanced down, only to find Izzy slipping a make-shift weapon into her hand. The gnarled piece of wood was no longer than a rolling-pin, but it had weight to it, so she gripped onto its hilt until her knuckles turned white. Giving a final nod of reassurance to Izzy, she rose from the ground, facing the direction of the noise. The second she got to her feet, Emily let the branch fall beside her, startling Izzy, who then warily joined her.

"It's beautiful." Emily whispered as she let out a tremendous sigh of relief.

There, in a small clearing on the other side of the hawthorn, was a deer. Majestic and unfazed by its audience, it tilted its head, twitching an oversized ear momentarily as it sized them both up. Its reddish-brown coat boasted an array of creamy coloured flecks on its back, which brightened the gloom of the woods. Above its head, a velvety crown of newly grown antlers elegantly reached up to the sky like two outstretched arms waiting to cradle a newborn baby.

"What's it doing here?" Izzy murmured as the deer strolled over to get a closer look at them both.

"I'm not sure Izz…I've never seen one so tame before… not even at the zoo."

With just the hawthorn separating them now, the deer bowed its head low, and with a trembling hand, Emily reached out to stroke its brow. Its fur was soft and warm, as she'd always imagined, and for a moment she let go of the fear she was harbouring. For a moment, it was Emily and the deer: respite from the madness. But that moment wasn't to last, as suddenly the deer jerked backwards. Glancing over their shoulders at the hole in the ground behind them, it seemed to sense the impending danger, and that was when the screams broke out.

The unearthly, tormented cries of all the tortured souls trapped within Crooked House suddenly erupted from the ground, rattling the birds from their trees, and turning Emily's knees to jelly. Before she could react, the deer fled, galloping off into the distance, leaving Emily and all her worries far behind it.

81

Peter saw the flames flickering in the darkness and recognized them instantly. He'd spent half his life dreaming of them, despite never witnessing them in person. They danced and swayed in the distance, the way they always did, haunting, hypnotic, their amber glow deftly revealing the burned-out carcass of an old Mini Cooper as it slowly expired.

"J..James..." He muttered, stumbling over to the burning wreckage, just as he'd done so many times before.

He knew how this played out. His kid-brother's lifeless body behind the wheel, melted to the driver's seat, his face charred and contorted in the kind of agony only a fifteen-hundred-degree fire can inflict. In some sick way, he wished he had been there that night, had seen poor James with his own eyes all those years ago. Surely that would have been an easier image to carry than the grisly scenes his mind had conjured up in its absence. The image that confronted him now.

"James!" he cried, as the heat from the crash site covered him in ash and sweat, but the car was empty. For twenty years, Peter's brother had always been there, disfigured and unrecognizable from his injuries, trapped behind the wheel of his car and staring out through a smouldering hole where the windscreen had once been.

"*Peeeterrr…*"

His long-dead brother's rasping, gravelly voice permeated the soft crackling of the dwindling flames and sent icy shockwaves charging up Peter's spine. Holding onto his breath to steady his shredded nerves, Peter closed his eyes before turning to face the one ghost that had always eluded him. Upon opening them, he was startled by how close James' apparition was standing. A matter of millimetres separated him from his blackened sibling, and he could feel his wheezy breath as it rattled its way out of his scorched lungs.

His brother had always been handsome, more so than Peter when he was his age, but now he looked like a Halloween waxwork, half-melted and twisted into something hideous and full of sorrow. The only trace of his childhood best friend were his bright green eyes, which glistened in fire's light, like two emerald orbs floating in the abyss.

"*Wheeere weere yooou Peeeterrr?!*" He hissed. "*Yooou weere meant tooo take caaare of meeee!*"

His slurred accusation was like a dagger to the heart, and the decades of tears that Peter had held at bay all came pouring out at once, bringing him to his knees. He wanted nothing more than to hold his brother close, to cradle him in his arms, but the guilt he'd carried for so long prevented him, as if he'd forgone the right.

"I'm so sorry James!" he sobbed. "I didn't know…how could I?!"

"Yooou left meee....tooo die. My ooown brother...tooo busy."

His brother's words were like shrapnel, stuck in his seared throat, and Peter could no longer bring himself to look.

James Higginsworth had the world at his feet by the time he was eighteen. A gifted athlete headed for stardom, courtesy of a basketball scholarship. He had always been the brawn to Peter's brain, and with only a single academic year between them, they had been inseparable since the moment James was born; that was, until one night, he was tragically taken from him. Snuffed out in a cruel twist of fate.

"I'm sorry..." Peter wept. "It should have been me."

It had been the briefest of journeys, one he and his brother had made countless times. The convenience store had been a little over a mile away, and whenever they went, Peter would let his brother drive. It was their secret, at least until James had passed his test. Between training and practice and trials, he never quite found the time, but still Peter taught him enough: the basics.

Until one night Peter wasn't there.

Caught up at the library studying, he'd lost track of time and James' impatience got the better of him. The mini was a work in progress, a restoration project Peter worked on at the weekends with their dad. He could still remember the day he took it out for a spin. The sense of pride he felt, building a car from scratch. He'd intended to give it to James as a gift when he eventually passed and told him as much while he worked on it. If he'd just looked at that damn library clock. If he'd not been so caught up in his thesis, he would have been there. He could have told him it wasn't safe, and James would still be alive today. Not like this. Not this carbonized husk that was once so full of life.

"*Yessss!*" James's voice was laced with acrimony. "*Yooou did thisss to meee...and now it's yoour turn to suffer!*"

His words were like gasoline, rekindling the flames surrounding them and igniting the room once more. Higher and higher the fire raged, devouring the oxygen and engulfing everything until it was all Peter could see.

In many ways James's death had been Peter's making. It was in pursuit of James's ghost that he'd ventured into the paranormal, and so in some strange way it was only fitting that he would be his end too.

As the blaze intensified, Peter remained on his knees, alone once more, a broken man, accepting of a fate long overdue.

82

Meridia shook her phone and tapped its screen to restore some kind of light, but it was completely dead.

"Peter? Father?" She called out into the darkness, but neither replied. It made no sense, they had been right beside her just moments ago. "Where are you?!" She snapped, her voice trembling as frustration took hold.

The truth was, she didn't quite know where she was either. Caught in a quandary, she wasn't sure whether to move or stay still. While Meridia deliberated, she noticed a dramatic shift in the atmosphere as the smell of rat excrement and mould abated, making way for a familiar floral scent she couldn't quite place. Before she could recall what it was, an amber speck of light materialized in front of her, making her jump. What at first looked like a tiny pinprick in the fabric of the darkness, soon spread its way down to the ground, forming an opaque vertical line from her head to her toes. Meridia wondered if she might be dreaming again, backing away from the strange glow, only to clatter into a wall of fabric.

Clank! Clang!

The racket of metal scraping against metal rang out above her, and although Meridia jumped again, it didn't take her long to realize where she was. That sweet cozy smell of fabric softener, and the clatter of metal coat hangers coming together on the rail, she was standing in her bedroom wardrobe.

"What the..." Her sentence was cut short by another all-too-familiar word that struck fear into her heart the moment she heard it.

"*Sweetheart?*" The thin beam of light flickered as her father, Gregor, entered her bedroom. "*I know you're in here.*" His voice slurred from the booze. He instantly set about trashing her things in his drunken rampage.

Meridia knew it would only be a matter of time before he discovered her, cowering behind a flimsy panel of MDF. Pressing her face to the crack of light leaking in, she tried to steal a glimpse. It felt like a lifetime since she saw him last, or heard his voice. Every account her mother had imparted since that brutal afternoon had eroded any happy memories from Meridia's childhood. Now, whenever she tried to look back at him in the rearview window of her mind, all she saw was Gregor, the monster, the wife-beater, the coward.

"*It's ok sweetheart...you can come out. Daddy's not gonna hurt you...Daddy would never hurt you.*" His voice was shifting through the gears as he spoke, eventually settling on a snarl as the light flickered again, faster this time, before going out completely. "*There you are!*"

Meridia swallowed a mouthful of his warm whiskey breath as it blew through the gap in the door and coughed. In a matter of seconds, her coughing turned to screams as Gregor wrenched the door off its hinges and yanked Meridia out into the open by her arm.

The brute force sent her hurtling towards the bed

where she crashed into the bedside table and smashed her treasured nightlight into smithereens. Gregor loomed over her, fists clenched and looking like a man possessed.

What he lacked in stature, he made up in muscle, filling the decimated boxroom with his powerful frame and trapping Meridia in the corner furthest from her only way out. Consumed by rage, he just glared at her. Polluting her room with the smell of stale liquor as he huffed and puffed like a wild animal psyching itself up to pounce. His bright blue eyes were wild, ablaze beneath his bushy raven eyebrows.

"This is all your fault!" He bellowed from beneath his unkempt beard. The slur had gone now, and all that remained was anger and contempt. *"You're the reason we came here! YOU!"*

Meridia could do nothing, still shaken from her fall and paralyzed by fear. All she could do was cry.

"Why...*sniff*...why are you doing this? You're supposed to be my dad..."

"I came for you that day." Gregor, wired now, rubbed his face and waved his arms around like a crazed lunatic as he continued to spiral. *"Imagine my surprise when I found out you were at an after-school club? Ha! I was so revved up by the time I got there... so your mum got it instead! Either way, I figured I'd be doing her a favour in the long run...you see, we're not that different, you and me. The apple didn't fall far from the tree at all, did it, sweetheart? You think I didn't notice? That rage inside you. I can see it right now. I can see me! Your mum never deserved any of this, not you or me. She was the best thing that ever happened to me, and we ruined it. YOU ruined it! You're going to break her heart one day, you know that? Just like I did. So here I am! Back to finish what I started..."*

Meridia flinched, her lips trembling in terror as Gregor took an aggressive step closer. Every one of his poisonous words struck right at the heart of her deepest and darkest fear, that she would one day end up just like him, but deep down, she knew. She wrestled with it every single day, suppressed it, pretended it was just hormones and growing pains, but she knew.

Her father was right.

Meridia curled herself into a ball and closed her eyes as she braced herself for the first blow.

She was done fighting now.

She was done with everything.

83

Father Alexander's entire body tensed up as he felt the ear-splitting screams surge past him like a gust of wind in the darkness. A shooting pain raced up his forearm, once again reminding him of his shattered wrist, and the muffled whimper that escaped his lips as a result was swept along by the final echoes of the god-awful cries as they made their way out of the tunnel. Ears ringing and unable to see, he called out to the others whilst fumbling for his phone.

"Meridia? Peter? Is everyone ok?" But all he heard was a woman's gentle sobbing. "Meridia? Is that you?"

He tried to resurrect the light from his phone, but it was dead, leaving him no choice but to hazard a step forward towards the source of the noise.

"Meridia? Peter?" He whispered, shuffling his feet along in the dirt in the hope he might find them. Before the lights went out, Peter had seen something that shook him, but he had no clue what it was. Had they stumbled upon the witch's lair he wondered?

CLICK!

A loud hollow sound echoed overhead as a sudden burst of blinding light rained down on him from above.

"Grrr!" Father Alexander flinched, clenching his jaw to curtail the short, sharp dose of pain that followed. Whilst his eyes adjusted to its intense glow, the ethereal shaft of light revealed a woman up ahead, crouched on the ground with her back to him.

Her waif-like body quivered beneath the cool white beam as it sliced its way through the darkness, and Father Alexander recognized her instantly. A cold sweat broke out beneath his cassock as he staved off the urge to faint. Everything around him swayed, as if he was now standing on the deck of a sailboat, and he felt his knees give way beneath him.

"Melissa?!" He mumbled in disbelief. He'd not said his wife's name aloud since her funeral all those years ago, and now here she was, weeping before him.

"*It's so cold...*" she lamented, "*here in the dark...I'm so lonely Martin.*" Her voice, once velvety, now sounded fractured. Crackling through the static in Father Alexander's head as he wrestled with his grief.

He stumbled towards her, knees still weak from shock, and was greeted by the fleeting aroma of her favourite perfume. She was wearing nothing but her long satin nightdress, its thin grey straps barely discernible against her pallid, bony shoulders, whilst her tousled chestnut brown hair looked dry and matted up close under the glaring light.

"*You lied to me Martin...you told me the lord would take care of me...Why would he abandon me like this? Condemn me to darkness...what did I do wrong Martin? What did I do to deserve...this?*" Melissa gestured towards the gloom that lay beyond the spotlight's gaze and cried. "*It's all a lie*

Martin...there's nothing here...no heaven...no utopia, only darkness and solitude."

"I'm so sorry Mel!" Father Alexander finally succumbed to gravity and broke down beside her.

Still lacking the courage to look at her face, he rested his weary head on her icy shoulder for a moment and closed his eyes to slow the steady flow of tears. They had only been married a year when Melissa had fallen ill.

Childhood sweethearts, they had waited and waited before tying the knot whilst Martin pursued his childhood ambition of a naval career, but as the constant separation and desire to start a family became too much to bear. He eventually resigned at the age of twenty-five, after seven years of service. From there, they wasted no time in marrying, holding an intimate ceremony the following summer surrounded by close friends and family.

They had no idea of the heartache and suffering that awaited them, and by the next fall, Martin found himself lost and alone. That was almost thirty years ago now, yet from what he could tell, the frail woman trembling next to him, although pale and malnourished, looked like she was still in her twenties. The sight of her brought everything flooding back to him. The endless hospital appointments and failed treatment plans, the feeling of utter helplessness, until eventually they had no-one else to turn to but God. When Melissa finally lost her battle and passed into the night, Martin remained by God's side, and he had been with him ever since, knowing he could never love again.

"Hold me Martin... I'm so cold..."

Father Alexander cuffed his tears away and shuffled round, opening his body up to her. Raising his left arm, he reached around to feel her once more, and that was when the creature screamed. All it took was a single drop of holy water to touch her forehead, and the witch's game was up.

He'd been preparing for this moment the whole journey there, playing it out in his mind over and over. He knew all too well of the demon's trickery, fully expecting his grief for Melissa to be twisted and used against him. Still, he could feel the overwhelming compulsion to do as she asked, to comfort her, but he had to stay strong. No matter how convincing, whatever this thing was, it wasn't Melissa.

"I cast you out, unclean spirit, in the name of the Father, and of the Son, and of the Holy Spirit." Father Alexander rose to his feet in front of the witch and traced the sign of the cross on top of her tangled hair.

Head bent, as if she'd been shackled to the ground at his feet, her ferocious screams rang out around them. Hundreds of voices all at once, each one roaring in suffering and torment. Their terrifying cries were deafening, but still Father Alexander continued with his prayer.

"Depart and stay away from this servant of God. For it is the Lord Himself who commands you, accursed and doomed spirit..."

"*Look around you priest!*" The witch spat back, raising her head in defiance, and as she did the mask of his beloved Melissa contorted into something new and altogether horrifying.

The brown wig of deception she'd been hiding behind melted away, as did the youthful, pale skin that sat beneath it until all that remained was the gaunt, skeletal face of pure evil, marred by centuries of decay. Her eyes were sunken, shrouded by thick black leathery skin that had hardened over time, and she continued to spout her protests through cracked and rotten, yellow teeth.

"*Where is your god now?!*" She screamed, and the temperature suddenly rocketed.

The alcove became hot like a furnace as the light above them flickered and danced, painting shadows on the walls around them as countless corpse-like silhouettes rose from the ground. The legion of shadowy creatures slowly staggered to their feet, like long-dormant zombies clambering out of their muddy graves until Father Alexander was completely surrounded.

"*Your precious god has abandoned you! Left you all to choke on the sickening stench of your own petty and meaningless existences. Your kind are nothing more than a plague in this world! A plague that has now run its course. Your time is up holy man. You will join your wife soon enough. She belongs to us now! As below, so above! You will all join her in hell! Hahaha!*"

Her venomous ramblings lit a fire around him, a raging inferno of gold and amber which engulfed the shadowy figures, swallowing them whole. Their crackling, tortured screams filled his every thought as the witch condemned them all to a fiery hellhole.

He could feel his head spin, his body drenched in sweat, as the temperature continued to rise and the witch's show of power threatened to overwhelm him, but he had to continue. He had to finish the prayer.

"H...he...He who walked on the sea and reached out His hand to Peter as he was sinking. So then, foul fiend, recall the curse that decided your fate once and for all. Indeed, pay homage to the living and true God, pay homage to Jesus Christ, His Son, and to the Holy Spirit."

"*Nooooooo!*" the witch cried out again in contempt as she was violently thrust against the back wall of the dungeon with a bone-crushing,

Crack!

There she stayed, pinned two-feet from the ground by an unseen force. The fire diminished, and what little flesh she carried on her withered frame was then brutally stripped away. Her eyes viscously erupted, bursting within their sockets, until all that remained was a pile of putrid bones and a fractured skull where her vile face had once been.

Still, she fought, snapping at the air with her jagged, broken teeth like a wild animal, and so, sensing the shift in power, Father Alexander found the strength to go on.

"Keep far from this servant of God, for Jesus Christ, our Lord and God, has freely called him to his Holy Grace and blessed way and to the waters of baptism." He fervently waved the sign of the cross in front of her, spraying her with what remained of his holy water. Each droplet that struck its target released a needle-thin stream of smoke, as if it scolded her cadaverous body, and she sank further and further down the wall until all that was left was the witch's crumpled, decomposed carcass.

Still trembling from the rush of adrenalin, Father Alexander stepped through the sulphurous stench that hung in the air and approached the lifeless pile of bones on the ground in front of him. Kneeling, he reached into his coat pocket and retrieved a tiny wooden crucifix, then rested it against the witch's remains.

"In the name of the Father, and of the Son, and of the Holy Spirit. Amen. I commend you, my dear Molly Harding, to Almighty God, and entrust you to your Creator. May you return to him who formed you from the dust of the earth. May Holy Mary, the angels, and all the saints come to meet you as you go forth from this life. May Christ, who was crucified for you, bring you freedom and peace. May

Christ, who died for you, admit you into his garden of paradise. May Christ, the true Shepherd, acknowledge you as one of his flock. May he forgive all your sins and set you among those he has chosen. Amen."

As he finished his final prayer, the shrinking flames around him dwindled and died, making way for the artificial light of Meridia and Peter's phones that lay scattered around him in the dirt. Their owners also had returned with Peter knelt, dejected in the room's entrance, whilst Meridia cowered in the opposite corner, as if under attack.

Both awoke with a start, shrieking and flapping at phantom thoughts; the final remnants of their own personal nightmares the witch had conjured up to turn their minds against them.

"It's ok! You're safe now," Father Alexander assured them, unable to mask his exhaustion, as he wobbled back to his feet.

"The demon is gone."

84

"WHAT IS THIS PLACE?" EVERYONE JUMPED AS EMILY burst into the dungeon with Izzy in tow. "And what is that god-awful smell?"

"Mum!" Meridia rushed towards her, swamping her in the biggest cuddle she could muster.

"We heard the screams..." Emily explained as she fought to stay on her feet from the impact of her overzealous daughter.

Peter registered the commotion but couldn't think straight. His mind was still reeling from his hallucinations. He could only assume Meridia and Father Alexander had suffered similar ordeals going by how rattled they both appeared. It had all seemed so real, and he could still feel the heat from the burning wreckage of his brother's car.

"So, is anyone going to tell me what's going on here?" Emily's impatience bumped him out of his daze.

"It's...err...some kind of crypt, by the look of it." He finally answered. "My guess is we're all standing directly beneath Crooked House..."

Peter spotted the pile of bones in the corner and trailed off. When he'd first inspected the room, he had seen the witch standing there in all her gruesome glory. Her body coiled and ready to attack like a giant praying mantis. He could still see her eyes, ablaze in the darkness and full of hate, as if he was looking at the devil himself. Now all that remained was a fractured skull with a simple-looking crucifix propped up against it.

Peter turned to Father Alexander to thank him and remembered how badly injured he was. Clearly in agony, he looked deathly pale and as if he was on the verge of collapse.

"Truth is, I don't quite know what's going on here either Emily. I can only assume Father Alexander will tell us when the time is right, but for now I think we need to get him to the hospital." Peter flocked to him in support, throwing an arm around the priest's waist to help steady his rickety legs.

"I'm ok Peter." Father Alexander's pride piped up. "I just need a moment's rest before we leave...just to steady myself and catch my breath."

Peter helped him over to the nearest wall so he could use it as a crutch and recover some.

"Emily, can you keep an eye on him while I take a look at something? We may not get another chance like this." Peter glanced at his watch and noticed at best they only had another thirty minutes of daylight left. "I'll be quick, I promise."

They were still yet to help Father Alexander climb out of the tunnel and get to Emily's car.

"Of course, go...just be careful." Emily swapped places with Peter as he strode out into the main passageway.

"Wait!" Meridia took chase. "The others are here," she blurted. "I saw them before it all went dark."

But Peter wasn't interested in the others right now. There was only one room he wanted to investigate. The one the missing owners believed was at the centre of everything sinister going on in Crooked House: Room 4.

<h1 style="text-align:center">85</h1>

Meridia felt sick to her stomach the moment Peter's flashlight struck the rusted brass number 4 and promptly stopped. Beneath it, another ominous dungeon beckoned.

"Wait here," he whispered, tiptoeing towards the opening, but there was no way on earth Meridia was going to do that. Still on edge after her run in with her dad, she had no intention of waiting anywhere on her own for the foreseeable future.

Flanking Peter on their approach, she felt the nerves in her neck twitch from left to right almost involuntarily, forcing her to scour the shadows in case her deranged father jumped out on her again. She wondered how much truth there had been to the witch's narrative, had her dad really come looking for her that dreadful day?

'*Stop it M*' she reprimanded herself.

There would be plenty of sleepless nights ahead of her to reflect on the witch's claims, but right now, she had a far bigger problem. Peter, in his infinite wisdom, had decided to actively seek out the most terrifying denizen of Crooked House.

On their approach, Peter kept his light directed firmly at the ground, as if there was still a part of him that opposed looking inside. When they arrived at the opening, they both clung to the neighbouring wall like armed police about to make a drugs bust.

Crackle!

Meridia's heart almost burst through her ribcage as she felt someone beside her.

"What are you doing?" Izzy whispered, having joined the party.

"Shit, Izz, you almost gave me a heart attack!" Meridia rested on her knees to catch her breath as Peter risked a quick peek around the doorframe and immediately hauled himself back.

"I think there's someone in there." He blurted underneath his breath. "I saw a shadow by the entrance."

"Let's get out of here. I've got a bad feeling about this room," Meridia begged, tugging at his sleeve.

She racked her brain to recall if she'd caught a glimpse of the monster from room 4 before the lights went out. It all happened so fast, but she was sure she would've remembered had he been there. But if it wasn't him standing in the doorway, then who was it? Before she dwelt on the matter any longer, Peter plucked up the courage to look again and disappeared into the room.

"Oh god. Stay there M, don't look." But she'd come too far to be denied.

The first thing that hit Meridia as she stepped inside was her gag reflex, as the overpowering stench of rotten eggs violently assaulted her airways. She was amazed that none of them had noticed the smell sooner, as it was so pungent.

In the centre of the oppressive room, under Peter's shaky spotlight, was the grisly source. A vast pile of human remains dominated the enclosed space in every way, like a slimy pyramid of death. It towered above them, almost touching the ceiling. Dozens of bodies, all hideously fused together by the onset of decay, cast a macabre shadow on the opposing wall.

Beneath it, carved deep within the earthy ground and spanning the entire room, was the same style pentagram they had found etched into the tree at the tunnel's entrance. Its sharp trenches were filled to the brim with whatever blood and gunk had oozed its way down from the mound of decomposing victims at its centre. A mishmash of adults and children, all twisted together, the base of the sticky mass comprised of nothing more than a glistening collection of skulls and broken bones. The summit, however, featured a smattering of rotting flesh as it clung to the tortured faces of those who'd died more recently.

"Peter, what is this place?" Meridia broke the stunned silence, covering her mouth to stem the invasive stink.

"I...I don't know...some kind of kill room? Or catacomb perhaps? Maybe both. Look!" Peter pointed to an old wooden trapdoor in the ceiling above the mountain of bodies. "That must lead back into Crooked House. It looks as old as the house, yet some of these victims, they look..."

"Fresh," Izzy joined them, her eyes bulging behind her glasses in a state of shock.

"We need to get everyone out of here. Now!" Peter whispered, snapping his light back to the exit and slowly retreating. "I...I don't know what we're dealing with anymore..."

Still in shock, he ushered both girls away from the horrific scenes in room 4, but Meridia needed no convincing, taking Izzy by the hand and dragging her out into the main tunnel. Nervously bouncing his light back and forth, Peter signalled to Meridia's mum and Father Alexander that it was time to leave.

"What did you see? You look like you've all seen a ghost," Emily quizzed, as she helped the wounded priest to his feet.

"We need to hurry!" There was panic in Peter's voice now, and Meridia was convinced he'd seen something she hadn't.

Whatever it was, his fear was infectious, spreading throughout the group like wildfire and spurring them all back down the tunnel.

"Don't look back!" he kept saying, pushing them onward towards the ladder, their only way back to the land of the living. "We need to get to the car whilst we still can."

One by one, they climbed out of the hole while Peter waited at the bottom, still frantically wielding his flashlight, as if he was expecting someone to follow. When it was his turn to scramble to the surface, he hurried them all toward the car, checking over his shoulder as they rushed through the murky woods. The day was passing its baton to night, and the thick grey clouds that strangled what remained of the evening sun did nothing for their cause.

A brisk walk soon turned into a jog as Father Alexander, looking frailer by the second, got swept along by the tidal wave of fear as they all raced towards the clearing up ahead.

Click, click!

Emily unlocked the car as they approached, and Meridia felt a huge swell of relief rise within her as they scrambled to climb in. Father Alexander flopped into the passenger seat with a loud *thud* and Meridia couldn't tell if he was still conscious. Her mum paused to check on him.

"Father? Father, can you hear me? We need to get him to the hospital!" she cried, turning to Peter for guidance.

"Quickly, go!" Peter's voice grew louder as he barked out the order from the back seat, where he sat squeezed between both girls. He kept looking out the back window feverishly and as her mum started the car, Meridia could hold her tongue no more.

"What is it Peter? What did you see in there?!" Peter began muttering, still looking out the rear window as if in a daze.

"There was someone else in there... with us, the man in a hood. He was sitting in the corner of the room...in the shadows, as if he'd been waiting for us. At first, I made out like I hadn't noticed him...he just stayed there, silently, watching us like he had all the time in the world. But then I noticed the others..." He pointed out of the window, back at the woods, and Meridia twisted to see what he was looking at.

There, scattered amongst the trees, was a swarm of people in hoods, just like the ones she had seen in her dream. There must have been at least two-dozen of them and counting. The more Meridia watched, the more they kept multiplying, like an infestation of roaches crawling out of the woodwork. Each one stopped just shy of the clearing and stared intimidatingly beneath the cover of the trees, a legion of stone-faced guard dogs seeing off their master's unwanted visitors.

As they shrunk into the distance, Meridia understood what had spooked Peter so badly and an intense feeling of dread set its anchor down in the bottom of her stomach.

Crooked House was a terrifying hornets' nest of murder and menace, and she couldn't help but feel they had just naively given it another kick.

86

"Wait! Something's wrong," Kane whispered, impeding JJ as they approached the street door to his house.

It had been a long, tense walk back to Shawbrook, and despite the cold weather, they were both sweating beneath their winter coats.

"Look, the door isn't shut properly." Kane felt a strange tingling sensation between his ears, like he might faint as the edges of his vision began to blur and cloud over.

He'd thought about this moment the entire way back, dreaded it, and now the moment of truth had finally arrived. He felt sick to his stomach and weak at the knees. His dad's silver Kia Sportage was still parked on the drive, and the house was silent as he delicately pushed the door open wide enough so he and JJ could creep inside. The first thing he noticed was that someone had roughed up the plush cream entrance rug, as if they had kicked it across the hall. Its matte grey rubber lining was folded back on itself, revealing the varnished wooden floor beneath. This was not a good sign.

"Mum...Dad?!" he called out and then instantly

regretted it when he realized any intruder may still be lurking somewhere in the house.

They both waited a moment, listening for anything unusual, before cautiously proceeding to the living room.

Kane felt his heart sink the moment he peered around the doorframe, and then bundled his way inside, fighting the impulse to vomit.

"Nooooo!" he cried in angst, as JJ rushed in behind him.

It looked just like a crime scene from a slasher movie, with overturned furniture and white wispy cushion innards sprawled all over the plush beige carpet. In front of the bay window, his dad's favourite yellow armchair was drenched in blood from the top down, as if someone had cut the throat of whoever had been sitting there. Left of that, where his mum usually stretched out on their lazy royal-blue sofa, was the carcass of a fluffy teal cushion, slashed and gutted. Its stuffing strung out like the bargain-basement cobwebs you buy at Halloween. Just above the sofa's headrest, the magnolia paintwork had been spattered with blood in the shape of a down-turned mouth that was now trickling its way further down the wall.

Floods of tears rushed to the surface of Kane's eyes, pouring down his cheeks and blurring his vision as he soaked up the aftermath of what could only be his parents' brutal murder. He felt JJ grab him from behind in a mix of consolation and sorrow, their sobs bumping up against each other as they struggled to accept the surrounding bloodbath.

Numb from shock, Kane stood motionless in the centre of the room. A room that had been the family hub for as long as he could remember, filled with love and laugher, yet now resembled a butcher's workshop. The coppery smell of his family's blood conspired with his sticky, salty tears until he could no longer keep it all in. Shrugging JJ off, he rushed toward the tiny wicker bin between both chairs and filled it with his breakfast.

"Zach! Zach!" Behind him, JJ fell to his knees, screaming out in search of his adopted brother, but as his desperate pleas echoed up the staircase, deep-down Kane knew there would be no answer.

The house was empty and had most likely been that way most of the day now. Whoever was responsible was long gone, as was Kane's entire family. Zach included.

It was over.

They had lost.

EPILOGUE

Peter raced ahead, pushing Father Alexander's wheelchair towards A&E. He'd been unresponsive since they left Crooked House, and his pulse felt weak.

Since their last visit to Chase Side Hospital, Izzy had vowed never to step foot in its halls ever again, and yet here she was, about to do just that. Meridia and her mum had left for the Jackson's house, having failed to reach Kane or JJ the entire journey there. Since the sinister cult's unsettling show of force everyone was on high alert, and the fact they'd now lost contact with Zach's rescue party didn't bode well.

Luckily for Father Alexander, the hospital stood deserted, but as the nurses flocked to Peter at the reception desk, Izzy caught sight of a sudden movement from the corner of her eye. She was quick to recognize the back of his flat cap as he entered the elevator.

"Mr Richards," she muttered, and rushed over to see which floor he was headed to. Gazing up at the lift's tiny digital display, she watched as it counted to 4 and then stopped. She glanced back at Peter, who was now immersed in hospital paperwork, and figured she would take a look.

Given everything they had witnessed, she was now convinced Mr Richards was involved somehow, and knew the opportunity to spy on him might not present itself again soon.

Ding!

The next lift arrived and as the nurse passed Izzy in its doorway, she noticed a sudden waft of floral antiseptic which transported her back to the last time she was there. Staring into the claustrophobic metal cube, she wondered if this was a good idea, but when the doors began to close, she quickly made up her mind and slinked inside.

"If he sees you, just run for the stairs...run back to Peter..." She repeated the mantra all the way up to the fourth floor, and when the shiny elevator doors parted ways and split her nervous reflection in two, she came face to face with an empty reception desk. Behind it, scribbled on a whiteboard, was a range of numbers; one through twelve. Each number had a corresponding name, and it didn't take long for her to spot '*Richards*' scrawled next to the number five in blue marker.

Getting her bearings, Izzy crept along the glistening laminate corridor towards the cubicle in question, being careful not to make so much as a squeak. The corridor was fenced in by thick blue curtains, and it came as no surprise to find cubicle five was closed to prying eyes.

Izzy looked around to make sure the coast was clear before pressing her ear to the curtain. The slow and muted sound of a heart monitor bleeping, accompanied by the gentle whooshing of breathing apparatus, was all she could make out at first, but as she listened closer, she detected a lowly whisper. It was a man's voice, and although Izzy couldn't discern what was being said, she could tell from its delicate timbre it was devoid of any emotion, almost robotic.

This wasn't the sweet nothings of a devoted husband, more the droning monotone of a stage hypnotist.

With her curiosity piqued, she looked for the curtain's hem so she could steal a glimpse inside. Izzy carefully peeled back a layer of the blue polyester wall, just enough for her to get a peep. Mr Richards was sat with his back facing her when she discretely peered in. Perched on the edge of a tiny blue plastic chair, he was leaning over towards the head of the bed and softly babbling as if he was delivering a message. Over his shoulder, the fully equipped hospital bed was a mass of plastic tubes and flashing machines, but at the heart of it all was an old woman, unconscious and frail. Izzy recognized her at once, and the hairs on the back of her neck rose to attention as her logical brain tried to make sense of what she was seeing.

There, laying in the hospital bed, was the old woman from room 8 of Crooked House.

Mrs Richards...was an echo.

"Can I help you?" A nurse's voice rang out behind her, and Izzy froze. Overcome by fear and confusion.

"S...sorry...wrong floor." And with that, she turned and bolted. Puffing and panting, she sprinted all the way down to the ground floor, just as she'd promised herself. She had to find Peter and tell him.

When she reached the reception area in A&E, Peter was nowhere to be seen, so she sheepishly approached the receptionist.

"Excuse me...I'm looking for my friend. Father Alexander? He was brought in here a few minutes ago in a wheelchair."

The plump, middle-aged woman behind the desk frowned over the top of her glasses as she forced her eyes to readjust from the screen she'd been staring at.

"You must be Izzy," A man's voice came from behind her, bright and bubbly.

She turned to find a nurse standing in front of her. He wore blue scrubs and carried a clipboard under his arm. Somewhere in his mid-twenties, he had a kind face framed by jet-black hair that was slicked back away from his forehead. The sight of him put Izzy at ease as he smiled at her with bright blue, welcoming eyes.

"I'm nurse Grady." He said, offering out a hand. "But you can call me Silas. Don't worry about Father Alexander. I'm going to take good care of him."

AUTHOR'S NOTE

When I was 12 years old, I spent almost every Monday after school watching 80's horror movies with my best friend Scott. Although we gradually drifted apart as we grew up, those groundbreaking and iconic scares still fuel my imagination to this day.

The excitement and anticipation each time we got our hands on the latest *Nightmare on Elm Street* or *Evil Dead* movie is something I'll always cherish, so this book is for you.

ACKNOWLEDGMENTS

I'd like to thank my wife and son for their continued support and encouragement. I really couldn't do any of this without you.

I'd also like to thank Ray and Adam, for continuing to believe in me and for helping me realize a childhood dream.

Last, but not least, I'd like to thank all the readers who have chosen to join me on this journey. I hope you enjoy this second instalment of the Crooked Tales series.

About the Author

© Chris Harrison

Chris Harrison, born in North London, is not just a writer, producer, and author of the *Crooked Tales Series*; he's a storyteller on a mission. Graduating from Middlesex University with a degree in Film, Chris turned his fascination with the art of storytelling into a lifelong exploration of literary and cinematic horror. Having previously written for film and education, he's now dedicated to realizing a dream—crafting immersive worlds filled with spine-tingling terror for a young adult audience.

Chris's creations fuse classic supernatural themes with contemporary urban mythology, re-imagining our deepest fears for a new generation of horror enthusiasts.

www.chris-harrison.com

instagram.com/chrisharrison1975

threads.com/@chrisharrison1975

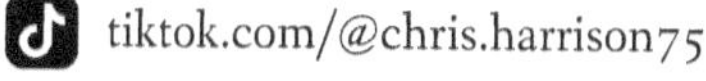
tiktok.com/@chris.harrison75

x.com/CHarrison22975

www.ingramcontent.com/pod-product-compliance
Lightning Source LLC
Chambersburg PA
CBHW022300310726
48973CB00001B/152